PARADISE

THE PARADISE CLUB SERIES

JA LOW

Paradise Club Series

Cover Design @ Book Nerd Fan Girl
www.booknerdfangirl.com
Editor @ Swish Design & Editing
www.swishgrafix.com.au

❀ Created with Vellum

FOREWORD

Please note this book is extremely hot.
If you do not like lots of sex and sex with other people then do not pass go.

1

CAMRYN

O kay. Maybe the trench coat was not the greatest idea. I've been propositioned a couple of times as I've walked down 5th Avenue. Add in the dirty looks from the women who think I'm a hooker. Let's be real, if I were, I would a be a goddamn expensive one, that's for sure. I'm high-end all the way, baby. They can clutch their pearls and designer bags because I'm not after their husbands. I'm actually on my way to cheer up my man, who has been working extra hard at the moment. Poor guy is so stressed, in fact, he's so stressed he hasn't had time to pop by my office and give me my afternoon delight like he usually does.

A man in an expensive suit holds the glass door open for me as I enter Harris' building. My heels click-clack against the marble floor. The rush of a warm breeze floats over my goosebumped skin. The days have cooled down as winter slowly creeps over New York City. The leaves have changed from the lush green foliage to the burnt orange of fall to the decaying brown pile of crap littering the sidewalks. Pulling out my swipe card, I smile at the security guard who lifts an inquisitive eyebrow at me with the tiniest of smirks crossing his lips. He knows exactly what I'm up to and wholeheartedly approves. I hit the elevator button to take me up to the top floor, where thankfully, the majority of people have finished for the evening, only the last of the workaholics are still active in their cubicles. The bell dings as the elevator doors open into the foyer of Harris' company.

"Evening, Janice," I say, greeting the receptionist, who's still working after hours.

"Good evening, Miss Starr." The older lady smiles at me, taking in my not-too-subtle outfit.

"How's he doing tonight?"

Janice rolls her eyes. "He's in a mood," she warns me.

"Let's hope I can ease him into a better one," I say while giving her a cheeky wink.

"You're going to need something more than a sexy outfit hidden under that coat to get him out of the funk he's in. His father stopped by."

My shoulders sink. Harris doesn't get along with his father, who he describes as controlling and overbearing, but as he holds the purse strings to his trust fund, he has to do what good old daddy tells him to. Otherwise, he'll be cut off. All I can say is I'm so glad I am self-made—I want to be the one in charge of my purse strings.

"Why don't you pack up for the night? I'll take care of it from here."

She gives me an appreciative smile as she quickly tidies up her workspace, then rushes through reception into the waiting elevator. Janice gives me a thumbs-up as the doors close. Silence now filters through the work area. Taking a deep breath, squaring my shoulders, I untie my trench coat and let it loosely hang in front of me, exposing my very expensive lingerie. I make my way down the corridor, passing the empty offices until I reach the one I'm after. My knuckles knock against the wooden door two times.

"What, Janice? I'm busy," he bellows from behind.

You certainly will be in a minute.

I twist the doorknob and slink into his office. His head is

down, busily scribbling something onto paperwork in front of him. I let my coat slip off my shoulders and fall to the floor. It takes him a while to look up. Obviously, he's waiting for whoever entered his office to speak first. When he finally does look up and sees me standing there in nothing but a gorgeous black lace outfit, those gorgeous sea-green eyes widen in a moment of shock before heat starts to burn behind them. He drops his pen and sits back against his chair, and his large hands begin to loosen his tie as his eyes roam hungrily over my near-naked body.

"What do I owe this pleasure?" His voice deepens as his eyes zero in on my breasts, spilling from the cups of my bra.

"I've been worried about you." Walking closer to his desk, my hips move side to side, hypnotizing him. "You've been working so hard lately, and I haven't seen you in a while."

"I'm sorry, baby. Work's been…" He forgets his words and trails off as I stop right in front of his desk.

"I've missed you," I purr.

Harris bites his lip as his eyes stay firmly set on my breasts.

"I've missed you, too."

"Good." Placing my hands on his desk and leaning forward, I continue, "I've come to help you release some of that tension I can see building all over your body."

"You have?" His voice rising, just like the tent in his pants.

"Yeah. I've come to make you feel better. You want me to make you feel better, don't you?" He nods his head quickly. "Good." I smile at him. "Sit back, relax, and let me make you feel better," I state as I drop to my knees and crawl under his desk.

"Fuck, Camryn. You know this is a fantasy of mine."

Looking up between his legs, I smile. "I know. I just wanted to say goodbye before you went away on your business trip. You know, so you don't forget about me."

His large hands cup my face. "How could I ever forget about you? You're perfect." Well, that's good, I'm glad to hear that.

"Fuck it! Let me cancel my weekend. I want to spend it with you on your knees instead."

Licking my lips, that sounds like a great idea. "As much as I want to say let's do it, you said it was important family business."

Harris' hands fall from me, a slight look of pain flashes across his face. *What did I say wrong?* He pushes back on his roller chair, moving away from me.

I scramble forward, slowly getting to my feet. *Has he lost in his mind?*

"Hey, what is it?" Trying to gain his attention again, I continue, "Whatever it is, you can tell me." Moving closer to him, his large hands wrap around my waist as he picks me up and deposits me on his lap. My legs straddle his large frame.

"I don't know how I ended up with you in my life, but I am so damn thankful." He kisses me, it's slow, tender, with a hint of sadness. *What's going on?*

"I'll be right here waiting for you when you get back," I say, reassuring him, but it feels like there's an element of goodbye to his kiss.

"I know you will be. I don't deserve you." There's that look of pain again across his face. He's actually scaring me.

"Babe." Running my hand through his lush, thick hair. "I'm here for you. No matter what. You know I'm your ride or die."

He lets out a heavy sigh. "I know you are. That's what I love about you. No matter what, you're always there for me."

"That's because I love you."

"I love you, too, Camryn." Kissing me again, this time with heat and a sense of urgency, his palms roam over my skin, curving around my ass as his fingers sink into the fleshiness of it. Pulling me hard against him, I feel his arousal. "I need you, Camryn. I need you hard and fast. I need to be inside of you."

"Yes." Wrapping my arms around his neck, I reiterate, "Yes."

Harris' fingers make quick work of the fly on his suit pants, then a quick flick and his boxers have been pushed down too. His dick is standing at attention between us. I move myself to my knees, then center myself right over him, his fingers move the edge of the lace to the side, allowing me to sink down on him.

We both hiss at the connection between us.

Harris buries his face into my neck as he begins to move inside of me. His thrusts are manic as if he's soaking up every last drop of me like I'm going to disappear on him.

"I love you, Cam," he chants over and over again, which ordinarily would set my heart on fire, but tonight, it's filled with unease.

Something is going on, but he can't tell me, and it feels like when he does finally tell me whatever it is, I might not want him. There's isn't anything in this world he could tell me that would make me think any less of him. I love him with all my heart. He's the first man in a long time where I have let my guard down.

He's buried himself deep inside of my heart—it is all his.

I am his—forever.

How wrong was I?

I should have listened to my gut.

I should have asked more questions.

Because I had no idea what was coming next.

2

CAMRYN

Thankfully, the commute to Greenwich, Connecticut, wasn't bad from Manhattan. As the city gives way of its concrete urban jungle to the green oasis of suburbia with its picture-perfect streets, there are beautiful burnt orange leaves decorating the paths perfectly as if someone has placed them there. The gated estates of billionaires start to come into view as I make my way to this evening's event.

We had a last-minute party to organize this weekend, and because they were willing to offer double our normal charge, how could we say no. Plus, Greenwich is full of extremely rich and affluent people, so expanding from our core demographic of Manhattan to the suburbs seems like a good idea.

Starr and Skye Events is still a new business in the highly competitive world of high-end event planning. We don't have the luxury to turn down high-paying clients. Kimberly, my business partner, and I hustle. We will work twenty-four hours straight if we have to, to get our name out there to the society queens and upper crust of New York.

Finally, I pull into the driveway of the estate where we're working today and press the buzzer.

"Camryn Starr from Starr and Skye Events." Talking into the static, there is a buzz, and the gates begin to open. I follow the long winding driveway through acres of trees until I finally emerge feeling like I've just set foot in the French countryside. I notice Kimberly waving me off to the side and follow her directions away from the house, pulling into a car space, obviously in the employees' area.

"Hey." She smiles, opening my door.

"Hey." Grabbing my bag from the passenger's side and pulling out my phone, I'm ready to get going.

"Everything's on track." Kimberly brings me up to speed on the progress of the party. "The clients would like to meet us, now that you're here."

Nerves flutter in my stomach. This isn't the first time we've worked for celebrity guests who don't want their identities given away until the day of the party to curb any media interest and especially leaks. Kimmie and I are used to the hoops these kinds of clients put us through, but still, it's always nerve-wracking meeting them. You just hope that you've done a good enough job for them —it takes one client to undo your reputation you have worked so hard for.

"Right." Quickly checking myself in my car's mirror to make sure I haven't smudged my lipstick, or I have a bird's nest on the top of my head, I continue, "Let's go meet these mysterious clients, then."

Pressing the golden doorbell of the main house, we both wait nervously. The wooden door opens, and we're greeted by a man in a three-piece suit.

"Miss Skye, Miss Starr, welcome to the Van Kamp Estate," he greets us. "My name is Carlton. I am the butler of the residence." Of course, they would have a butler, a house this size probably needs one. "If you would like to follow me inside, I will escort you to the library where Mr. and Mrs. Van Kamp will see you."

Carlton holds the door open with his white-gloved hands while

Kimberly and I step into the grand house and instantly feel like we have stepped into a museum. Walls are lined with old paintings and tapestries. Along the marble corridor, priceless vases and antiques stand. I don't think our insurance will cover a priceless Ming vase if we knock one over this weekend.

Finally, Carlton escorts us into an antique-styled library. Persian rugs are scattered across the floor, and what looks to be first edition leather bound books line the walls. The room has a musky old person smell with a hint of maybe cigars about it. A large mahogany desk sits to one side and a green velvet chaise to the other. Carlton steps out of the room and closes the door.

"This place is kind of creepy," Kimberly whispers, our eyes scanning the room around us.

"I bet it's haunted." I give her a nudge.

"Shit! Don't say that. You know how I feel about ghosts and haunted houses."

Kimberly comes from a good, old Southern family. She grew up in one of those *Gone with the Wind* plantation homes, which she swears is haunted. She often tells me strange things happen around her home. I've stayed there and never seen anything, though. I've known Kimberly for years. This gorgeous, southern belle debutante, who looks all apple pie and sweet tea, is actually a bulldog underneath that outside appearance. Don't let the blonde hair, big boobs, and accent fool you, she has turned into a true New Yorker and will rip your balls off if she has to.

We met when I moved to New York after leaving a bad situation in Los Angeles behind me. My best friend, Vanessa, was attacked by her then-boyfriend in our home—I found her covered in blood and almost dead. It was a traumatizing situation. After that, I couldn't stay in town anymore. The therapist told me it was Post-Traumatic Stress Disorder from the attack. It's taken me a long time to finally get over the nightmare that haunted me afterward. I made sure Vanessa was safe before I left. Her best friend, and now soon-to-be husband, Christian Taylor, from the uber-famous band Dirty Texas, took her in and nursed her back to life.

I needed a fresh start for my own sanity. So, I packed up and headed to New York. Got a job working with the legend, who is Diane Black from Noir Events, the top events company in the city. Unfortunately, my idol turned out to be Cruella Deville in disguise. After being short-changed one too many times on our holiday bonuses and finding out our boss was pocketing it all instead, Kimberly and I decided enough was enough and started our own business. When we launched and began to gain attention, Diane tried to get us blacklisted in New York society. Thankfully, we had enough connections that it didn't work. It also helped that we had so many ex-Noir employees who wanted to work for us that we expanded quite quickly. It wasn't long until we were nipping at Diane's heels for being the top luxury events company in Manhattan.

After being shown into the library, only a few moments later, our mystery clients arrive. Two sets of older couples enter the room, dressed in tuxedos and ball gowns, dripping in diamonds and furs, looking utterly fabulous and keeping in theme with the grandeur of the home. Behind them is a woman, maybe in her mid-twenties, dressed in a deep red evening gown, her dark hair pulled up into a perfect French twist. She too is dripping in diamonds. With a white fur stole wrapped around her ivory shoulders, she looks like a beautiful porcelain doll.

"Miss Starr, Miss Skye," Carlton introduces us. "This is Harvey Van Kamp and his wife, Linda, and their daughter, Isabelle, whose engagement party you have organized."

Kimberly and I quickly look at each other, mentally checking over the party we've just planned. Dammit! Nowhere in the paper-work did they mention an engagement party. Fuck!

Isabelle flashes her huge diamond ring as we shake her hand. It's utterly mesmerizing.

How the hell is she going to wear that all day? Isabelle doesn't look like she has the strength to hold herself up, let alone a boulder on her hand.

Carlton pulls me from my thoughts again with his monotone voice. "And this is Byron, his wife, Patricia, the parents of the groom-to-be."

We shake their hands also.

"Thank you so much for organizing everything tonight," Mr. Van Kamp addresses us. "Sorry, we had to keep the engagement portion of tonight's festivities a secret. We couldn't chance the media finding out about it."

Understandably, as we both nod our heads in agreement. Putting on our most professional smiles, while quickly calculating everything that's been organized downstairs and how we can make it more engagement-looking, I state, "It is our pleasure." Thanking them and giving them all a smile, I continue, "It looks like a fairy tale downstairs. We hope you're happy with it?" Fingers crossed because I know what these East Coast princesses are like—we can't afford to have some spoiled brat tarnishing our reputation.

Turning toward Isabelle. "And Miss Van Kamp, congratulations on your engagement. We hope we will make this a night for you and your future husband to remember."

She nods, giving us a perfect smile. "Oh, I've already had a peek outside." Oh God, I hold my breath waiting for her verdict. "It looks magical, thank you." Phew. "My fiancé is just finishing up a business call and should be here at any moment."

That's when I hear his voice, strolling through the wooden doors dressed in a tuxedo, which clings to his hard body. The material is cut to perfection on him. His blond hair is slicked back, and there's no hint of a five o'clock shadow that he was supporting earlier. His sea-green eyes twinkling as he looks at the lady in red, his fiancée.

I have to be dreaming because this can't possibly be happening.

"Sweetheart, sorry I took so long, just finishing off some business. I promise I'm all yours tonight." He nuzzles into her neck, affectionately.

"Darling, this is Camryn and Kimberly. They have organized our engagement party."

The groom-to-be turns to us. His green eyes register who is standing in front of him.

Me.

The woman he spoke to only hours earlier. The woman who he told was having a horrible time on his business trip. That he missed me. Oh, and also that he loved me.

Me.

The same woman who was screaming his name as he pounded into me on his desk the night before.

Me.

The man who I had finally handed over my heart to for the first time in years. The same man who told me he was never going to let it go. The man who promised plans for a future together.

With me.

The same man who's now standing in front of me with his fiancée wrapped in his arms. The man whose engagement party I've just fucking organized. My heart stops. I've just organized my boyfriend's engagement party to another woman.

Harris' face pales, realization sinking in, that his mistress is standing in front of him with his fiancée and family around him.

I could totally make his life hell.

Fuck, that noise.

I've worked too damn hard to throw my business away on some cheating scumbag. No, fuck him, he will *not* make me crumble.

Before I know it, the words are tumbling out of my mouth, "Congratulations." I lean forward, shaking his hand, putting on the performance of a lifetime.

"I'm sorry, could you please excuse us? We have to attend to something downstairs. We will be ready for your entrance in the next hour," Kimberly says, handling the situation.

The group all nod their heads in agreement.

My eyes never leave Harris' as I walk out of the room.

3

CAMRYN

I can't breathe.

    I can *not* breathe.

Rushing back to the employee parking area, I am nearly hyperventilating.

Shit.

Fuck.

How the hell does this happen?

How did I not know?

"Breathe, Cammie, breathe," Kimberly tells me, sitting me down on a plastic chair at the entrance to the catering tent. "I need a bottle of vodka, stat," Kimberly yells at some hapless staff member who happens to be in her sights.

How stupid am I not to know my boyfriend has another woman on the side?

Or fuck! *Am I the side piece?* Of course, you are, she's the one with the fucking diamond on her finger.

Six months I have been with this man. We've been on holidays together. We've spent every waking moment together when we both are not working. I never questioned his late-night business meetings or dinners. Even his weekends away. I had blind faith in him.

Damn! How could I have been so stupid?

"Here, drink this." Kimberly shoves the bottle of alcohol into my hand. Taking a swig from the bottle, the liquor burns my throat. The burn feels good instantly, and so I take another sip, embracing the pain. I stare out over the gorgeous party Kimberly and I have planned. It's magnificent, like a magical fairy tale. One of our finest parties to date.

A giggle catches me off guard, and then another, and another.

"Cammie, are you having a breakdown?" Kimberly asks when worry lines set in.

"Kimmie, we just organized my boyfriend's engagement party." Taking another swig of the vodka, I can't help but giggle again.

"I know, sweetie." Pity is written right across her face.

"He's not marrying me." That realization hits me like a ton of bricks, turning my stomach, the effects instantaneous. "The life we planned..." looking up at Kimberly, "... he's going to have it with *her*." Pointing the bottle in the direction of the house, I continue, "How could I be so stupid... *again*, Kimmie?"

"Hey." Kimberly kneels in front of me. "There's nothing stupid about you. This is not your fault. Do you hear me?" she scolds. "He's the cheating scumbag. He's the one who's been fucking around with two girls. He's the one who's been living a double life. I want to rip his balls off and shove them so far down his throat he chokes." This makes me smile. I love her so much. "What do you want to do?" Kimberly asks. Tilting my head in confusion, she resumes, "We can have this party packed up in an hour."

"Wait! What?"

"Babe, we don't have to do this. We can just pack up and go."

"And ruin our business?" My voice raises, "We've worked too fucking hard to let some cheating scumbag take that from us. No. The show goes on. Fuck him!"

"That's my girl." Kimberly wraps her arms around me, giving me a supportive embrace.

"This party is going to be the talk of the social pages. I want everyone to know that Starr and Skye Events put this on, and we fucking nailed it."

"Cammie," Harris calls from the darkness.

"You fucking asshole," Kimberly screams at him. "I don't care that you're our client. You can fuck off." Kimberly points her long-manicured finger at him. She never liked Harris, always saying someone that perfect had to be hiding something, and she was right.

"It's okay." Grabbing her wrist, I stand and take a deep breath while squaring my shoulders. He doesn't deserve to see me cry. Turning to face him, I hate that he looks so bloody perfect. The man was built for tuxedos, like James fucking Bond. The worst part is I know exactly what is under the tuxedo, the way my tongue used to love licking every dip and plain of his six-pack stomach. The way his strong hands used to thread through my hair as I worshipped him from my knees. The way I could tease him until he nearly blacked out with ecstasy.

But now? Now he looks like a stranger in the dark to me.

"Cammie, please let m-me explain," his voice wavers.

"There is nothing to explain, Harris," I state calmly. "You have a fiancée. Any other explanation is null and void."

He takes a couple of steps forward toward me. "Baby, please. Let me explain. I don't love her. I love you."

The vodka turns rancid in my stomach.

How can he say that?

Here. Now. Rage bubbles to the surface, and there is no way I can keep it under control now. Picking up the bottle of vodka, I throw it at Harris. The glass bottle hurtles toward him while I mentally debate whether or not I actually want to cause him harm with the projectile, but it's a little late now for second-guessing. He easily dodges the bottle moving to the side as it hits the gravel parking area with an unimpressive thud. The damn thing doesn't even smash. Utterly unsatisfying.

"How dare you say those words to me!" Raising my voice at him, disgust twists around each syllable. "This is your engagement party, Harris. Your fucking engagement party."

He stands there in shock, my words hitting him like tiny little arrows. In the six months we've been together, we have never fought. Never argued about anything.

It was all so easy.

Simple.

I thought it was perfect.

I was wrong.

"You have some nerve telling another woman who isn't your fiancée that you love her at your engagement party to another woman. Who the hell are you?" My body is shaking with contained rage, which is at the point of exploding.

"Baby, please?" Harris coos, stepping closer to me. "It's a business deal." My lip curls in disgust. "Cammie, don't shut me out," he pleads.

Shut him out!

Shut. Him. Out?

The man is engaged, and I had no idea. He's the one shutting *me* out.

"I should have told you earlier and explained my situation, but I didn't want to lose you."

"You're a coward." Harris' shoulders slump. "Of course, you were going to lose me. Do you seriously think I was going to be okay with you running off and marrying some heiress? That I was okay with being your mistress?" Harris slowly steps closer to me, but I hold up my hand in front of Harris for him to stop. "Don't you dare come anywhere near me." The hurt on his face pierces my heart, the last bit that's still alive. Never again. This is why you never let a man have access to your heart because they will eventually rip it out.

"I didn't sleep with her."

As if that makes it all okay.

"I don't care," I scream at him.

"So, I've never cheated," he tries to reason with me.

"Don't forget, I saw the way you walked into that room and looked at her. You may not have slept with her yet, but I think that would have changed tonight." There's a flash of something across his face that assures me I'm right before he schools his features again.

Why am I even standing here listening to this asshole?

Turning on my heels, I make my way toward my car. I need to get out of here. I can't stand to look at him anymore.

"Camryn," he calls after me.

"It's too late, Harris. It's over. I'll send you your stuff." Digging through my bag for my car keys, I state as I walk, "Don't call me. Don't come over. Nothing. Live your life with your new fiancée." Stopping, I glare over my shoulder at him. "Isabelle seems lovely. She really looks like a woman in love tonight. Guess you're fooling her as you did me." Grabbing my keys quickly before Harris can reach me, I swing around and unlock the car door. But the door slams shut as Harris presses himself against me, his body heat seeping through my skin.

"This isn't over, Camryn," he tells me, his lips touching my ear.

"Don't, Harris," I warn as he presses himself harder against me, my hands bracing themselves against the steel for support.

His lips graze my neck. "I have no choice. My father made sure there was no way I could say, no." Biting my lip, I hate there's a portion of my heart that flutters at his confession. "I told him last week I wanted to marry you."

What! No. How dare he say that.

Pushing back against him, I free myself from his grasp. I whip around and face him.

"I told him I wanted to marry Camryn Starr. This beautiful,

amazing, workaholic event organizer who stole my heart the first time I set eyes on her."

"Wait. What, did you say?"

"That I want to marry you?"

Shaking my head. "No, no. The bit where you told your dad I was an event organizer."

The penny drops for Harris too. "No. He wouldn't do that." His face screws up, and he slams his hand against the car.

Folding my arms across my chest, I say, "I think your father chose my company for a specific reason." Staring directly at Harris, I notice his shoulders slump.

"I can't believe he did this. I knew he wanted our families to merge for the good of his business… but to hurt you like this in the process. I can't ever forgive him for that." Harris rakes his hand through his blond hair.

"You can tell dear old daddy, I've gotten the message loud and clear. I'm no longer in your life."

"Cammie, I'll fix this. I'll fix us." Cupping my face with his palms, he persists. "Please, just give me some time. I'll give up everything for you." His comment catches me off guard, which gives him enough time to lean down and kiss me. Harris' kiss is desperate—he knows he has lost me, but he's giving it one last shot at trying to convince me to stay, to maybe even manipulate me into being his side piece, all because he doesn't love *her*. But he has to for the sake of the family.

What happens when he has to produce an heir?

Is it going to be an immaculate conception?

I think not.

Stupidly I kiss him back, one last time.

Harris rests his forehead against mine before he begins to speak. "I knew you still loved me." Giving me a cocky smile, he actually thinks that his kiss is so powerful that I will simply forget all this bullshit that's happened tonight. I move out of his grasp and to the side, which isn't far as I'm still pressed up against my car.

"Loved. As in past tense, Harris." The confusion on his face is kind of laughable. "You think I'm that easy that one kiss from you wipes away everything that's happened tonight?" Harris takes a couple of steps back as if I've just slapped him. "That was good-bye, Harris. I was saying goodbye. Because that's the last time you will ever have me in your life." With that, I push forward, knocking him back, then pull open the door of my car and jump in before he can stop me. Putting the key in the ignition, the roar of my sports car comes to life.

Harris knocks on my window. I hesitate for a moment but press the button to lower the window.

"This isn't over, Camryn. I'll fight for us," Harris warns me.

"Please, don't. It's a fight you won't win," I tell him. "Enjoy your night, Harris. Congratulations." And with that, I put the car in reverse, which makes him jump out of the way before I run him over, then push my foot down on the accelerator, which kicks up the gravel, and I get the hell out of there, leaving Harris behind in my dust.

4

CAMRYN

"Hey, Liv." My greeting is hollow. I'm exhausted. Defeated. Humiliated. Lady Olivia Pearce is my sister, Ivy's best friend back in England. She owns this gorgeous castle on the England-Scotland border that's been in her family for like five hundred years. We've hired out her family home for my best friend, Vanessa's wedding, to rock star, Christian Taylor, from Dirty Texas.

"Are you okay?" These damn tears haven't stopped falling since arriving back in the city. "Cam, are you okay?" Olivia asks again when I don't answer.

"Harris and I broke up."

"Oh, babe… I'm so sorry. What happened?"

"I organized his engagement party." Olivia falls silent on the other end of the phone.

"Um… what did you say?"

"He's engaged to someone else." The words stab me in the heart, thinking about it.

"What! No. How? I don't understand."

See, even she's confused, so imagine how I feel?

"It was a last-minute party… the clients were particular about not wanting the media to find out that it was being held. It wasn't until the happy couple were introduced to us by their family that I realized it was a party celebrating Harris and a girl called Isabelle's engagement."

Olivia gasps and falls silent, obviously processing what I've told her.

It takes a moment before she finally says, "What did you do?"

"I pretended I didn't know him in front of them. I've worked so hard building up this business, I wasn't going to ruin it over a guy."

"You're so much stronger than I would have been. I would've punched him in the face." Olivia giggles.

"Believe me, I pictured it over and over in my head. But instead, Kimberly faked an emergency and got me the hell out of there. But he came after me."

"Oh no, Cam." Olivia gasps.

"He confessed he still loves me. That his family is forcing him to get married."

"I know what that's like," Olivia's whispers.

In my anger, I forgot she too agreed to marry a guy for her family's business. She's royalty, they have different traditions than some rich guy from Connecticut.

"But you weren't dating someone and leading them on," I tell her.

"No, but…"

I know she's thinking about her time in Monaco. She had a holiday fling with Axel Taylor, Christian's twin brother, who's also in Dirty Texas. We were there for the bachelor and bachelorette parties. I know it sounds bad, but we all encouraged her to have a fling before she marries her womanizing fiancé to meet her family's obligation. I mean, her fiancé's running around town hooking up with every supermodel under the sun. It's all over the tabloids, so why shouldn't she have some fun. It is only fair.

"But you and Axel are not dating, are you?"

"No," she quickly adds. "I gave him a fake number for that very reason."

"A fake number?"

"Yes. Because I'm betrothed to another. What happened in Monaco was a weekend of fun. That's all," Olivia quickly adds.

"But he asked for your number?" I push further.

"Yes. But it was a holiday fling. I told him that."

"Is it going to be awkward... you know, at the wedding?" I'm pretty sure Axel isn't used to a girl giving him a fake number.

"Um..." Olivia hesitates. "I hope not." I place a mental note to keep an eye on that situation. "Enough about me," she says, changing the subject.

"I'm humiliated, Liv." I let out a heavy sigh. "Thankfully, the media didn't know about Harris and me dating. They have seen us pop up here and there together, but not 'together'..." I use air quotes, "... if you know what I mean." And that was my choice, not his. Harris wanted to shout it from the rooftops, but I didn't want me dating one of New York's most eligible bachelors to interfere with my business, or for people to think he's the reason why our business has been so successful. Now with hindsight, I guess it was for the best. Otherwise, I would have page six on my doorstep salivating over what's just happened. It's hard enough seeing the news this morning covering their 'surprise' engagement party, the speculation on how she snagged New York's hottest bachelor. Seeing their smiling faces just makes me want to rage out. "They are everywhere."

"Oh, Cammie... that's horrible."

"It is, but there is a silver lining. We have been inundated with new business." Which is one giant finger in the air to Harris' father. "I can't get away from it all, Liv."

"Why don't you come here," Olivia asks. "I can give Ivy a call. She could come up from London to see you. We can have girl time. You shouldn't have to put up with seeing them running around town as if nothing's happened."

Maybe Olivia's right. I was going to England anyway in a couple of weeks to start setting up for Vanessa and Christian's wedding, but this simply gives me more time to make it perfect. Plus, I haven't seen my sister for a long time, and I miss her.

Ivy lives in London, where she runs her own interior design business. We haven't caught up recently because she's been busy jet-setting around the globe for her celebrity clients.

Maybe this is exactly what I need—girl time.

"That's it. I'm jumping onto the next plane. He can pander to the paps with his new fiancée, but I don't need to see it."

"We can raid the cellar when you get here," Olivia offers.

"Sold!"

Olivia has fancy stuff in her cellar. Royalty always has the good stuff locked away for that special occasion.

"I'm excited," she squeals. "I mean not 'cause Harris is a dick, but we get girl time." Her words make me smile. "Text me your flight details."

We both say goodbye to each other while I scramble to change my flight.

Hitting Kimberly's number on my phone, I place it on my bed, putting it on speaker while I grab my suitcase and madly start throwing clothing and other items into it. I wish I had more time to pack because I honestly have no idea what I'm putting in there.

"Hey," she answers the phone, the sadness in her voice tells me she's worried about me.

This is why I need to get out of town.

"I just wanted to let you know I'm leaving for Olivia's today."

Silence greets me on the other end.

"Excuse me?" Kimberly eventually asks.

"I can work remotely. I'll have my laptop." Grabbing a second suitcase to throw my shoes into, I continue with the job of packing.

"I'm not worried about that. You're going to England... *today?*" I can tell she's thinking I'm being dramatic.

"I can't stay here. I can't pretend nothing's happened while they swan around town as if they're the fucking king and queen of New York society."

"I understand, babe. But it's our busiest time leading up to Christmas."

Dammit! My stomach falls, she's right. I'm being utterly self-ish. The lead up to Christmas is our crucial time and our most lucrative, I will be leaving her in the lurch.

"I can cancel my flight." Guilt hits me like a tonne of bricks.

"Babe, don't do that. I don't want you to cancel. If you need to get away from everything, then go. I can delegate. I'll hire more interns. I'm sure, Seth will love to step up as will Margot," Kimberly adds.

Of course, they will love more responsibility, they're our best planners. I know the company will be in great hands, and I feel less stressed about leaving Kimberly in a mess.

Stopping my frantic packing, I reply, "Thank you."

"I don't blame you for leaving. Just look after yourself, okay?"

"I promise. I'm going to sit in front of the fire, probably cry a million tears and drink a thousand bottles of wine."

"You know he's not worth your tears," Kimberly advises.

"I know. He deserves nothing from me. But I do need to get it out."

"I get it," she says sadly. "Have fun. Don't behave, and I love you, Camryn."

"I love you, too. I owe you big time, Kimmie. I'll see you soon."

"Introduce me to some of those hot rock stars, and we'll call it even."

I laugh. "Consider it done."

My Uber is waiting to take me to the airport, so I make my way downstairs.

"Miss Starr," Billy, my doorman, halts me. "Um... there's been some deliveries for you." I frown because I wasn't expecting anything. "There are a couple of large vases of flowers that have arrived."

I look up and stare at the beautiful bunches of flowers and know exactly who they're from. True to his form, Harris isn't going to let me go. Heading off early to England is most definitely the right idea.

"Billy, I'm on my way to Europe for the holidays. I won't be back for a while. Keep them, and any more deliveries like this give them to your wife." His eyes widen.

"Miss Starr, are you sure?" I nod. "Thank you. She will enjoy them so very much. Would you like me to keep the cards?"

I shake my head. "I already know what they will say, and I'm not interested. Happy Holidays."

And with that now final, I make my way to the airport.

5

NATE

I'm back in New York, finalizing things with Sam Rose, my oldest friend and silent partner, in my latest venture, The Paradise Club Resort. I've decided to turn my extremely successful, ultra-exclusive sex clubs into an island paradise. Let's be honest, living your fantasy for one night sometimes isn't enough. Sam and I have been working on this venture for five years together. He knows resorts, and I have the same experience with clubs. Unfortunately, due to his family's business being of the wholesome variety, he's had to come in as a silent partner.

The resort will be ready to launch over the next couple of months, and we have so much to do. We're planning on a soft launch next year for a select few hundred of our trusted clientele to see if the resort will run smoothly. The hardest part so far has been hiring employees. Good employees. We've moved some from our city locations to the island, but we need to hire so many more. You want the right caliber of employees—discreet, sexy, and most importantly, love having sex. I know some people can fake it for the money, but I want genuine people who love it and are not simply sex addicts. All staff must pass a strict psychological test to make sure we are not employing people who have a dependency or who have had past traumas, which might trigger a bad memory. So, it's been hard.

"Morning, Teresa, you look beautiful this morning." I smile my biggest smirk at Sam's receptionist because I love watching her flustered features when I'm around.

"Morning, Mr. Lewis," she mumbles. "Mr. Rose is waiting for you." Giving her a wink as I pass, I stride on into Sam's office.

"Are you flirting with my receptionist again?" Sam chastises me as I take a seat opposite him.

"Maybe... I love making her blush."

Sam grumbles something which makes me chuckle, then continues with, "Don't touch my staff," he warns, which he does every single time I come into his office.

"Not my fault, I'm irresistible."

Sam rolls his eyes and huffs. "Coffee?" he asks, changing the subject.

I nod.

He busies himself with his fancy coffee machine, then hands me a mug of some Italian concoction, which is actually pretty good.

"So, next month, we have the soft launch of the resort." I nod in agreement. "We will iron out all the kinks then."

"Well, I hope we don't get rid of all the kinks," I add.

Sam glares at me. Geez, someone woke up on the wrong side of the bed this morning. Come on, my jokes are hilarious. "And it's all ready to go?"

"Yes. There will be about two hundred visitors spread out over the month. I think that will give us a good idea of their experiences."

Sam nods as I take a sip of the piping hot liquid.

"And you think Camryn and Kimberly will be ready?" I ask.

Sam suggested Camryn and Kimberly from Starr and Skye Events would be the perfect company to help organize the soft launch and the Grand Opening of the resort. Kimberly's mother and Sam's mother are the best of friends. She's family. He trusts her, which is what we need when dealing with a top-secret resort like ours.

I've met Kimberly a couple of times over the years, and she's great, loads of fun, actually. I haven't met her business partner, Camryn, before, but as she hangs out frequently with Sam and his sister, Harper, I believe she's trustworthy too. Sam and Harper suggested we all go out to dinner to make sure we're all comfortable working together. What I wasn't expecting was for this gorgeous blonde bombshell to walk into the restaurant and knock me off my feet. It's been a while since anyone's done that to me. She's beautiful, intelligent, funny, but most of all, she understood our vision for the resort.

We agreed that before finalizing the contract, we need to take the girls to the New York club to make sure they understood what they're getting into. The last thing I want is for the event planners to freak out over watching people fuck on the beach.

We'd tried to sync our calendars, but there just wasn't a day free for all of us to go. So, Camryn suggested that Kimberly should go as she's single. Sam's face lit up at the prospect.

Of course, a woman like Camryn wouldn't be single.

Lucky bastard, whoever he is.

So, when I saw Camryn Starr walking into the high rollers section of the Monte Carlo casino looking like a fucking Bond girl during my friend's bachelor party a couple of weeks later, I was fucking shocked. I had no idea Camryn was friends with the band, Dirty Texas. Christian Taylor, whose bachelor party I had organized, his fiancée, Vanessa, is best friends with Camryn, something about working in London together.

"Of course. Trust me. They are professionals." Hearing the confidence in Sam's voice.

If only I were a professional in Monaco. I've always lived by the rule 'never mix business and pleasure,' even if my business *is* pleasure. I never mess around with clients. Technically, Camryn isn't a client, but I have hired her to do a job for me. I don't fuck around with people who I've paid to do a job for me because let's be honest, if things head south, she could fuck with my business. I've worked too damn hard to have a disgruntled fling fuck it all up. I'm careful about which staff I hook up with for that exact reason.

Maybe it was the bachelor party vibes, or that she's close friends with mine, that it sort of took away the professionalism. Or maybe it was seeing her walk into my club in Monte Carlo, those green eyes wide and filled with excitement at what was happening before her that made me do it. I'm not proud.

"Kimberly was fine when I took her the other night." This grabs my attention. I've long suspected Sam's had a crush on Kimberly, but they both keep saying they're just friends.

"And?" I push my friend.

"She was fine."

That's not quite the answer I was looking for. "Fine?" I question.

"Yeah. She didn't freak out. She thought it was fun."

My eyes narrow in on him. "And did you help her explore everything the club had to offer?"

Sam looks down at the papers on his desk and uncomfortably begins to fidget with them. "No. I did not," he replies through gritted teeth. But something did happen, though. Before I even get a chance to push him about anything further, his office door swings open and slams just as quickly.

"That motherfucker," Harper curses. Sam and I both look at each other with concern as she slumps in the chair beside me. "That motherfucking bastard," she repeats.

"Are you okay?" Sam tentatively asks.

"No, I'm not." She waves her hands in the air dramatically.

"Did someone hurt you?" The protective brother comes to life, and his face changes from amused to stern.

"Not me. Camryn."

Now Harper has my attention. "Is she okay?"

"No. Her asshole boyfriend just got engaged."

"Camryn's engaged?" The question coming out before I have a chance to hide my reaction.

Sam frowns in my direction, his eyes bore into mine.

"No. He's engaged to another woman."

"I'm not following?" Sam's attention returns to Harper as he jumps in.

I'm as confused as him.

"Harris fucking Edwards…" Harper seethes. Shit! I haven't heard that name in years. Please don't tell me Camryn was dating that douchebag? "… just got engaged to someone else." Harper grabs a newspaper from her bag, slamming it on Sam's desk.

"Camryn's dating Harris Edwards?" My gaze goes to Harper while Sam's reading the paper.

"She was. But not anymore. I mean, the fucker hired her to plan his surprise engagement party. Who does that?"

"He what?"

The door to the office swings open and in walks an exhausted-looking Kimberly. "It was his father, not him who hired us," Kimberly corrects Harper. I stand up, offering her my chair. "I had no idea it was coming. It was a last-minute booking, and we were sworn to secrecy as they didn't want the paps to get hold of it."

Slumping into the chair, I let out a long sigh.

"I'm going to fucking kill him," Sam threatens.

Stand back, buddy, me too.

"Camryn's on her way to England as we speak," Kimberly adds.

"I don't blame her," Harper muses. "He's been all over the social pages this morning with his 'surprise engagement.'"

Grabbing the paper from Sam's desk, I have a look at the black and white photograph of the smiling couple. Looking every inch like the society darlings the newspaper is screaming about.

Sam and I went to college with the dickhead. We never liked

him, and the feeling's mutual. He especially hated me. I totally understand why, finding me in bed with his girlfriend will do that to a guy. To be fair, though, I didn't know they were together. She never mentioned anything, so how was I to know?

"I can't believe she was dating that douche." Not realizing I've said it out loud until three faces look up at me with eyes wide and eyebrows drawn together.

"We went to college with him. He's not the biggest fan of Nate." Sam chuckles. "Especially finding him in bed with his girlfriend."

"She told me she was single," I attempt to defend myself.

"You're just so irresistible," Harper teases.

"She's going to be okay, isn't she?" Sam asks Kimberly.

"Yeah. She just needs to get out of town. So, sorry she's missing the meeting today."

"Totally fine," I add, which is highly unusual for me because bailing on a business meeting for personal issues, I don't normally have time for that shit.

"We'll see her in a couple of weeks, anyway, for the wedding," Harper adds.

That's right, the wedding.

The one we're both friends with.

The same wedding, she will be single at.

Not like that means anything.

6

CAMRYN

We are all drunk and sitting around the open fire in Olivia's cottage, dressed in our pajamas. This is the perfect spot for me to wallow in my misery, it's dark and cold outside, and Olivia even thinks there might be a light dusting of snow overnight. If I weren't so heartbroken, this place would be utterly romantic.

"Men fucking suck." I take a long swig from my glass, the red liquid warming me, my throat, and then my stomach.

"Tell me about it," Ivy cheers in agreement.

"Who needs them?" Olivia adds.

Ivy and I look at her. "What? I am not going to use my vibrator for the rest of my life, Liv. I need a fucking man. I need dick. Cock. Balls even. I need strong arms and whiskers," I tell her. The damn alcohol starts playing with my emotions, and the stupid tears fall down my cheeks again. I try and compose myself before I say, "I could have cheated on Harris when we were in Monaco, but I said no," I confess, the girls all looking at me to continue.

"Who?" Olivia asks.

"Nate," I tell them.

"Who's Nate?" Ivy asks.

"Nate owns The Paradise Club. They are these exclusive sex clubs…" Quickly, I cover my mouth as I'm not meant to say anything about them. I've damn well signed a non-disclosure agreement. Stupid wine.

"I… I wasn't supposed to say anything." Panic laces my body as I try and open the bottle of wine in front of me, but the cork won't budge.

Ivy gives me a look. "I won't say anything, Camryn."

I know she won't, she's my sister, and I trust her with my life.

"So, sex club?" My sister's eyes widen at the mention of it. Ivy's been so busy building her multimillion-dollar interior design business that she hasn't had time to date in recent history. She definitely doesn't have one-night stands, not even to relieve the ache from not being pounded in such a long time. My sister likes to be wined and dined. She needs to have a connection with someone before sleeping with them, which is usually around the fifth date or some weird rule like that. So, the thought of a sex club is probably blowing her mind right now.

"Oh, yes, and it's so fucking hot. Isn't it, Liv?" Smiling as I take a sip of my wine, dropping my friend right into it.

Olivia shoots me an are-you-fucking-serious look from across the room.

"You went to a sex club?" Ivy questions Olivia, who's just as innocent as she is.

"Um… yeah. They took us there." Olivia's cheeks are now bright red, and it's not from sitting beside the fire or from having one too many glasses of red wine either.

"Who?" Ivy asks.

"Dirty Texas," I tell her.

Ivy's eyes widen.

"And Liv here most definitely had some fun. Didn't you?" I give Olivia a wink.

"Um…" Olivia squirms. "She totally banged Axel Taylor," I add.

"What? *The* Axel Taylor." Ivy stares at Olivia as if she doesn't know who her best friend is anymore. I'm finding this all rather hilarious, least it's making me laugh instead of sobbing in a heap.

"Um... so Camryn, what happened with Nate?" Olivia tries to change the subject. "You said you nearly cheated."

Touché, little one. She changed the subject well.

"Nate's my new client." I hiccup—that's not ladylike at all. "And he's so hot. Like *GQ* model hot. Christian Grey, sexy, kinky, billionaire hot." I giggle, like a goddamn schoolgirl, not a thirty-something-year-old woman. "He's a flirt. I loved Harris at the time, and he respected that. Until he described in great detail all the dirty things he would have done to me if I were single."

Ivy and Olivia's jaws drop at my admission as I reminisce about my night...

"I have a confession," I tell Nate as he escorts me away from my friends.

"Really?" Nate raises his brow at me.

God, he's gorgeous, chocolate-colored hair, sapphire blue eyes, wears the hell out of a suit. And flirting comes second nature to him, his deep, timbered voice is made for sin, and he knows what his effect on women is.

"I hated this place."

This grabs his attention.

"I thought Sam said you'd never heard about this before?"

"Sam doesn't know about my past." Nate folds his arms across his chest, those piercing blue eyes trained on me, his body's tense.

"I'm assuming you know about Vanessa, and what happened to her?" I ask him.

"Yes. Christian called and told me what her ex did to her while she was in the hospital."

Nodding my head, I'm glad I don't have to explain that horrific scene again.

"My ex was Lance Burrows." His eyes widen as the name sinks in. *My ex was Vanessa's partner's best friend. He's defending that prick, over him nearly killing Vanessa.* Not only did he defend the violence, but he'd also been cheating on me throughout our entire relationship with the women of The Paradise Club. *"So, I had some reluctance to work with you."*

"You did?" He seems surprised.

"It was a horrible time for me." A shiver runs down my spine thinking about that time.

"Why did you change your mind?" He tilts his head in curiosity.

"Sam and Harper." He nods his head in understanding. *"Plus, I'm the fucking best."* This makes him chuckle. *"Which means someone will mess up your Grand Opening, and I can't let that happen to my friends."* I can't take my eyes away from his smile, his whole face is lit up.

"I like a woman who's sure of herself." The smile falls from his face as his voice drips with heat.

"You might not be saying that when I'm bossing you around," I reply, raising a brow at him as I take a sip of my cocktail.

"I don't mind a woman on top." Those blue eyes stare at me intensely. We are veering into dangerous territory, but a little flirtation doesn't hurt anyone.

"Good. It's my favorite position."

"I think you're going to fit in well around here."

That delicious smirk doesn't leave his face, the first signs of his five o'clock shadow mar it.

"Come on, let me show you around." He moves fluidly, his long legs eating up the distance between us, his hand reaches out and touches the small of my back. It ignites a fire within me, my skin prickles with goosebumps. I know we both feel the spark and look at each other, equally confused by the connection. Nate is the first to break the tension between us, moving me back from the office to the bar area.

Our friends are long gone. I wonder what they're doing?

"This way... I hope you're prepared for what you're about to see? If at any moment you feel uncomfortable, let me know, and we can leave."

I turn and look at him with an irritated posture, my hands resting firmly on my hips. "I'm a big girl. I can handle it."

"I'm sure you can." He grins. "Safeword for the club is Paradise. You can use it anytime you want." My eyes narrow on him. He thinks I won't be able to handle this, I'll show Mr. Sex Club what I am made of.

I'm no prude.

As we enter, I am a little more shocked than I thought I would be. I considered myself as sexually adventurous, but seeing it in front of me in Technicolor is a little confronting. You feel like you've intruded on someone's personal space, but once you get used to seeing people in various stages of undress and sexual positions, you understand how beautiful it all is. How safe everyone feels. How free they all look knowing no one is there judging them for liking or doing something that normal society won't or can't accept.

"It's beautiful, isn't it?" Nate's breath is warm against my skin, prickling it with goosebumps. Every nerve ending in my body is overstimulated, and just the action of the gentle brush of Nate's arm against my body makes me throb with need. My skin is almost itching with desire.

"I can see it on your face, you want to be a part of this. Right?"

"Yes," I reply without hesitation, my voice breathless.

"I bet you'd look beautiful letting go. Men would rush to feast on you. Every part of your body would be touched, caressed, adored. They would try and wring out every last drop of your orgasm."

Yes. Yes. Yes.

Nate's hand runs down my side. "I would give anything to see you let go, Camryn."

My chest rises and falls quickly, with my heart rate accelerating. "Nate." My voice is soft as he presses himself against me. "I'm seeing someone." My teeth sink into my lip, almost causing it to split while my body silently curses me for not taking him up on his offer.

"I know. Sorry." But he doesn't move away from me, I can still feel his heat at my back. Silence falls as we try and compose the desire swirling between us. "But if you were single, the things I would do to you…" he whispers in my ear.

"What? What would you do?"

I'm playing with fire now.

Coming back to the now, I continue, "I wanted to come right there and then."

Ivy and Olivia simply stare at me, I know they're judging me.

"I'll be looking after the Grand Opening of his first sex resort."

Both girls nod their heads, mesmerized.

"I can't stop thinking of Monaco." I take a sip of my wine. "I bet he knows how to fuck." Waving my glass around in the air, I continue, "You don't own a sex club and be shit in bed, right?"

"I guess he would have lots of practice," Ivy adds.

"Are you slut-shaming my client?" I turn to my sister.

"What? No!" She raises her voice with each word.

"Do you think he sleeps with the staff?" Olivia asks.

"Probably. The staff is hot." Shrugging my shoulders, I smile.

I wonder if he uses the perks of his job? Of course, he does.

I wonder if I can too? No. Probably not.

But I am single now. If I can't sleep with Nate, can I at least sleep with one of the staff? I bet they know how to fuck, seeing as it's their job.

"You have a funny look on your face," Ivy questions.

"I was just pondering if I could sleep with any of the staff."

"Cam," Ivy chastises me. "No more wine for you. You've turned into a horn dog."

"Horn dog?" I frown at my sister.

"You've just broken up with your boyfriend, and now you're thinking about screwing around with prostitutes."

"Are you fucking serious?" I raise my voice.

"Guys." Olivia tries to bring down the simmering tension.

"When was the last time you had sex, Ivy?" My sister instantly turns red at my question. "Exactly. Maybe if you got laid, then you wouldn't have a major stick up your ass."

"Cam!" Olivia warns me.

"I'm off to bed." Throwing my hands up in the air, I keep going. "Jet lag." As I stumble over the couch, trying to walk away in a huff, but for some reason—mainly alcohol—I fail miserably at it.

Lying on my bed, I'm staring up at the dark ceiling. The only light filtering through my room is from my cell and the person I am texting.

"Cam," Ivy calls from the door.

Shit! Throwing my cell to the floor, it's as if I've just been busted doing something I shouldn't have been doing. *That's because you were doing something you shouldn't have been doing.*

"Go away." Yes, I'm acting like a child.

My sister ignores me and comes into my bedroom. She jumps into my bed and shoves me over to the other side.

"I'm sorry," she says into the darkness. "I didn't mean to judge."

I stay silent for a little bit, stewing because she hurt me, then I whisper, "I'm sorry, too." Sitting up on my bed, I turn and look over at her through the darkness.

"I don't mean to be a prude." She lets out a quiet sigh. "I wish I was more like you." *Huh! What did she just say?* "I wish I was more carefree. More adventurous. I admire you, Camryn."

"Ivy."

She shakes her head. "It's been two years since I've slept with someone," she confesses to me.

Holy shit! My poor sister, she is about to burst from all that pent-up sexual frustration.

"You were right. I do have a stick up my ass."

"Maybe you should stick something else up there instead." I let out a small giggle and elbow her. This makes us both burst out laughing.

"Maybe! I'm sorry about earlier."

"Ignore me, I'm drunk."

"I was being judgmental." She nervously plays with her hands. "And maybe... a little jealous."

"Jealous?" I am seemingly surprised by my sister's admission.

"I've never done anything adventurous. Sexually, I mean," Ivy whispers the last bit. "And now Olivia's done something crazy." Oh, I get it. She's feeling a little left out. "And now you've been to a sex club."

"There's going to be a stack of single rock stars at this wedding. Why not branch out a little with one of them?"

Ivy turns to face me. "But it's a wedding." She seems a little shocked, which makes me giggle. *Oh, this poor little thing.*

"Exactly. Perfect time for a little sexual exploration, right?" I give her a nudge.

"I doubt a rock star will be interested in me."

Is she serious? My sister's a knockout.

"Babe, they're going to be all over you." She shrugs my compliment away. "You're gorgeous, even if you are dressed like a Victorian marm."

"No, I don't," she argues.

"Let me give you a makeover..." I flutter my eyelashes at her. "It will make me feel so much better." Ivy doesn't seem convinced.

I can tell by the lines that are forming between her eyebrows and how she's tilting her head. "Please... come on."

"Fine," she says through gritted teeth.

"Yay. We're going to have so much fun."

Ivy grumbles beside me, but then I see the flicker of a smile in the darkness. "We cool?" Ivy asks.

"Yeah, we're cool."

"Okay, then, night." Ivy jumps out of my bed and heads off out the door.

"Night, Ivy."

My sister closes the door behind her with a soft click.

Picking up my cell, I continue texting with someone I shouldn't be.

7

NATE

*C*amryn: *Hoping the offer is still on the table.*

I stare at my cell, not quite believing what I'm reading. It's late here, so it has to be really late over there. I'm assuming she's had one too many glasses of something, and she'll probably regret it in the morning.

Me: *I heard what happened. I'm sorry.*

The little bubbles dance across my screen, then disappear. I wait and wait to wonder what she's going to say. Twenty minutes go by, and she hasn't messaged me back. You need to leave it Nate. She's just had her heart broken, you shouldn't be thinking about all the things you promised to do to her if she was single. That was a momentary blip in Monaco when I stepped over a line that I shouldn't have.

My cell beeps, alerting me to her message, so I grab my phone quickly.

What am I doing? Waiting for a girl to message me. That's not me. That's not me at all.

So then, why is my body tense while I am waiting for her to message me back? Because Camryn Starr intrigues you.

Something about her has hooked you, and now you want to know more. You're not supposed to want to, but you do. Maybe it's because I'm so used to women being gold diggers, calculating my net worth by the assets I have. Or they see me as some kind of trophy—having sex with the king of sex clubs, thinking I'm some kind of fucking porn star.

Look, I never leave a woman unsatisfied, but just because I own sex clubs doesn't make me some kind of sexual deviant. Camryn Starr is a beautiful woman, blonde hair, curves, legs that go for miles, and the most mesmerizing green eyes. But it's not just her looks, it's her intelligence that turns me on. Someone who can keep up with me in the business stakes with her drive and determination to be the best, it's a fucking aphrodisiac for me.

I think as soon as I met her, that I'd met my match. She didn't take my bullshit, she wasn't afraid to disagree with my ideas, and she was always one step ahead of me, and that was fucking hot. This life I live is a lonely one. Yes, I am surrounded by beautiful people on a daily basis, people who are always up for some fun, but I don't know, it would be nice to share what I have with someone.

I've tried to date while in this business, but either the women are jealous and think I'm cheating on them all the time, or they think because I own sex clubs, I'm not into monogamy.

Camryn Starr can't be the woman for me, especially as she's currently nursing a broken heart.

Camryn: I'm drunk.

. . .

Me: Don't blame you.

Camryn: I'm in England.

Me: I heard.

Camryn: Does everyone know?

Me: No. I was having a meeting with Sam when Harper and Kimberly popped in.

The bubbles appear again only to disappear. What surprises me next is the fact that my cell begins ringing, and 'Camryn Starr' is flashing across the screen. I panic for a couple of moments, then pick up.

"Hey." *Yeah, real smooth, Nate.*

"Hey," she says sadly. "I don't know why I called you. I'm drunk," she tells me again. There's a light slur in her words. "I shouldn't have sent that text to you."

"I probably shouldn't have replied."

Silence falls between us.

"I have a question?" She's changing the direction of the conversation.

"Shoot."

"Is the resort going to be like the clubs?"

Well, that wasn't what I thought she was going to ask.

"Yes, but better." This I can do, talk about work. "Think of the

most luxurious island you've ever seen… crystal blue water, white
sand… then think about your most forbidden desires."

She lets out a little moan.

No. No. No.

Please don't make those kinds of sounds, Camryn.

My dick twitches as if he's been summoned.

Now is not the time.

Work! Think of work.

"The resort caters to anything you want."

"Anything?"

Why is there curiosity in her tone?

Is she after something?

"Yes… anything."

Silence falls between us again.

I'm going to hell for the question I'm about to ask, "What is it
that you desire, Camryn?" I can hear her heavy breathing on the
other end of the phone.

"I…" she hesitates.

"It's my job to deliver desires, yours are safe with me." I am
pushing her for my own personal perversion.

"I want to be surrounded by men."

Crap! That's not what I had in mind, but this isn't about me.

"But…" she hesitates. "I want them to have control."

This is a common theme for very successful women. They
control so much in their real life that in their fantasy life, they want
someone else to take the reins.

"I want to be blindfolded." My dick throbs as she continues, "I
don't want to know who's fucking me or how many." Fuck me
dead! "Does that make me a slut?" Her question is almost a
whisper.

"Never. You're a woman who knows what she wants." A tiny
huff echoes through the phone. "I could easily arrange this." *As
long as I am one of the men,* I think. But she doesn't need to know
that.

"Really?" She doesn't seem convinced. "How many men?"

"As many as you desire. We have staff on call to cater to your desires." Her breathing increases as silence falls between us. I wonder if her nipples are hard. Do they ache pressing against the fabric of her clothing? I bet if she sunk two fingers into her cunt, it will be wet. "It's their job to serve." I hear her swallow, hard. "Is this something you would like to try?" *Or is this just a fantasy she uses to get off*, I continue the question in my mind.

"I don't know." I can hear the hesitation in her voice. "I don't think it would be professional of me."

Oh, so she does want to try, but it's because she's working her moral compass, and it's telling her no.

"During the soft opening, we are welcoming all comments and reviews of our facilities."

"Wait! What?" she questions me.

"During the soft launch, I'm fine with you enjoying the facilities. But, for the Grand Opening I would like you to refrain. Is that okay?"

"Of course. I would never leave a client."

Why is her professionalism getting me hard?

"Would I be able to bring someone with me?"

Interesting.

"Female or male?"

"Female." Relief floods me. I have no idea why.

"I think that would be okay, but only for the soft launch."

There's a slight giggle which makes me smile.

"Have you tried the facilities?" Her voice is becoming more confident now.

"At the resort? Not yet. But at my clubs? Yes, of course."

"Oh... which has been your favorite?"

Wait. What? How did we get to me?

"I don't know." I am feeling a tiny bit flustered, which is very unlike me.

"I told you mine... now you tell me yours?" Flirtation is peppering her tone.

I am crossing over a line. It's something I never do, but she's intrigued me now. Plus, we're only talking. Not doing.

"We offer a BJ wakeup call at the resort. I wouldn't mind trying that."

"Really?" She seems surprised, and I can tell by the higher inflection at the end of the word.

"I'm a simple man. Nothing beats a good blow job."

"Okay, noted. Continue..."

Hang on. What does she mean 'noted'?

"The outdoor showers at the resort might be fun. A glass wall is exposed in the rainforest so anyone can watch as they pass."

"So, you're an exhibitionist, Nate?"

"Depends on the woman." *Stop flirting, you moron.*

"What else?" Camryn's voice lowers, and I am questioning if this is turning her on?

"There's the dark room."

"The dark room?" Camryn repeats.

"It's not for everyone." I continue by telling her, "It's a room, shrouded in darkness. You have no idea who or how many people are in the room with you. Every couple of minutes a light turns on for a couple of seconds, and you can see for a moment the naked bodies around you, then you are sent back into darkness. It heightens all of your senses."

"Oh." Well, that sounded more like a moan. "And you have tried this?"

"A couple of times. At first, it's a little daunting, but as soon as the sounds, the hands, the mouths touch you, you're lost to your senses."

"How do you know if it's male or a female mouth on you?" she questions.

"You don't," I tell her truthfully.

"Oh."

"You have to try it for yourself. Then you will see what I mean?" Because in the end you don't care, need has taken over, and your desires are fulfilled.

"If you take me, I will. I trust you."

Her words hit me hard. *She trusts me.*

"I wouldn't let anything happen to you, Camryn."

"I know you wouldn't." I can hear the smile in her voice. "What else does the resort have?"

"Our bungalows each have a designated host, who will cater to anything you desire... a bottle of champagne, a massage, a fuck." She inhales a sharp breath, but I continue, "Each host is hand-picked for that guest. They are matched exactly to your desires. Nothing, within reason, is off-limits."

"So, I could ask for a massage with a happy ending?"

"And they would deliver it for you," I tell her.

"There is a grotto hidden under a waterfall where anything can happen. There is a whole section of the resort dedicated to BDSM and other kinks and fetishes. There are whole areas for voyeurs and exhibitionists. Anything goes at any time of the day, just not in the restaurants. No one needs to see that while sitting down to a three-course meal."

This makes her giggle.

"Clothes are optional everywhere except for the food areas, you must be clothed to eat in the restaurants."

"Exactly! Who wants to see balls at breakfast?"

We both laugh.

"It's nice hearing you laugh."

"The last twenty-four hours haven't really given me anything to laugh about."

"He's going to realize what a mistake it was to let a woman like you go."

"Thanks," she replies quietly.

"I hope you realize how incredible you are, Camryn."

Silence falls between us. Perhaps I have overstepped the mark.

"I better go… jet lag and one too many wines have kicked in. Thanks for the chat."

"Anytime."

"I'll see you at the wedding. Safe travels, Nate."

"See you then."

And with that, she's gone, and my dick is standing at attention.

I'm going to have to do something to relieve that.

8

NATE

C amryn and I haven't stopped texting since that first initial night. Weeks of flirtish text exchanges, always stopping short of phone sex. Sometimes we talk about work or the updates with the resort. I tell her about the day a monkey jumped onto a boat from the mainland and caused havoc on the island, and the videos were pretty funny. Or the time someone found a green tree snake curled up under the lid of the toilet. We laughed over these crazy stories.

Then there are the funny memes we keep sending to each other. Honestly, I feel like I'm in high school again. Every time my phone beeps, I jump and open the text message right away.

It's my addiction.

She's my addiction.

I know it has to stop because, let's be honest, nothing is ever going to happen, but I actually enjoy her company. Well, her digital company anyway.

We chat most nights as she's going to bed. The time difference is pretty good, and usually, I'm still in my office in New York. Thankfully, over the last few days, I've been working from home, and no one can see my stupid ass while I'm talking to her.

Camryn's a friend. A super sexy, funny, beautiful, intelligent, hypnotic, flirty friend. I think you get the idea.

Due to some drama down on the island, I had to fly down there before heading to England, which meant I've missed the rehearsal dinner and didn't arrive until very late.

Camryn asked me to text her when I arrived in my room.

Me: Made it. I'm here. It's fucking cold.

I'm not expecting her to answer me as she has to be up early tomorrow for the wedding. Thankfully, someone turned the heating on in my room. Otherwise, I would probably freeze.

Looking around at the medieval stonework, I didn't get to see much of the castle as I arrived because it was so dark. But, walking through the hallways and seeing all the priceless artwork and tapestries hanging on the walls, it's pretty cool to know that your ancestors before you walked the same halls.

Fine—I'm a history buff.

Camryn: Yay. You made it. Hope you got everything done. You're so dramatic it's not as cold as New York.

Me: Why are you not asleep? GO TO BED.

Chuckling as I look at my watch, it's past midnight.

Camryn: Bossy, much?
Her texts make me smile.

Me: Just worried about your beauty sleep.

Camryn: Are you saying I need beauty sleep? ;(

Me: You know you don't.

Camryn: Is that a compliment Nate Lewis?

Me: GO TO SLEEP, CAM

Camryn: Fine.

Bet she's rolling her eyes at me. I can hear it in her tone. Then there's a knock at the door. *Who the hell could that be at this hour?* Opening up the old wooden door, the last person I thought I would see standing there is Camryn Starr.

"Hey."

"Hey."

Awkwardness falls between us. She has a woolly robe wrapped around her. Her blonde hair is pulled up in a messy bun, and there's no sign of makeup. As I look down, she's wearing fluffy slippers.

I shouldn't find any of this sexy.

But for some reason, I do.

"I just..." She seems lost for words, so I wait for her to continue. "I've had way too much champagne, and I just wanted to see you." She bites her bottom lip while those green eyes look up at me through her lashes, and I'm instantly hard. Shit! Fuck! This isn't good. "Now, I have.... I've got to go." She turns on her heels and hurries to walk away.

"Camryn." I take a few steps, reach out and grab her arm, spinning her around to face me. The silence of the castle falls between us. "It's nice seeing you again."

My heart is thumping in my chest. There's this invisible line between us, and we're skirting around it, tiptoeing the edges. We haven't taken that leap yet.

She's so beautiful.

I want to kiss her.

I can't.

Not until after the Grand Opening, then it's game on.

"Nice seeing me?" Confusion crosses her face when she tilts her head to the side as she frowns, then she pulls her arm from mine.

Dammit! She's hurt.

"It is," I tell her.

Which now, judging from her high chin and glare was the wrong answer.

"Right. Better go. Got to get my beauty sleep," she says sarcastically.

I'm missing something, and I don't know what?

Camryn begins to turn to walk away.

"Cam?"

She lets out a sigh as she turns back around. "It's late, Nate."

Reaching out, I let my hand caress her face. She closes her eyes for a second as I let my thumb fall across her lips before letting my hand fall away. "I can't cross the line, Camryn."

She nods in understanding. "I can't either, Nate."

Shit! This sucks.

"No matter how much I want to."

There's a weak smile followed by a sigh. "I better go."

"After the Grand Opening," I blurt out.

She fumbles then grimaces. "There won't be a line?" A small smile falls across her face. "After the Grand Opening," she says, slowly nodding her head.

"Night, Camryn."

"Night, Nate."

I watch her sexy as fuck ass as she shuffles back to her room.

That's only a couple of months.

I can wait. I think.

✤✤✤✤✤✤✤✤

Fuck!

This is going to be so much harder than I thought.

Camryn looks so beautiful walking down the aisle, so much so I couldn't keep my eyes off her. No offense to the gorgeous bride, Vanessa, she looked radiant, of course, but Camryn dressed in her bridesmaid dress, which made her tits push up, well, it made me uncomfortable that's for sure.

I hate going to weddings! Mainly because any single woman at the event has hearts in their eyes, and they are looking for a man to drag down the aisle next. That's not for me.

"Hi." A pretty blonde slides up to me as I sit at my table, alone. I smile at her, but I'm not in the mood to flirt. I can't take my eyes off another blonde that is currently in another man's arms. Cam's laughing and having fun as he swings her around on the dance floor. I notice his hand is sitting way too low near her ass.

I don't fucking like it.

My anger is brewing as I sip on my tumbler of scotch, the liquid sliding down way too easily right now.

"Did you like the wedding?" The blonde tries to gain my attention, but it's not working.

"Yeah. It was good."

"How do you know the couple?" she continues to probe.

"I'm friends with Christian," I tell her. "Who I see is free. Please excuse me." Standing before she can even protest, I head on over to the bridal table.

"Congratulations, you two." I lean forward and kiss Vanessa, then slap my friend Christian on the back. The man's utterly besotted with his new wife.

"Thanks, man. Best day of my life," he tells me with a beaming smile on his face. "Maybe one day it'll be you." He gives me a smirk, and I roll my damn eyes.

"Yeah, right, don't hold your breath." I chuckle, my eyes looking over to where Camryn is laughing and flirting with the guy who's way too close for my liking.

Vanessa pulled away from our conversation, and as she leaves, she says, "Sorry. Excuse me, guys."

"That's Johnny from Sons of Brooklyn," Christian points out.

I don't care.

"Right," I reply and take a sip of my scotch.

"I think they've hooked up in the past."

Why do I need to know that?

Looking at the two of them, seeing the familiarity between them, I can see he's right. Johnny's hand is running all over her as she looks up at him with flirty eyes. There isn't a line between them, and if there was, I could tell he's happy to cross over it.

Fuck!

"That's got nothing to do with me."

Christian eyes me suspiciously. "You sure about that?" He chuckles. "Because you haven't been able to take your eyes off of them."

"We are working together."

"So, I've heard."

He takes a long drink of his beer. "That's all?" he asks.

"Christian," I warn him.

"She's beautiful," he tells me.

"I have eyes." Not meaning to get cranky with him on his wedding day, he just laughs at me. He sees the lies behind everything that I'm saying.

"Vanessa and I worked together." Yeah, I know this. "Five years of this push and pull between us made for a difficult time."

"Does it get easier?" Looking over at him, I am questioning if maybe he can tell me how to handle this situation building between Camryn and me.

"Fuck, no. The pull was too much. So, I married her." He roars with laughter as he slaps me on the back. *Well, that's no fucking help.* "But I feel ya, buddy." His voice lowers to a whisper, "Cam's a nice girl. She deserves someone who wants to look after her. Especially after that douche she was with."

I remember Camryn telling me about her ex, the one who defended the man who attacked her best friend. Then I remember what Harris did to her.

"If you don't think you can be that man, then move along."

Turning my head, I stare at Christian. "We can't."

He nods his head. "Then let her go until you can."

Christian's right, I need to put some distance between us.

The music has slowed down, and Camryn has wrapped her arms around the guy's neck. His palms are gripping her ass cheeks, and his fingers are digging into her flesh.

Fuck him! I am drowning myself in scotch.

"Whatever happens tonight," Christian begins. "Don't hold it against her."

He's right. Just because I can't have her doesn't mean—

Well, no, I don't want to think about her sleeping with that young douchebag.

"Congrats again, man." We shake hands, and I head out of the ballroom.

Camryn can do whatever she wants.

I'm simply not in the mood to watch.

9

NATE

Once I let my ego go, I had a pretty awesome night. Christian's friends are fun. We watched the fireworks in the back garden just before midnight while drinking scotch. A light dusting of snow had fallen, and the garden looked like a Christmas wonderland.

I decide to leave the group I am with and explore a little more of the castle. The history nerd inside of me is getting the better of me after one too many scotches. Running my hand along the cold stone, I think, *if these walls could talk.* I wonder if this wedding was as crazy as the ones that may have happened here previously.

Rounding the corner, I stumble upon Camryn, shivering as she's watching the snow fall from the darkening sky.

"Cam?"

Turning at the sound of my voice, I see the tears falling down her cheeks.

Shit! I rush toward her, pull off my tuxedo jacket, and wrap it around her trembling body, then pull her into my arms. She nuzzles my chest with her face.

"You're frozen," I state the obvious.

We stay like this for some time, quiet, until she stops crying.

"I'm sorry." A flush creeps across her cheeks as she pulls herself back from my arms. "I've ruined your shirt." Looking down at the makeup smudges right across the front of my white shirt. It's ruined. Who cares? I have a million more.

"Are you okay?" My hands rub her freezing arms, trying to get some warmth back into her body.

"I just..." She looks around as if realizing where she is.

"Come." I grab her hand, pulling her back inside. Stepping down the hallway, which thankfully is empty, then up the stone staircase to the next floor, she follows without question. I reach my room and push the wooden door open, then slam it shut behind us. I let go of her hand and walk over to the mini-bar, then pour each of us a glass of whiskey and hand her the crystal tumbler. "Here, this will warm you."

She takes a tentative sip, then she throws back the entire contents of the tumbler stunning me.

"I must look like crap?"

"You've looked better." I smile at her while she stares at me for a couple of beats, then laughter falls from her lips.

"Thanks for not bullshitting me." Camryn walks over and pours herself another glass. She catches her reflection in the mirror as she passes. "Jesus, I do look like shit." She licks her finger and tries to rub off the smeared mascara.

"What's going on?"

Camryn lets out a heavy sigh, turning back to me, sipping hers slowly this time. "I guess the whole wedding, love, happily-ever-after vibe kind of got to me."

"Harris is a dick."

"You know him?"

She's seemingly surprised by my outburst, so I nod. That dickhead is the last man I want to be talking about, but I will answer her. "Yeah, we went to college together. He was your typical spoiled rich kid."

"And you weren't?" She raises a brow at me.

"Oh, no," I smirk. "I was definitely a rich kid... I just wasn't a dick." Camryn laughs. "We never got on. Didn't help that I slept with his girlfriend." She chokes on her drink. "In my defense, I didn't know they were dating at the time." I am trying to redeem myself, but she simply shakes her head. "Years later, he still holds it against me." Camryn takes another sip of her whiskey. I watch her pink lips moisten with the amber liquid, then watch in slow motion as her tongue comes out and swipes across her lips collecting the residue. My body groans internally in appreciation. "How did you guys meet?" Curiosity's getting the better of me.

"We literally ran into each other outside a coffee shop. We both ended up covered in coffee." She smiles at the memory. "He asked me out as the hot coffee soaked through my clothing. I thought it was kind of ballsy after he ruined my suit." She shrugs. "I decided to take a chance, and well... we all know what happened."

"It's not your fault."

"I know." She lets out a sigh. "Just shit taste in men, I guess."

"Hope that doesn't include me?"

"Jury's still out." She smiles, and it's warm. "I'm sorry you had to see me like this." She moves her hand around, waving it up and down her body.

"You don't have to apologize."

"I do." Standing and straightening her shoulders, she continues, "You've hired me to do a job. I've overstepped so many boundaries I wouldn't normally overstep with clients. For some reason, Lord only knows why, I have with you." She lets out a sigh.

"Cam, look around..." She glances about the room seeming confused by my statement. "We are at our friend's wedding." She nods her head. "Who suggested I hire you?"

"Sam and Harper."

"And how do I know them?"

She shrugs her shoulders.

"Sam is my partner and best mate. Harper I've known just as long, and your business partner, Kimberly, I met over the years through Sam." She nods her head. "We don't have a normal business relationship. Our worlds are too intertwined without us even knowing it."

"True." She gives me a small smile. "I've worked so damn hard to be taken seriously in my industry. I just…" She sighs. "My reputation is everything."

Ah, now, I understand where she's coming from.

"I think you're brilliant. Honestly, from our first meeting, it was your intelligence that attracted me." Moving toward her, I say, "Then Monaco happened." Camryn looks up at me. "I had no idea you were going to be there. But I was happy you were."

"You were?" she questions.

"Yeah." Nodding my head. "I was looking forward to talking to you again. Mainly about business but—"

"But?" she interrupts.

"You looked like a fucking goddamn Bond girl walking into the casino that night." I run my hand through my hair. "I'm ashamed I forgot all about your business qualifications and could only think about how attracted I was to you." Stepping closer. "Then I saw your face light up with curiosity as I took you around the club. I could see the way your body responded to what you were watching. I knew you had a partner, but I didn't care in that moment." Camryn bites her lip. "You're one of the most beautiful women I have ever seen."

"If I were single then…" Camryn lets the words fall away. She doesn't have to finish them.

"I'm glad you weren't." Her mouth falls open, and her head jerks back, but I notice her surprise. "If we had slept together that night, I don't know if I would have taken you seriously."

Oh shit! Her back straightens, and a slow disbelieving head shake is followed by, "Are you serious right now?"

"Not like that, Camryn." I realize straight away how bad that sounded. She crosses her arms across her chest. "Let me explain! I meant I wouldn't have let this friendship develop between us." She softens a little dropping her arms to her sides. "I like what we have." Quickly, I add, "I like I can call you when something happens at work, and you get it. I like how you tell me about your day and about the disasters that occur. It actually helps my mood." This makes Camryn smile. "I like getting your text messages before you go to bed. Even the crazy memes you send me."

"They're good, right?" She chuckles.

"Yeah, they are."

"I feel like you're about to give me the whole... it's-not-you-it's-me speech." Her eyes narrow. "Are you?"

"No." Quickly defending myself, "I'm just saying..." I push my fingers through my hair. "Honestly, I have no idea what I'm saying. Other than... I like and respect you." My hand falls to the back of my neck, and I give it a rub because I have no idea what the hell is spilling out of my mouth anymore.

"Thank you." Camryn smiles at me. She then takes a couple of steps toward me. My body tenses as she wraps her arms around me, but slowly, I do the same. We stay like this for a while. Her floral scent swirls around my nose as I subtly try and breathe her in without her noticing. The longer the embrace continues, the thicker the sexual tension becomes.

Camryn's fingers grip the back of my white shirt and hold tight. Closing my eyes, I attempt to think of anything but the feeling of her against me.

My hands run along the curve of her back, subconsciously.

No. What am I doing?

The night air shifts around us, the large room feeling like with every tick of the clock, it shrinks a little more, closing in on us. Both of us not daring to look at the other because if we do, I'm not sure if I will be able to stop.

I let my hand move further down her body and over the curve of her ass. She doesn't move, nor does she push me away. I let my fingers dig into the flesh, pulling her hard against me.

My dick springs to life, feeling her warm body against mine. Shit!

"I shouldn't be touching you like this," I whisper my meek objections into her ear with a warm breath.

"Me, either." Camryn's hands slide down my back until she has my ass in her palms, pulling me closer to her until there is no space between us. "As long as there are clothes between us, we're fine. We aren't doing anything wrong, Nate." Her lips move across my chest as she speaks, the warm sensation sending goosebumps over my body.

As long as there's a barrier between us, we can't go too far.

Can we?

10

CAMRYN

W hat the hell am I doing?
But he feels so good.

So warm.

So hard.

I can feel every muscle tense under my touch. His hard planes press against me. Even his ass is tight.

What are we doing? We keep giving each other mixed signals.

We push and pull against the other—I want you, I can't have you.

We know we shouldn't be doing this, but there are so many words that have been spoken between us.

I respect you.

I like you.

Let's be friends.

I think you're beautiful.

In all honesty, I just want to fuck him.

I shouldn't be thinking about that after breaking up with Harris.

It's been over a month, Camryn. Harris is definitely not thinking of you as he fucks his fiancée.

That image instantly churns my stomach.

But there is something about Nate. If you take away the kinky sex club owner, the expensive suits, the cocky attitude, underneath it all, he seems relatively normal.

You have only been texting with him for a month. The stupid voice inside my head is being all rational and shit.

Seeing Vanessa and Christian get their happy ever after after so many difficulties—from the night he saved her from a handsy executive to rescuing her from her violent ex, to sitting by her side telling her how beautiful she is after she'd had a double mastectomy to save her life—it made me feel like anything is possible. This is Christian Taylor, rock star, and famed womanizer, the last man you'd think would want to settle down and stay faithful to Vanessa. But he does, and he loves her. Now, Ness is knocked up with twins, and their family is going to be complete.

Yeah, okay… I'm jealous.

I thought I was going to have a happily ever after with Harris, except he's now having that with someone else, the scumbag.

Too much champagne, coupled with heartache during a wedding, led to my mini-breakdown in the fucking snow. I thought I could have a little cry and then walk back inside and let Johnny take me back to his room so he could finish what he promised me he would. Except now, I'm here in the arms of the one man I shouldn't be, and, in all honesty, I don't know if I care. I just want to feel something, anything again.

Moving my hands from his delicious ass, I run my nails up his back, which makes Nate groan. I can feel him hard against my stomach. Still, we both refuse to look at each other because I know when we do, the spell will be broken.

Turning my head, I bite his nipple through the white tuxedo shirt.

"Cam…" he groans. "Fuck!" The tortured words coming from his mouth are turning me on. A man like Nate Lewis, who has access to anyone in the world, is coming undone under my touch.

It's an aphrodisiac and drives me more. I move my head and bite the other nipple. "Jesus," he groans appreciatively.

His fingers grip my ass tightly.

"As long as we have clothes on, nothing's really happening, right?" That's the moment I look up and into those blue eyes, which have turned a deep sapphire color as desire swirls behind them.

"Right," he agrees.

My hand moves over the bulge in his tuxedo pants, and I grip onto his thickness.

"Fuck," he curses, biting his lip. His chest heaves as he tries to gain control of himself.

"Tell me to stop, Nate."

Those sapphire eyes widen with lust. "I don't want you to stop, Camryn." A smile falls across my face as I rub him harder with my hand. I don't stop. Our eyes are locked. Next thing I know, he's pushing me back against the wooden desk. His chest is heaving while my heart is racing. He picks me up and places my backside on the edge.

Fuck! That was hot.

"What are the rules?" he questions me.

Huh? What does he mean?

"The rules, Cam? How much clothing are we allowed?" Pushing his hips between my legs, I can feel his length against me. "What can go?"

"Take off your shirt," I tell him. He has a tank on underneath that still counts as a shirt. He quickly takes off the makeup-stained tuxedo shirt and throws it to the side, showing his bronzed, toned arms. "Pants, too." He raises a brow and slowly begins to unbuckle his belt. It disappears behind him somewhere. Then he's pushing his tuxedo pants to the floor. He kicks his shoes off, then his socks, and steps out of the pants. He's wearing black boxer briefs, and the head of his dick is poking out the top of them.

Biting my lip, I appreciate the thick tip.

"What are you wearing underneath?" he questions me.

"Just underwear."

"Take off your dress, Camryn."

Oh, demanding Nate is hot.

Slowly, I unzip the back of my bridesmaid's dress. He moves away and starts shuffling through his bags until he finds another tank top. "Here."

I let the straps of my dress fall, exposing my barely-there lace bra, giving him a glimpse at my ample chest. I know men appreciate boobs, but those eyes darken even more as he catches my breasts. He moans as I slip on the white tank over the top, taking away his view. Nate steps forward and helps me shimmy out of the dress. It ends up on the floor with all the other discarded items.

"I want you in my bed, Camryn."

Damn him and his demanding ways, but I like it. Jumping off the desk, I make my way to his wooden bed. It's a gorgeous four-poster, hand-carved heirloom, probably centuries old. I wonder how many people have fooled around in this bed.

Nate slaps me hard across my ass as I pass him, which makes me stop, and slowly I turn to him. He simply smirks at me.

Fine. I liked it. But still.

Crawling onto the bed, I position myself in the middle, waiting for what he has planned.

"We both agree, we have fun with our clothes on, right?" he questions me.

"Not sure how much fun we can have with our clothes on," I answer. I think I've fucked myself trying to be all I-want-you-but-we-have-to-be-professional bullshit. There is nothing professional or friendly about what we're doing. I should have said fuck it and let him fuck me.

"You have no idea." Raising a brow at me, I can see the hunger written across his face as he moves toward me. Nate takes a knee on to the duvet, and like a damn panther, he stalks me, moving closer and closer. Far out, I've never been so turned on in my entire life.

Nate reaches my legs and pushes them wide.

"I will only touch your skin through your clothes, Okay?"

No! That's so not okay.

I want his lips on my thighs. I want his tongue to be sweeping along my vagina. I want his goddamn fingers inside of me. He doesn't wait for my answer before his face disappears between my thighs. His nose runs along the lace seam of my panties, making me jump.

"Fuck," he groans.

Did he just sniff my vagina?

He takes in another deep breath, humming as he does. I want to reach out and touch his hair, but he just said only where our clothing touches. So, instead, I grip the duvet beneath me. His hot breath blows against my aching pussy, and it's making my clit throb. He's going to kill me like this.

Over and over again, he rubs his nose across the seam of my panties, pushing the fabric against my clit. *Oh. Yes.* My panties are becoming wetter with each stroke, making it easier for him to get the friction I need. His fingers dig into the bed beside him as he's unable to touch me. Then I feel his tongue against the lace. Holy shit, that feels so good. He maneuvers the lace of my panties just enough so he can get to my clit. Then he sucks. Hard.

"Holy, fucking shit." The sensation is insane. My hands almost launch myself off of his bed. He hums, moans, and groans as he works over my tiny bud. He's using every bit of his mouth to touch me everywhere, while he pushes me higher and higher.

Fuck, this is so good.

More.

I need more.

He keeps finding the perfect amount of friction even with the barrier between us, and he works his magic mouth until I can't take it any longer, and I come so hard that I swear I want to pass out from the intensity.

He moves up my body, pressing himself against me. I can see his chin is wet, but he doesn't wipe me away. He presses himself harder against my body. Wrapping my legs around his hips, I pull him closer. Our faces are so near, I can smell myself on his lips. He hovers over me, rubbing himself against the lace. Over and over. He leans down and bites one of my nipples through the material. Arching my back at the sensation overload, I moan.

Who knew dry humping could be so—so hot.

He does it to the other one giving it equal attention, all the while rubbing himself against me, using me to get off.

"Cam," he groans, and he sounds close. If he keeps going the way he is, I think I can come again. He rubs against me furiously, pushing the damp lace against my clit, stimulating it, until I feel the need building again. Nate pushes and pushes until I feel wetness across my stomach, and his animalistic groans fill the room. But I don't care that he's just come all over me because he continues rubbing himself on me until I come again.

Holy shit.

Fuck!

This was so… unexpected.

Nate's forehead rests on my shoulder as his whole body slowly comes down from his orgasm. He reaches out and opens a drawer where a box of tissues are located. He pulls out a couple and wipes my stomach, then does the same again and cleans himself. He throws the tissues into the bin beside the bed and rolls onto his back.

"That was…" Nate's face turns to me, worry lacing his wrinkled brow, now that the glow of what we've done is starting to fade.

"Hot, Nate. So, fucking hot." Rolling onto my side, I smile at him.

"Felt like being back in high school again." He smirks.

"I should go." My eyes are becoming heavy, and I am feeling awfully sleepy.

"No, stay," he murmurs.

"You sure?"

"Yes. We can freak out about it in the morning."

Nate wraps his strong arms around me, pulling me to him. He rests his chin on my head, and I nuzzle into his warm chest. The next thing I know, I'm asleep.

11

CAMRYN

Waking up beside Nate isn't the worst thing in the world. But it's also not the smartest thing, either.

"Can we freak out now?"

Nate smiles as he opens his eyes, his hand is resting on my hip. My leg is wrapped over his, and we are entwined with each other.

"I really wish I could freak out, but I don't feel like it."

Nate seems surprised when he asks, "Do you regret it?"

"No, not at all." Reaching out and running my hand across his stubble, I continue, "Couldn't regret those orgasms."

"I don't either," he adds.

"We aren't going to make this weird between us, are we?"

"I sure hope not."

"I feel like I'm giving you mixed signals," I say straight out, confessing what's been worrying me.

"I thought I was doing the same thing to you." We both smile at our similar thoughts. "I've gone on and on about not mixing business and pleasure and all that shit, and..." He looks between us.

"I gave you that whole speech last night of... 'respect me, I'm a professional woman' and then threw myself at you."

"Well, I caught you." He chuckles. "And, I do respect you."

"I was horny."

"So was I," he tells me. "I feel like a month full of messages and calls kind of led us to this moment."

He's right. It was probably one of the longest foreplays ever. We just couldn't help it.

"So, what do we do?"

"I don't know, Camryn." At least he's giving me an honest answer. "I have to leave this afternoon. I need to head down to London to check on my clubs, then fly to the resort to get ready for our soft launch in a couple of weeks."

We're both very busy people.

He runs a sex empire. He's a client. He's also a friend.

Are you bothered if he sleeps with anyone else? I'm not sure.

"Can I be honest with you, Nate."

"Of course, you can."

"I like you." Biting my lip, then I continue, "I like our chats. I like what's inside of you, not just what's on the outside." This makes him chuckle. "But I don't want more..." I pause. "Harris, broke me," I tell him. "What he did to me... the lying, the cheating, the damn well everything..." I am waving my hands dramatically in the air. "He's gouged a big scar on my heart."

"Camryn..." I can hear the sincerity in that one word.

"I know you both have issues. And you probably don't want to hear this, especially not while we're both half-naked, but I honestly thought Harris was the one." Nate tenses beside me. "Maybe that makes me a selfish bitch for jumping you last night, for pursuing you straight after Harris cheated on me. I felt so lost."

"Cam, you don't have to apologize." Nate reaches out and caresses my face. Like the bitch I am, I lean into his touch, lapping up the affectionate move. "Not going to lie, hearing you talk about Harris like that, it riles me. But I understand what you had together, and I can respect that." I like Nate's honesty. "I like this..." Nate waves between us. "I like getting your text messages.

I like hearing your voice. I like hanging out with you. But like you, I don't want more." *Oh, well, that's good.* "I'm about to open the world's largest sex resort. I have two more islands that Sam and I purchased, and we have started on. Also, I'm looking at expanding The Paradise Club into luxury yachts. Most women I've dated don't like it when my attention is elsewhere. They don't understand that unfortunately, business does mean more to me than them."

"I totally get that. That's where I'm at, at the moment, too. My business has one hundred percent of my focus, and men hate that fact." Letting out a sigh, I close and open my eyes. "I let Harris take my focus away for a while. I won't do that again."

Nate nods in understanding.

That's why I can talk to him. He gets it. He gets me.

"Guess we're more similar than we thought."

"Guess we are." Smiling up at him, I state, "So that leaves us as what? Friends?"

"Yeah. I hope so. Someone you can depend on any time, day or night," he tells me.

Those words appeal to me.

Somehow, I feel lighter for them being said.

"That sounds nice. But what about this?" I wave my hand between our half-naked selves.

"Um..." Nate frowns. "Would it destroy all the things I've just said if I told you that I wouldn't mind fooling around with you again?"

"Oh, you would?"

"But I understand if this is a no-go zone now."

"Let's not be hasty now." Nate raises his eyebrow and wiggles it. "I mean... we both just said we're super busy people." Nate nods his head in agreement. "And we both agreed we're not looking for anything more." Again, he nods his head in approval. "But a girl has needs." I run my finger down his bronzed bicep. "I'm also going to be really honest with you right now." He nods his head, waiting. Moving quickly, I push Nate back against the bed and straddle him. "If you have time before you go. I would like to fuck you properly. No clothes this time."

His eyes widen, and his mouth falls open. He seems utterly shocked but also pleased at my forwardness when his lips turn up in a smirk. "But…" holding up my finger, I halt him from talking. "When you go, there's a high probability that I might fuck someone else, too."

Nate tenses below me.

Shit! Maybe that's a little too forward, but it's the truth.

"I have a high sex drive," I state while rubbing myself against him. "If I'm not in a committed relationship, then I have no problems finding a release when and where I want to." Nate's fingers dig into my hip, holding me against him. "Can you work with that?"

"Yes," he groans as I rub myself against him. "Fuck! Yes." He closes his eyes for a brief moment then continues, "It's only fair I warn you now… there's a high probability I might fuck someone while at the London club."

I tense a little hearing his words, but it's only fair I take them on board because he took mine.

"And I most certainly will when I get to the resort. You know… for quality measures."

This makes me burst out laughing. "Of course. No one wants a crap blow-job wake-up call."

"So, we will be each other's scratches when we have an itch?"

"Yep." Moving over him, I start to grind.

"And no jealousy?"

I shake my head. We aren't in a committed relationship, so there's nothing to be jealous of.

He hesitates, not sure if he believes me.

"If you need to fuck someone in front of me, Nate, to prove I won't be jealous, then that's fine."

"Don't say those things to me, Camryn. You're giving me all kinds of ideas."

My eyes widen, feeling him harden against me. "Does that turn you on, Nate? The thought of fucking someone else while I get myself off watching it."

"Fuck, Cam," he groans. "Don't say it if you don't mean it."

Leaning forward, my teeth sink into his ear lobe. "Oh, I mean it," I purr into his ear. "I wouldn't be opposed if the woman wanted to eat my pussy while you fucked her."

"Goddammit, Camryn. Do you want me to come in my pants?"

"Just like last night."

Nate growls, before grabbing and throwing me onto my back.

"I'll warn you one last time, Camryn." Nate looks like he's seconds away from losing control. It's hot, and I am extremely aroused. "Don't test me, woman."

Oh, he's turned all alpha on me.

Hot. Hot. Hot.

"I want to try everything you have to offer, Nate."

He reaches over and grabs a condom from the drawer next to the bed. Nate takes off his white tank top, and my hands instantly reach out to touch him. Running my nails down his stomach, I watch his bronze skin turn red with my marks. He pushes his briefs down exposing his dick.

Dammit, Nate Lewis, you have a pretty dick.

A tiny bead of pre-cum sits on top. I take a finger wiping the bead off and place my finger into my mouth. His eyes darken to an almost black with need.

"I have the darkest fantasies living inside of me that I've never been able to explore before… until you."

Sheathing himself, he nudges my legs wider, then moves my panties to the side and runs the tip of his dick through my wet folds.

Shit. Yes.

"I can give you what you want, Camryn." He pushes inside me

slowly. "I can deliver your wildest fantasies." Pushing further, he's now stretching me, and it feels so good. "You want me to find a woman that can eat your pussy as good as I can? Done." Closing my eyes, I listen to his dirty words. "Want me to blindfold you, tie you up, and offer you as the resort's personal sex toy, leaving you spread open so anyone can fuck your perfect little cunt? Done!"

Oh my God, Nate's dirty talk is on point.

"Yes. Yes."

"I want to fuck you in the rainforest where everyone can see. I want them to wish they were me... wish they were the ones making you come."

Shit, Nate! I claw his back as he pounds into me. His teeth sink into my shoulder as I hang on for dear life.

"After you've fucked that rock star, which I know you will, I want you to call me. I want to hear how wet your pussy got for him?" Lord, help me now, Nate is going to kill me via his dirty talk. "I want you to tell me over the phone exactly how he made you come." Nate's able to find some nuclear button deep inside of me, which sets me off.

He pounds into me over and over again. His hand covers my mouth as I scream the place down as I come undone. Doesn't matter that the walls are ten inches thick because the entire castle is going to hear me come.

"Take it, Camryn. Fucking take all of me."

My eyes widen, I don't think I can come anymore.

Nate flexes his hips, and fuck me dead, somehow he finds another bundle of nerves that sets me off like a fireworks show. I've never been so wet in my entire life. Should I be embarrassed?

Nate's hand moves from my mouth to my throat. Thick fingers wrap around my neck, and he squeezes ever so gently. My eyes roll back into my head as I think about this man being a sex wizard. How does he know what I want or need?

"Trust me, Camryn."

Oh, I do.

Looking him straight in the eyes as he puts more pressure around my throat, giving me just enough, he continues fucking me, but his stare never leaves mine. A smile forms on his face as I take everything he gives me.

"More, Nate. I want more."

"Fuck, Camryn. Jesus, fuck!" His eyes roll into the back of his head as I squeeze myself around him. "Do it again?" those almost intense dark sapphire eyes tell me. "Make me feel that tight cunt wrapped around my dick."

I do it again, and again, and again until Nate loses himself in me. His hand falls from my throat as he turns feral with need. I hold onto his broad shoulders while he gives me his all until he falls forward and screams his release into the bed.

Holy fucking shit!

We're both breathless and covered in sweat.

Nate looks over at me. "Where the fuck did you come from, Camryn Starr?"

12

NATE

"Earth to Nate…" My brother, Alex, kicks me underneath the table, as we watch three women having fun in the cube. "You've been lost in your mind for the past ten minutes. There are three beautiful women eating each other out, and you are not even the slightest bit interested." I can tell he's growing annoyed with me.

"Sorry. There's something on my mind."

More like a someone.

My attention is turned back to the three beautiful women having fun in the cube. The cube is a giant glass-walled room that anyone can enter and basically entertain the people around them. It's one of our most used rooms.

One of the women is blonde, and my mind begins to wander to another blonde. One I left behind not forty-eight hours ago. One that's been sending me naughty text messages ever since, telling me how many times she's touched herself after she left my bed. I've jerked off over her words too many times to count.

I'm addicted.

I know it!

What happened that morning took me by surprise. One minute

we were talking about the fact that we shouldn't cross the line, that we should be friends, then next thing I know, we're fucking each other's brains out, and she's asking me for the dirtiest things.

There's been a lot of women who have told me things they want done or to do, but they have never affected me the way Camryn's requests have. I like a confident woman, but most of the women outside my world, who are unaware of my business, try too hard. They try to be something they aren't. Whereas, Camryn, I think she's a woman who has had to hide her true self. Because let's face it, there are a lot of men out there who cannot handle a successful, driven, intelligent woman like Camryn Starr. All they see is the gorgeous blonde, big tits, and legs for days. They don't care that her business intellect is sharp as a tack. They only care about getting a woman like her on her knees to service them, when really, they should be the one on their knees servicing her.

"You okay? You're acting weird," my younger brother tells me.

Alexander is a couple of years younger than me, and he's taken over the family's real estate empire. He likes what I have created. No, he enjoys the benefits of being my brother, but he isn't that interested in the business. He's happy building his empire in another field. My dad was happy when my brother told him he wanted to take over from him. My father always thought it would be me, but I had other plans. Yes, my parents know what I do. They're not keen on it as it doesn't interest them, but they're proud of my achievements even if it's in a field perhaps they don't entirely approve of.

"Did something happen at the wedding?" I know my brother, he's annoying as fuck and won't give in until I tell him what's on my mind.

"What happens if you meet someone—" I don't get to finish.

"What the fuck, you've met someone?" he raises his voice.

"Not like that, dipshit. And lower your fucking voice."

Alex picks up his drink and takes a sip.

"There's a girl I've been talking to. We move in the same

circles but had never met. I also hired her to do a job for me." Alex raises a brow. "She runs her own business. She's crazy smart—"

"So, she's ugly?"

"Alex!" I roll my eyes at my brother.

"Hey, you led with smart brain instead of hot tits like you normally do, so what am I to think?"

Do I? I'm such a dick.

"She's smart. Beyond beautiful. Yes, she has great tits. She's also sexually compatible with me. Basically, she's a fucking unicorn."

My brother takes my comments in and mulls them over for a little bit before saying, "You like her."

"Duh."

"No. I mean you actually like her! Not just because she might be a good lay but because you like hanging out with her."

"Yeah. We talk all the time. Even before we slept together."

He nods his head while taking it all in. "You're not ready to be monogamous, is that it?"

"She doesn't want to be monogamous."

"Hang on… what the fuck?" My brother's question surprises me. "You telling me this woman ticks all your boxes and more, plus she's happy to let you screw other people?"

"She'll be sleeping with other people, too."

Alex waves his hand in the air as if it's a given. "Why are you not marrying this woman."

"Be serious, Alex."

"Fine." He rolls his eyes. "If you don't plan on marrying the woman, or getting serious with her, then what's the problem?" Maybe he's right. "Oh…" he claps his hands loudly, "… the problem is you can see yourself falling for her, but she doesn't want anything more."

"Don't get yourself carried away there, brother. It hasn't been that long."

"But she's told you she doesn't want anything, right?"

"Yes. But I told her the same thing."

"Ah... interesting."

"Stop analyzing me," I grumble.

"Then you need to stop analyzing everything. You're so caught up in your own head. If you believe her when she says she doesn't want anything, then take her word at face value and don't feel bad about fucking around."

He's right. This is the first time I've believed a woman when she's told me she wants no-strings-attached fun. Most women think they want it, but then feelings develop and 'boom,' they're crying because they found you fucking one of your staff in your office, or so I've heard.

"Can't believe I'm saying this, but you're right," I tell my brother.

Alex puffs out his chest triumphantly with a big dirty smirk. "Now, that I've got my wingman back... do you think you could arrange for those three women in the cube to come play with me?"

"I'll see what I can do."

🌴🌴🌴🌴🌴🌴🌴🌴

"Mr. Lewis, you asked for me." The beautiful blonde walks into my office.

"Yes, Jade, I did."

"What can I help you with, sir?" Those bright red lips look deliciously plump, and I wouldn't mind seeing them wrapped around my dick. I've played before with Jade—she's one of our senior girls at our London club. She loves sucking cock, and she's brilliant at it. She knows when I call her to my office what I'm after.

Sitting on the edge of my desk, I'm ready for her. My dick twitches to life.

"The usual, please, Jade. I want to see my dick painted red from your lipstick. Do you hear me?"

"Yes, sir." She gives me a smirk before dropping to her knees.

"Tits out, Jade." She undoes the top few buttons of her tight shirt, then unclasps the front of her bra, exposing her tits. Men are visual creatures. She undoes my suit pants dragging them to my ankles, then she pulls down my boxer briefs, and my dick springs to life.

Licking her lips, she begins to suck my dick as she settles herself before me. I watch as those bright red lips sink to the base of my cock while she sucks me to the back of her throat. No gag reflex. That's why she's the best. She leaves a bright red ring around the base of my cock. *Good girl.* She continues slowly up and down my dick until it has red ring marks all the way around.

My phone starts ringing, and I curse whoever's on the other end.

"Don't stop," I warn her, and she doesn't flinch. I answer the phone without looking at who it is.

"What?" I answer hoarsely.

"Did I catch you at a bad time?"

Shit! Camryn. My body tenses.

Jade notices, she hesitates before continuing her assault on my dick.

"Nooo." My answer comes out a little more like a moan as Jade works her magic.

"I interrupted something, didn't I?" Camryn's quick to catch on.

"No. Um..."

"Don't lie to me, Nate." She sounds angry as silence falls between us.

Camryn's jealous.

Dammit.

I knew it.

Then phone line goes dead.

13

NATE

"F uck!" Slamming my hand on the desk, Jade pulls back.

"Is everything okay, sir?" she asks.

"Yes... I ..." As I am running my hand through my hair, my phone starts ringing. It's Camryn wanting to FaceTime me.

"Hey," I answer the call tentatively.

"Are you in your office?" she asks.

"Um... yeah." I am feeling a little confused right now, not understanding what she's up to.

"Good." She smiles. "Do you have somewhere you can put your phone, handsfree."

Huh, what?

"No. Why?"

"Because I want to watch. Whatever it is you're doing." Those green eyes of hers twinkle with mischief.

"Really?" I question because I'm not sure I hear this right.

"Yes. Unless she doesn't want me to watch."

My eyes flick down to Jade, she's remaining silent, waiting for my command.

"Nate, I can see you're looking down at someone."

I nod my head at Jade, she gives me permission, so I move the camera down, so she comes into view.

"Oh, she's cute."

"Thanks…" Jade smiles nervously.

"Oh my God, you have the best tits," Camryn tells her.

Realizing Jade's are still out, I am starting to feel like this is a little surreal.

"Nate, give her the phone."

I do as I'm told and hand the phone to Jade, who's blinking fast and fumbling.

"Sorry, I don't mean to be weird or anything, I just want a closer look at your boobs." Camryn giggles.

"Really?" Jade's face lights up. "They're real," she says proudly.

Honestly, what the hell is happening?

"I can tell," Camryn muses. "Sorry to interrupt your night, what's your name?"

"It's Jade, and no not at all." Jade waves Camryn's apology away.

Hello, what about me?

"I'm kind of glad I called when I did."

"Yeah?" Jade asks.

My ear pricks up wanting to know Camryn's answer.

"Means I can now watch."

Wait! What?

"Really?" Jade seems excited.

"If you don't mind," Camryn adds.

"No, of course not. I think you're beautiful," Jade adds.

"Oh, babe. Really? Thank you so much."

Shaking my head, I just can't.

Why are you not here? It would be so much more fun," Jade asks Camryn.

That gets my dick twitching.

"You'd want me there?" Camryn seems shocked.

"Of course, you seem fun. None of Mr. Lewis' girlfriends are ever this fun."

Camryn and I both say at the same time, "We're not dating."

"Has Mr. Lewis had many girlfriends?" Camryn giggles.

"Okay, that's enough." I take the phone back from Jade.

"Hey, no fun. I was trying to get the juicy gossip." Camryn smiles at me through the screen.

"Nothing to tell."

"Boo. You're boring." She smiles. "Jaaadddeee," she screams through the phone. "You can start sucking his dick again." Camryn bursts out laughing.

Jade goes to move, but then she hesitates, waiting for my signal.

"You sure, Camryn?" I check with her one last time.

"Yes. Now go get a selfie stick or something. And call me back when you're ready." Camryn hangs up.

"I like her." Jade looks up at me. "She's different from the others."

"You think?"

"Remember, what's her name?" She snaps her fingers a few times and then states, "Felicity. When you had your city office away from the club, and she walked in on us."

Nodding my head—yeah, that was bad. She had to be escorted from the building.

"You can hear it in her voice that she likes you." Panic grips me, and Jade must notice. "No! I don't mean it like that," Jade quickly adds. "That she likes you, but understands you, too. She gets you and all this."

"You think?"

"I hope she calls back and is naked because she's smoking."

"She is…" I let that little tidbit of information about how I feel slip from my mouth.

"If you want to bring her in, I'd love to play with her." Jade licks her lips, and with that, my dick twitches back to life.

"If I do, you'll know."

"Use the laptop…" Jade points out. "It gives you more width, and you can be hands-free."

Good idea. Turning my laptop on, I key in my password and bring up FaceTime on the computer, then I hit call. My heart thunders in my chest—I am nervous for some reason. Maybe if Camryn is really serious about this, then I *have* found a damn unicorn.

When the screen connects, I see Camryn's changed, and now she's in her underwear. Holy fuck!

"Thought I would make myself comfortable." Camryn smiles, holding the camera away from her, showing me that she's half-naked. *Fuck, she's beautiful.*

"Hot," Jade mumbles.

"Let me set this phone up. I think I'm going to need both hands for this." I watch as she places things in position. She has herself at the right angle, so I can see everything. I do the same and turn the laptop, so it gets Jade who's on her knees again in frame.

"Jade, what is that color on Nate's dick? It's gorgeous."

"Oh, it's Mac, Lady Danger," Jade tells her.

Seriously? This is the weirdest blow job I've ever had.

"Great. Must grab some. I'm sure Nate won't mind me giving it a try." She sends a wink my way, and my dick twitches wildly. "Sorry, continue." Camryn lays back and waits for Jade.

Jade looks up at me, gives me a wink, and takes my dick into her mouth. My eyes flick to the screen as I watch Camryn's reaction. Her eyes widen, and she moves forward just a fraction as if trying to get closer. Jade's giving one hell of a performance. I flick back to see Camryn again, and this time her hand has disappeared into her panties. Fuck! My dick throbs as my fingers dig into the desk. But I can't take my eyes off Camryn, and neither can Jade.

"Take your pants off, Cam," I growl through the screen. "I need to see how wet you are. See if Jade needs to work harder to get you dripping." Camryn does as she's told, and her pussy is right there for me to see. "Move the camera closer, I want a better view." She does as she's told. "Closer," I say through clenched teeth. "All I want to see is your cunt on the screen and your moans in my ears. Do you hear me?"

"Yes," Camryn moans.

The camera moves closer as her perfect little cunt fills the screen for me. All I can see is her fingers dipping inside, and they're slick with her wetness. Jade sucks harder upon seeing Camryn working herself over. I can't take my eyes away from her. Her cunt greedily takes her fingers in time with Jade's sucking.

Camryn moves her hand away and begins working on her clit. I watch in fascination as her wetness begins to drip down her lips.

Goddamn, I wish I was there to lick it all up.

Jade takes me all the way to the back of her throat.

Holy shit. Yes.

Oh my god, yes.

Camryn's strokes increase more and more. I notice Jade's hand has disappeared between her thighs—she's getting herself off too.

Fuck, this is all too much.

Camryn's beginning to moan and groan while Jade's humming around my dick. My balls are ready to explode.

Camryn's the first, her orgasm fills my ears with her scream, which is too much for me, and I blow my load down Jade's throat. Not long after that, Jade comes. Looking over at the screen, Camryn's pussy is still there on show, pink and perfect.

"Thank you." Jade gets up and leaves the office.

Fuck me.

Pulling up my pants and tucking myself back in, the camera moves, and I see Camryn's flushed face.

"That was fun." Camryn gives me a big smile.

"Fuck, yeah, it was."

"Where's Jade?" Camryn looks around the room as much as she can by the limitations of FaceTime.

"She left."

Camryn pouts. "I hope she came?"

"She did."

"So, you play with her a lot?"

"She gives the best blow jobs. But no, not a lot."

"That was hot, Nate. Watching the two of you." I can hear it in her voice that she means it.

Something inside of me switches, and before I know what I am doing, I say, "Come to London. Tomorrow."

Silence falls behind the screen.

"How?"

Well, at least that wasn't a no.

"When does Kimberly go home?"

"She left today."

"Say it's a work emergency."

Camryn bites her lip, and I watch as she thinks it over. "I can come for the day but not overnight."

Damn! I'll take whatever I can get.

14

CAMRYN

"Hey, babe, I have to pop down to London tomorrow." Olivia looks at me funny, a frown forming on her forehead. "That's a long way for one day. Why?"

"Just have to collect something for a client. They're holding the last one in Harrods for me." Hoping she believes me, I continue, "I'm going to be on the first train of the day and be back by dinner.

"Okay. I'll get someone to drop you off at the train station."

"Thanks so much." I lean over and kiss her on the cheek.

Okay, I'm the worst friend. Leaving my girls to go chase some dick, but technically, it's work, right? Not like anyone is even going to notice that I'm missing. Everyone is all coupled up and enjoying the afterglow of Vanessa and Christian's wedding.

The driver has dropped me at the train station, and I see Nate standing outside waiting for me. His dark brown hair is blowing in the winter breeze. He's rugged up in a stylish navy coat, wearing jeans and a white chunky knit sweater.

"You made it." Greeting me with a kiss on the cheek, I'm surprisingly nervous all of a sudden. "My car is over here."

We slide into the stylish town car.

"It's about a two-hour helicopter flight to London."

"Beats sitting on a train all day."

Nate reaches over and takes my hand. "Thank you for coming."

I look out the window and watch the green countryside pass us by. It doesn't take long until we're at the heliport and lifting off.

Reaching out for Nate's hand as we soar over the English countryside, Nate points out important places as we fly by. Especially as we get closer to London. It's different seeing your hometown from the air.

Eventually, we land at the city heliport, and we're whisked off again in a classic town car toward his club.

"I know I keep saying it, but really… thanks for coming."

We pull up to a nondescript building in a fancy part of town, slide out of the car, and walk to a door. Nate pushes some buttons, obviously a code, and the door opens.

Oh, that's very James Bond.

Nate takes my hand again, bypasses the reception area—the woman at the desk waves—as we walk past. He leads me up a darken stairway, which takes us up a couple of flights of stairs where we reach a mezzanine area along which the offices are located.

"This is my office." He points to the door as we stop, but we don't go in.

"Thought you might want to have a look around first. You can leave your coat and bag in my office if you wish."

Shaking off my coat, I hand it to him and my bag as well. Nate opens the door then places it on the chair. "Here, you will need these." He hands me some colorful bracelets, and I hold them in my fingers. "Everyone has to wear them at the club if they are playing."

"What do they mean?"

"Pink if you're into exploring with women. Blue if you're into exploring with men. White is no sexual intercourse, but all other play is okay. Red is if you're happy to explore sexual intercourse in the club. Yellow is looking to explore with just one person. Green is looking to explore experiences with more than one person. Purple is okay with playing in public. Orange if you would prefer to play behind closed doors. Black means no play at all, and a lot of the staff members will have one of those on, but you will also see some staff members with colored bands," he explains. "Which colors would you like for today?"

"Pink, Blue, Green, Purple." I give him a wink.

"Perfect." Handing me the bands, Nate closes the office door behind him, then he takes my hand once again. We head down a corridor, then through another door. When we merge into another area, the mood lighting casts shadows across the room even though it's dark.

"You're now in the club."

Looking around the room, it appears stylish. But there's an underlying kink element to the room. The dusty white lighting appears like water droplets cascading down. Comfortable looking benches with fluffy white cushions line the wall. There are a few people seated on them in various stages of undress, watching each other with hungry eyes. Modern black and white sketches hang on the walls, each one depicting a couple or more in various states of passion. The signature of the artist catches my attention—Louis Marchant, the famous French artist. These must be worth a fortune.

"You know Louis Marchant?"

"Yes, I like to collect art," he adds, not stopping to let me appreciate them.

It's all very modern, nothing sleazy at all.

"It's not as busy in the daytime as it normally would be at night."

Holy hell, if that's not busy, what must nighttime be then?

Nate pulls me through the darkened corridors which have gray wooden doors along either side of the corridor, looking more like a dorm than a sex club.

"See how each door has a light above it. Green means empty, red means occupied. Some people allow blinds up. Some people want privacy. You can tell by this little note here." He points. "Some people want you to watch but not hear, and some people want you to hear but not watch." Then he points to the speaker. "Or, some people want both."

"What's in the rooms?"

"Each one has a different theme. We can also set them up for whatever the customer would like. Would you like to check it out?"

Of course, I would.

Nate opens one of the rooms displaying a green light. It changes once the door is closed, the red light turning on. This one is a Moroccan-themed room and nothing like I thought a sex room would look like. The walls are painted a deep burnt pink. There's a blue velvet chaise in one corner piled with darker blue cushions. A Persian rug is on the floor under a coffee table. Tiny Moroccan tiles line the floor underneath. There's a gold arch mirror, as well as a large bed, with an intricate wooden carved bedhead, white linen duvet, and jewel-tone crushed velvet cushions made up in the corner.

"Not everyone wants kink," Nate tells me. "Some people simply want to escape and enjoy their partner away from their normal life," he explains why this room looks more like a lavish hotel than a sex dungeon. "We have rooms on the higher levels set up for specific kinks. But the bottom levels are a little more mellow."

"It's beautiful." I run my hand over the silky sheets of the bed. "I could stay in here all day."

"You can if you wish." Nate grabs the tablet docked on the side table. "Here is your in-room menu." He hands me the tablet. "You can order food and drinks. Toys. Extra people. Certain kinks.

Pretty much anything on the menu." My eyes run down the long list.

"You have happy ending messages?"

"Of course." Giving me a smirk, he continues, "Would you like me to organize one?"

Do I? I could do with a massage.

"If you swipe right, you'll see your options."

My fingers move over the screen. There are photographs of the masseuses, and if they do men or women or both. I'm like a kid in a candy store—this is so cool.

"Go on, pick one."

Biting my lip, I go through them, but I don't know who to pick.

"You choose." I hand him the tablet.

Tilting his head in confusion. "You want me to pick for you?"

"Yes. I trust you. Plus, this is all very overwhelming."

Nate appears concerned as worry lines mar his face.

"Not in a bad way," I reassure him. "I just…" nervously I twist my hands, "… I've always fantasized about something like this, but never in my life did I realize it could actually exist."

"Now, I understand." Nate smiles and then types a couple of things into the tablet and places it down. "Come… relax for a little bit."

"I can't." As I begin to walk around the room, I say, "I have nervous energy to expend. You know when you were younger, and you couldn't sleep because you knew you were about to do something so amazing the next day."

"I like seeing your enthusiasm."

"You do?"

"Yes." Walking over to me, he holds out his hand, and I take it. "The more I am showing you, the more I see you bloom."

My cheeks flush at his compliment.

"It feels like I'm getting to unlock something great in you, Camryn." He reaches out and touches my face. "Let me show you, guide you. Trust me to know what you can and can't handle."

"I don't like being told what to do."

Nate moves closer. "Oh, little one, I think you're going to enjoy me being in charge." He leans down and kisses me ever so gently before pulling away when there's a knock at the door. Nate opens it, and a man rolls in a cart filled with champagne, strawberries, chocolate sauce, and whipped cream. *What has this man got planned?* The man disappears before there's another knock on the door. Nate opens it, and the blonde from yesterday steps in, along with a gorgeous brunette man.

"Would you like me to set up your massage, sir?" Jade asks.

"Just the one today, Jade." She looks over at me, and my cheeks flush. Jade walks over to the cupboard and retrieves a massage table, which she and the handsome man set up.

Oh. My eyes widen at the table in front of me.

"If you would like to undress, miss, we can start your massage." The handsome man is retrieving a tray full of oils from the bathroom. The sound of a cork popping pulls my attention back to Nate as he pours me a glass of champagne.

"Here, take a sip."

Taking the glass, I gulp it down quickly.

Nate chuckles. "I'm going to take a seat here." He takes a seat on the other side of the table and then instructs, "Jade, would you mind helping Miss Starr get undressed, please?"

"It would be my pleasure." Jade's hands lift my sweater over my head, and she carefully folds and places it on the chair beside us. She then falls to her knees and takes off my boots and socks. Her fingers ever so gently glide along my skin as she moves around me, setting my nerves on fire. Jade lifts my camisole, which exposes my bra. Next, her fingers undo the buttons on my jeans, then she pulls them to my ankles, and I step out of them.

"Do you feel comfortable, Camryn?" Nate asks.

"Yes." My body is hyperaware of my surroundings.

"And, are you okay if I control the room?"

What does he mean?

Without actually asking the question, he answers, "That I tell Jade and Keo what to do... to you."

Biting my lip, I can see the way Nate's eyes darken at his request.

"I trust you."

Nate's shoulders relax at my admission. "The safe word in the club is Paradise. If at any time you feel uncomfortable, you say the word, and we will all stop."

Duly noted. But there is no way I'm stopping whatever's about to happen.

"Okay," I voice my acceptance.

"Good." Nate smiles, grabbing a strawberry and dipping it in the chocolate sauce. "Now, come here and open wide."

I do as I'm told, opening my mouth as he places the strawberry inside. Closing my lips around his fingers, the juice runs down my chin.

His eyes sparkle with desire. Nate wipes the juice away with his thumb then places the remnants in his mouth. "Turn around." His voice changes to a command, and I obey. His fingers unhook my bra and let it fall to the floor, exposing my breasts to Jade and Keo. Both are now watching me. Their own need is evident on their faces. "Jade, take Miss Starr's panties off, please."

Jade moves forward, her fingers hooking into the side of my panties, and she pulls them down in one fell swoop, then I step out of them.

"Keo, please help Miss Starr to the table." The large man comes over, his eyes falling to my exposed breasts. He picks me up in his strong arms, making me squeal, then he places me on my back against the table. Keo hovers over me, and I can almost feel the heat burning through his clothes.

"You both can undress now," Nate tells the two workers.

They do so swiftly, and as they do, I am entirely unsure where to look first. Should I check out Jade's magnificent tits or Keo's glorious dick? Damn, that man is hung like a donkey.

Nate leans over me, his eyes wandering my entire body. His finger trails over my skin as he walks around me slowly. A wicked grin falls across his face when he reaches my feet. Then before I have a chance to do anything, he's restraining my ankles.

"Nate…" His hand comes out and soothes me by touching my ankle and running it up my calf.

"Trust me, little one…" He keeps going up my thighs and then down until he reaches my other ankle and restrains that one. I'm not surprised this time. "You will enjoy it." Buckling the ends together, his finger trails up along my ribs then over my breast. He plucks my nipple hard, which makes my back arch.

Nate pulls my wrist out and buckles it in place.

This better be a good massage if I'm being locked in.

Nate's finger trails over me again as he moves to my left side, down over my breast. A quick pluck of that nipple, and then he buckles that wrist as well. "Perfect," he states as he smiles down at me. "I'm going to have so much fun with you, little one."

He leans over and kisses me hard.

I'm unable to move. Unable to touch him. Unable to control the kiss. That bastard! That's why he's locked me in position because he knows I'd want to control things, and he wants to be in charge.

Fine, Mr. Lewis. Just this one time will I allow it, but remember when these restraints come off, I *will* be in control again.

Nate moves away from me, smiling to himself. He takes a seat beside me, close enough but out of the way of Jade and Keo. My head is turned to the side, facing him. He unzips his jeans and pulls out his dick. My teeth sink into my bottom lip as I stare. Nate looks so hard.

"Jade." Talking to the blonde, she looks over at him, dick in hand, and instantly, she makes her way over, then falls to her knees in front of him. "Show Miss Starr how much you liked sucking my cock last night. Refresh her memory."

I watch as Jade's mouth wraps around Nate's cock.

Holy shit, that's hot.

Her mouth slides up and down his length while Nate's head falls back against the chair, and he closes his eyes enjoying the sensation of her mouth. Damn him! My pussy's throbbing, and I can't do anything to relieve it.

"Keo, check how wet she is with your fingers," he orders.

Jade doesn't stop sucking when he speaks.

Keo moves into position between my legs as he takes one thick finger and runs it through my pussy. I can't help but moan at his touch.

Nate chuckles beside me. "More," he commands Keo.

And he gives me more—his thick finger sinking inside of me. *Oh, dear Lord. Yes.* He curls it, finding the delicate little nerve endings easily. His thumb grazes my clit. *God, yes.* In the distance, I can hear Jade choking on Nate, the noises grabbing my attention, and I see Nate's fingers digging into her hair as he begins to fuck her face harder.

Nate's dark sapphire eyes meet mine. "Another finger," he orders Keo.

Dear Lord. Biting my lip as his magic fingers continue working inside of me, I don't take my eyes away from Nate. It's as if we're connected or on the same wavelength. He continues pumping into Jade's mouth, the girl is taking it like it's champagne, the gagging sounds she's making are making me wetter and wetter.

"How wet is she, Keo?"

"Dripping, sir."

15

CAMRYN

"That's my girl." Nate smiles at me as if I've made him proud. He slows his thrusts into Jade's mouth until he pulls her off of him. She leans back on her heels. "Stop, Keo." The man's fingers instantly disappear from my cunt.

"No," I call out, I was so close. So very close. Bring those magic fingers back.

What the hell is he playing at?

"Suck on her nipples, Keo." The man follows his orders and moves to the right side of me, so as not to block Nate's view. His lips wrap around my nipple as he nips and sucks the sensitive tip.

Nate's sitting there hard as a rock, and he pops a strawberry into his mouth. "Jade, pour some of this over Miss Starr's breast, please... for Keo." Jade grabs the chocolate sauce and stands on my right side. Keo moves his face out of the way as the cold sauce hits my nipple. Shit! I hiss at the sensation.

Keo goes back and starts to lap up the sauce. He's going to town, and holy hell, the sensation is amazing.

"Jade, stand at her feet," Nate commands, then he stands unabashed as his dick juts out. He grabs the bottle of champagne and moves south.

What's he going to do with that?

Nate stops, turning his head to look at me, and with a devilish grin, he slowly pours some of the champagne over my pussy.

What in the hell?

"Drink up, Jade."

That's when I feel the swipe of her tongue against my pussy. The sensations of the bubbles and her heated tongue are insane. Jade's working me over. Keo's sucking my tits, and Nate's smiling down at me. It's a sensory overload.

Closing my eyes, I can feel the tension inside of me building. I don't think I can continue holding on, it's too much. Jade's tongue is too much.

"Oh my God, yes," my scream echoes through the room.

Nate smiles and motions for Jade to stop.

"Keo, suit up." Keo moves from my breasts, grabs a condom from the tray and sheaths himself. He moves between my legs, and in one swift movement, he's entering me.

Oh my God. Fuck. The man is huge. I feel like I'm being split in two.

Then I hear another foil tear and Nate's putting a condom on. I watch as Jade walks over to where he's sitting and crawls on top of him. I watch as she slides down his dick, both of them hissing at the contact.

My attention is drawn back to Keo, who's literally pounding into me at the same time his fingers are twisting my sensitive nipples. I can hear Jade's moans beside me. Nate's grunts. The sounds are filling the room. It's making me go crazy with need.

This is insane.

I've never done anything so crazy like this before.

Yes, I've had threesomes and even attended some swingers' parties with exes, but this, this is on a whole other level, and I love it.

Closing my eyes again, I savor every gorgeous drop of this experience.

Goddammit! Keo is going to make me come again with his magic donkey dick.

"Yes. Yes. Yes." Arching my back as he continues to pound into me, I'm going to be walking funny if he keeps going the way he is.

Moments later, he comes.

Then I hear Nate and Jade.

The room grows quiet, only the sounds of our labored breathing can be heard.

When I open my eyes, Jade and Keo have disappeared, and I'm left with a happy-looking Nate, who's admiring me spread out against the table.

"How was that?" He runs his fingers over my already heightened body.

"Fantastic, except…" Smiling, I watch his face change to concern. "I never got that massage I was promised. Only the happy ending."

Nate bursts out laughing as he unshackles me. "Rollover, Camryn. Let me massage you."

Hell, yeah. I do as I am told, placing my face in the hole of the table. The cool oil drizzles down my back, and Nate's strong hands begin to massage my tender muscles.

"Does this feel good?"

"Yes." I am mumbling through the hole, but he continues using his magic fingers and hands all over my body. There's nothing sexual this time, which is a little disappointing.

"I believe you now," Nate confesses.

My body tenses. I turn my head to try to look at him, but I can't see him. "What do you mean?"

Nate's hands leave me, then he comes into my view, crouching down beside me. "I've had many women tell me they're okay with seeing me with other people, but in actuality, they aren't."

Oh, I can see why that would be a problem.

"I'm not like those other girls, Nate."

I'm not. I'm not wired like that. I mean it's human nature to have the tiniest bit of sting when you see someone you like with another, but for me, that's quickly soothed away with my need, and that need is more than being answered.

"I'm starting to realize that, Camryn." He reaches out and brushes the hair back from my face. I push myself up, swinging my legs over the edge of the massage table. I'm fully naked, and Nate is looking delicious in his casual gear of jeans and white long-sleeved shirt. He hasn't put his chunky sweater back on.

"I'm not here to hurt you, Nate. I'm not here to marry you. To date you. To run away with you and live happily ever after."

A slight frown forms on his face at my words.

Standing, I move to him, placing my hands on his hard chest. "I like whatever this is between us. I like talking to you. I like hanging out with you. I like fucking you." This makes him smile. "But we are two very busy, driven people. We don't have time to devote to anyone else. Shit! I hardly have time for myself these days." Wrapping my arms around his neck, I continue, "What I say is what I mean. I don't play games. We're both too old for that. If I want to fuck you, I'll give you a call. If I want to fuck someone else, I am going to. Same goes for you." He smiles down at me. "Not many men can handle me," I say while staring into his gorgeous blue eyes. "But I think you can."

Nate pulls me close to him. "Not many women can handle me either, Camryn. That is, until you." Raising a brow at me, his words give me a funny sensation in the pit of my stomach.

"All I ask for is honesty, Nate. If I call you, and someone is giving you a blow job, tell me. Don't hide it."

"Where the hell have you been hiding all my life?"

"Probably in my office..." I laugh. "I'm a workaholic, you know?"

"I'm sorry I lied yesterday about Jade," Nate apologizes.

"I get it. We haven't known each other for long."

"Here on out, things will be different, I promise." Nate presses his forehead against mine.

"Now, can we finish my massage?"

Nate chuckles before spinning me around and bending me over the massage table. He leans over me, pushing his full weight on my body as he grabs the oil, drizzling it all the way down my body. I feel the oil slide between my legs.

"It's my turn now, Cam," he growls in my ear. His knee pushes my legs open, and his hands run down my back, those magic fingers working out all my tension. Then they sink to my ass, his thumb massaging my puckered hole with oil. "Has anyone taken this before?" he asks while massaging the oil in.

"Yes. But they didn't know what they were doing," I confess.

It's the holy grail. Butt sex. But most men have no idea what they're doing.

"This is mine." He rubs his finger around the puckered skin. "Not today, but mark my words, I will have it." Teeth skim my shoulder as Nate reaches over and grabs a condom from the tray. The next thing, he's entering me. *Yes.* His hand wraps itself around my blonde hair like a rein and pulls me back against him. *Holy shit.* That pushes him deeper.

Nate moves slowly, getting the position just right as if he's testing where my sweet spot is located, and when he finds it, he doesn't let up. His hand falls from my hair and moves to my throat, lightly wrapping it around the thin skin as he continues to thrust into me.

Yes. Oh yes.

I fall forward, unable to stand, my legs are so weak.

Nate's fingers dig into my hips. I'm so blissed out while Nate continues to feverishly fuck me until we both can't take it anymore and plummet over the edge.

16

NATE

We are coming into land at the heliport, and honestly, I don't want Camryn to leave. We had so much fun today, and not just because we had unbelievable sex, but after, we hung out outside of the club. We went for a walk through Hyde Park and discussed the upcoming soft launch of the resort. We spoke about her plans for the new year regarding her business. We then talked about our lives and how we grew up.

My childhood was very different from hers. I came from a loving family, well- off, parents still together. Whereas with Cam, her parents divorced when her sister was born. Her mom lost everything when her father left them for his secretary. The comfy life they had vanished, and her mother bounced around from rich husband to rich husband. Camryn said she never wanted to rely on a man for anything other than her sexual needs, and even then, she said she didn't need them, she had plenty of batteries and an awesome vibrator which made me laugh.

She said that's why she and her sister have worked so hard building their businesses, they never want to end up like their mother. Who she said she hasn't seen in years, not since husband number six, when her mom up and moved to Europe somewhere.

It explains so much. Why Camryn works hard. Why she's the way she is.

We even spoke about her relationship with Harris. While she was speaking, all I could think about was, *How the fuck did this man not realize what an incredible woman he had right in front of him? How could he fuck up and lose her?*

I'm thankful he did—his loss is my gain.

Camryn explained she knew Harris was not into the same things she was into sexually, and that she could do monogamy. She also said she didn't need to have crazy sexy all the time with other people, and that just because she was monogamous with Harris didn't mean she would be vanilla.

"This is me." Camryn smiles, the wind whipping her hair around her as the town car awaits to take her back to the train station, so another car can pick her up from there. "Thanks for today, Nate." Camryn leans in kissing me on the cheek.

Ah, no. That won't do. That won't do at all!

My hands reach out and takes hold of her face, and I kiss her passionately. When we finally pull apart, my stomach sinks with the realization that I won't be able to do that again, not for a couple of weeks until the soft launch.

As we finally stop kissing, Camryn pulls away, then smiles at me. "I had fun."

"Me, too."

"I'm looking forward to you showing me everything at the resort."

Me too, because the lists of things I want her to try are endless. My dick twitches just thinking about that very long list.

"We're going to have fun."

"Is Sam coming?" The mention of my best friend's name stills me.

"He might. Why, do you want him, too?"

Camryn tilts her head and squeezes her eyebrows together. "That sounded like a bit of jealousy there, Mr. Lewis."

Fuck! I didn't realize how that sounded. I was trying to hide that sting of jealousy I felt at the mention of my friend's name.

"I don't care who you fuck… just not my best friend." She wants honesty, so I am damn well going to give it.

"As hot as Sam is, I would never do that to Kimberly. She's had a crush on that man since birth." My brows rise. *I knew it!*

"But, thank you for making your feelings heard." She wraps her arms around my neck again. "You haven't fucked Harper, have you?"

"Hell, no. Sam would kill me."

"Or Kimberly?"

"No way! Sam has had a thing for her since I've known him. I wouldn't do that either."

"Okay. So, our close circle of friends is a no-go zone, is that what you're saying?"

"Yes."

"Okay. Then I'm glad we've sorted that out." She kisses me hard before pulling away, then starts to walk backward toward the car. "We can't tell anyone about this." She moves her hand between us. "Especially not Sam, Harper, or Kimberly," she warns me. I nod my head in agreement. "You know they will have us married off in two point five seconds." I totally agree that they are vultures when it comes to relationships. "They aren't like us." That's so true. "Well, have fun." Camryn waves before disappearing into the car. I wait until she's driven away.

I'm still in London when my phone rings. I head out in a couple of days to the sunny beaches of my resort.

"Happy New Year…" Camryn giggles loudly through the phone line.

"Happy New Year," I reply. Sitting back against my chair in my office, I'm certain she's drunk. Currently, I am in my London club. Tonight's the night when our takings are through the roof, and that applies to all our clubs—our clients like to ring in the New Year in style. I can hear people talking in the background through the phone, and there's some cheering before it muffles.

"They're so loud," Camryn moans. "I wanted to call before things got crazy and wish you a Happy New Year."

"Thanks, babe." I still. *Oh, shit! I just used the word babe.*

I hear a little laugh, and then she muses, "I like it. I'll allow you to call me babe." I'm sure my eyebrows are meeting my hairline, they are so high, and my eyes are wide as I hear her continue, "Does that mean I can call you, babe, too?"

"I guess." I fumbled with the pen in my hand, eventually dropping it to the desk.

"Okay, babe. Have fun. I hope Jade sucks your dick hard as your balls drop."

"You mean as the ball drops," I correct her.

"Um… if she's doing it right, your balls will drop after you've filled her mouth."

I choke on my drink. *What the hell?*

Camryn bursts out laughing. "Goddamn, I crack myself up sometimes. I'm really good at this dirty talking, right?" She giggles again.

How much has she had to drink?

"Sounds like you're going to have lots of fun tonight."

"Oh, I am. Johnny won't leave me alone. He's persistent, but I know the man has stamina, so I'll allow it." This makes me smile. "Shit! Hang on, someone's coming into the library," she whispers.

"Hey, Cam," I hear a male voice exclaim.

"Johnny. Hey…"

"What are you doing in here all alone?" he asks.

I hear the need in his voice, that sound of desperation in his emotionally choked voice.

"I was hoping you'd follow me." Seduction laces her every

word. The phone makes a sound—it's as if she's placed it down on a surface somewhere.

"Did you now?"

"Did you lock the door?" she questions.

I don't hear a reply, so I'm assuming that was a yes.

"Good." I can hear the smile in her voice. "'Cause my pussy is feeling lonely, and she needs a friend."

My dick twitches to life.

"Oh, really?" The man's probably moments away from coming in his pants. I know I would at his age if a beautiful woman said those dirty words to me.

"I'm not wearing any panties," Camryn coos.

Fuck! My dick's instantly hard.

Needing relief, I unzip myself and pull my aching cock from its restraint. Pulling open one of my drawers, I grab a bottle of lube in case things escalate.

"Fuck me, Camryn," Johnny groans.

"On your knees, boy," Camryn commands.

Oh, this is new. I bet he's doing exactly as she orders.

"Fuck, you look gorgeous," he groans.

I bet she's lifted her dress and is showing him her perfectly pink pussy.

Grabbing the liquid, I squirt some onto my hand, the coolness of the gel is relief against the heat of my cock.

"Make me come all over that beard."

Shit. I grip ahold of my dick tighter.

I like dominant Camryn.

"Yes," she hisses.

He must have made contact.

Camryn's moans float down the phone line. "That's it," she tells him. "Don't move," she yells as he hits a perfect spot for her. "Fingers. I need your fucking fingers," she commands.

Johnny must do as he's told because she groans as they enter her.

"Yes. Yes. Keep going, boy. Keep going."

My hand moves furiously in time with her panting. I can hear how wet she is, the sounds are echoing down the line.

Yes. This is exactly what I need.

"Harder. Harder," she pants. The sound of her wetness increases until he pushes her over the edge, and she screams down the phone for me.

And fuck, if not seconds later, I'm coming in my hand.

"I need to fuck you, Camryn," the male voice grunts. "Flip over so I can slide my cock into that wet pussy." Camryn giggles— she's delirious from her orgasm and the alcohol.

I hear rustling then a loud grunt. He's inside of her.

"Fuck, yes," Camryn pants. "Give it to me, big boy."

Oh, fucking hell, I roll my eyes at that.

The phone fills with grunts, moans, and his balls slapping against her wet cunt. My dick twitches back to life, but I just listen, imagining what she must look like in the darkened library with her face pushed up against one of the antique chairs.

"Harder, Johnny, harder," she tells him, urging him on.

Does he fulfill her like I do?

Does he know how to make her scream? Like really scream?

His groans become more animalistic as he gets closer. Camryn's moans become louder, but they're different from the ones she gives me. He's not making her come—she's faking it. My dick's hard thinking about how I know I would satisfy her properly. What's the guy doing? He's getting himself off, and that's it. He thinks his work is done because he ate her pussy and made her come. Oh no, little boy, your job is far from over. If your woman is not dripping wet down your fucking dick while you are pounding her, then you're not doing something right.

Johnny comes with a grunt and Camryn fake pants.

"Fuck, Camryn, you're so fucking good."

"You're not so bad yourself, Johnny." She giggles—it's fake. There's a rustle. Obviously, they are straightening themselves up.

"You should leave first. Don't want anyone catching us or arousing suspicions."

"Oh, yeah. Right." Johnny seems a little put out by her words. "I'll come find you at midnight. That way I can ring in the New Year with my mouth around your dick."

"Fuck, yeah," he states excitedly.

There's a muffled sound—is he kissing her? Then, there is the click of the door shutting.

"You still there, babe?" Camryn asks.

"Of course..." I'm grinning like a Cheshire cat. "... but I'm curious to know why you faked it."

The phone goes silent for a few seconds, and then she mumbles, "How did you..."

"I know every tone of your orgasms, Camryn. I've heard you enough times to know when you *really* come."

"Good to know." She giggles.

"He was a mediocre substitute. But I know you're going to be hanging out for a real pounding by the time you get to the island."

"Really?" She sounds intrigued.

"Also, when I see you next, bring that dominant woman out. I liked hearing her."

"What do you mean?" she questions.

"The whole get-on-your-knees-and-eat-my-pussy thing." She laughs loudly. "I like it."

"Duly noted." I can hear the smile in her voice. "Have a fantastic night, Nate."

"You, too, Camryn."

The line goes dead.

And I realize I'm in so much trouble with this woman.

17

CAMRYN

M y New Year's Eve turned out great. At the stroke of midnight, fireworks went off in the gardens bursting luminous colors through the night sky, while everyone was outside having a great time. Next thing I knew, I was giving Johnny a blow job in the bushes, but the air was ice-cold. So, we quickly moved things inside when his dick started to shrivel up due to the snow starting to flutter down around us. Dicks and cold don't go so well together. I spent the New Year having Johnny ring my bell. But, by the time I woke up, shit had hit the fan.

Apparently, Olivia's cheating, dickhead of a fake fiancé, arrived for New Year's with her bitch of a sister Penny. Her fiancé and sister are totally banging. It's all over the socials because they're always together. Anyway, Olivia and Axel have been having a little winter fling, especially after the hotness of Monaco. But Eddie, her dickhead fiancé, showed up and crashed whatever was going on between Olivia and Axel. She should have been honest and told Axel she had a fake fiancé, but she never did. Now, her world has come crashing down around her. Olivia's decided to head down to London today with my sister, to stay with her until everything blows over with Axel. She doesn't want to ruin Vanessa and Christian's time at the castle.

I'm heading back to New York, which I'm not looking forward to. I've been away from home for a long time. The peace and serenity have been great, but I know there's a shitshow waiting for me. Everything I've pushed deep down inside when it comes to Harris is probably going to rear its damn ugly head.

"I'm sorry." I wrap my arms around Olivia to hug her, then she places her bags in the back of the car. I understand when you need to leave things behind.

"It's not your fault you told me to tell him. That he would understand." I watch the tears fall down her cheeks and drip off her chin. "I was too scared to tell him, and now it's blown up in my face."

"Everything will work out, I promise."

She nods, seemingly unconvinced.

"I'm just a phone call away. Okay?"

Olivia nods again. Her eyes are puffy, and to be quite honest, she looks like shit.

"Time to go," my sister tells her.

Olivia opens the door to the waiting car.

"Have a safe flight back." Ivy hugs me tightly—I wish I could have spent more time with her.

"We need to catch up again soon."

"I know. I know... I promise to make more time."

I could do the same. It's not all her fault.

"Good luck when you get home. Hope Harris doesn't harass you too much."

"I am hoping he will be over it by the time I get back. I mean, he has a gorgeous fiancé. He shouldn't be worried about me."

"Call me when you get home, okay?" Ivy asks me, and I nod my agreement.

"Welcome home from rehab, Camryn," the sign reads as I walk out of the arrival terminal and back into JFK airport.

Harper and Kimberly's blonde heads pop out from behind the sign.

"You fucking bitches." Giggling, I wrap my arms around them. It's so good to be back with my girls.

"You're looking good," Harper tells me. "Breakups suit you." Kimberly flashes her a what-the-fuck look. "What? Too soon to be joking about Harris?"

Harper looks between us.

Oh, how I have missed Harper's raw honesty.

"No. It's fine. I'm fine," I state with a smile as we head on out to the limousine waiting at the curb outside the doors. "It's good to be home."

As I walk out into the cold, I see the mucky snow pushed up along the barriers and hear the loud sounds of impatient cab drivers. Stressed parents rush around screaming at their kids. It's bedlam.

Home.

We jump into the back of the luxury car, then Harper pops the bottle of champagne and pours us each a glass.

"Welcome home, Camryn." We cheer, then take a sip of the bubbly liquid. "Now, tell us, did you fuck a rock star?" Looking up at Harper, I give her a sly smile. "Oh my God, you so did, you cheeky cow." She clinks her glass against mine, and without allowing me to answer, she continues, "Who. How. When. Tell me it was good?"

"Johnny from Sons of Brooklyn. He was good. Great! Young, loads of stamina. Great dick."

Harper and Kimberly are the last two girls who need to know about my hook-up with Nate, especially since they know him so well. We mix in the same circles—Harper's brother is best friends with him. No. They don't need to know anything about Nate.

"You lucky bitch." She rolls her eyes at me. "What I wouldn't give to mess around with a rock star."

"You're just going to have to wait till you finish working for Dirty Texas Records before you screw one." Vanessa runs the PR for Dirty Texas Records, but as she will be heading into maternity leave soon, they needed someone they could trust to help them out. I suggested Harper Rose. She owns one of the fastest-growing PR companies in New York to help, especially as they are expanding the label into New York.

"Thanks so much for recommending me. I have a meeting with some of the guys in a couple of weeks when they're here with Sam looking for commercial spaces for the label."

"Anytime. Got to support my bitches." Raising my glass, we continue catching up on everything I've missed, including all the gossip on how Harris and Isabelle have been swanning around New York like they own the place. I'm not surprised, really. Harris does have an ego. It sucks that I'm going to have to watch it all unfold until I head over to The Paradise Club Resort in a couple of weeks.

We pull up out the front of my apartment building, and Manny, one of the porters, opens the door for me.

"Miss Starr, welcome home."

"It's so nice to see your smiling face again, Manny." And it is, it's great to be home. We head into the foyer while the driver grabs my bags and passes them to the porter.

"Miss Starr, welcome home," Jonathan, the security guard, welcomes me as I enter the building.

"Good to be home," I tell him.

"Just to let you know, Miss Starr, Mr. Edwards has been around multiple times." Bile rises up my throat, and I turn up my nose. "He's been very insistent on seeing you. We have had to bar him from the premises due to his behavior."

"Oh, I'm sorry. But thank you. I never want to see him."

Jonathan nods his head.

"Miss Starr, your mail and packages are in your apartment, I will bring up your bags shortly."

"Thank you, Manny."

"We donated the flowers that came daily to the local retirement home," he adds.

"Thanks so much for doing that. I hope they enjoyed them."

"They did, ma'am."

This was the kind of shitstorm I wanted to avoid when I got home.

We jump into the elevator and head up to my apartment.

"You, okay?" Kimberly asks.

"I'm a little shaken if I am being perfectly honest."

"I think you should come and stay with one of us for a while," Harper adds.

"No. I'm not going to let him run me out of my home. Screw him!"

"He's been sending flowers to work, too," Kimberly adds. "And has shown up a couple of times."

Wait! What?

"I didn't want to tell you. We have it handled."

The elevator chimes and we get out. With shaky hands, I open the door to my apartment.

This isn't fair.

He doesn't get to affect me like this.

He's the one who messed up, not me.

I'm in shock at the number of boxes lining my dining room table.

"What the…" Harper walks over to them, wide-eyed. "They can't all be from him. Can they?" She runs her fingers subtly over each one.

"I don't remember ordering anything." Biting my lip, I am feeling uneasy in my own home. This is all a bit weird, even for Harris.

"Go, have a shower, freshen up, and we will open them for

you," Kimberly tells me.

That seems like a fantastic idea.

****

After running a hot shower and soaking my body, I feel a little better and come out to a table filled with expensive gifts.

There is row upon row of diamonds from Cartier, Tiffany, etc. Designer bags from Chanel and Hermes. Shoes from Christian Louboutin and Jimmy Choo. Sexy lingerie from Agent Provocateur.

What the actual fuck!

"Send it all back." The anger I am feeling is filling every inch of my body.

How dare he?

"This bag alone is worth one hundred thousand dollars," Harper says as she looks at a limited-edition Hermes bag.

"Have it."

Harper screws up her face at my suggestion. "I'll buy my own, thanks. But I thought if you sold it all, you could donate the money to charity in his name, something that would suit him. Like, I don't know, endangered African cockroaches or something of that nature." For the first time since stepping into my apartment, I burst out laughing.

Harper looks at me strangely as if I've lost my mind.

"That's brilliant, Harps." I am still unable to control myself. The laughter is coming thick and fast.

"I'll get some of the interns to sell all this stuff, and find a well-deserving charity for the money." Kimberly smiles.

"Thanks, guys." My friends wrap their arms around me. "I don't know what I would do without you guys."

"You can't get rid of us," Harper tells me. "You are stuck with us for life."

I'm so happy to be home.

18

NATE

C *amryn: I'm finally home.*

Camryn's text message comes through as I slide out of my pool from doing some laps to unwind. Wrapping my towel around my waist, I sit in one of my pool chairs and open my phone, then hit call, because in all honesty, I want to hear her voice.

"Hey." She sounds tired.

"You made it home safely."

"Yeah. I'm exhausted and freezing, but it's good to be back in my own space again."

"If it makes you feel any better, I've just gotten out of the pool."

Camryn groans. "No, that doesn't help or make me feel any better." She gives me a weak laugh.

"You okay?" Feeling like something is up, I wait, and she's quiet for a moment. The hairs on the back of my neck stand to attention as an uneasy feeling falls over me. "You can talk to me."

She lets out a heavy sigh. "It's Harris." Hearing that bastard's name is like a knife through my chest.

"What about him?" I ask through gritted teeth.

"I can't talk to you about it."

"Why not?"

Is he there?

Has he been there?

Camryn wouldn't mess around with him knowing he's engaged to someone else. The man is a charismatic asshole, and I know he could worm his way back in.

Fuck, no! I am working myself up. Calm down!

"I know how much you hate him."

Keep it together, Nate. Keep it together.

"He's a dick. I want to punch the smug look off his face every time I see him," I add.

"I..." she hesitates again. "I don't want Sam to do something stupid. He feels the same way about him that you do. I know how protective Sam can be."

Huh. What the fuck has happened?

Why would she need protection?

Fuck me, I'm fuming.

What the fuck has Harris done?

"Are you safe?" I'm concerned for Camryn's safety.

"Yes. Of course, I am. Shit! Sorry... I didn't mean to worry you," she says, quickly, putting me slightly more at ease. "I have a porter and security here at home and work. They've dealt with it."

Dealt with what?

"What's going on, Camryn?" Dammit, I am losing my patience with her.

"While I was away, Harris came to my apartment multiple times. He's caused a scene, and he's been banned. The same thing happened at work, too." That motherfucker! I ball my hands into a fist, and I close my eyes in an attempt to calm myself down. "I came home to all these extravagant gifts."

I've never wanted to harm anyone as much as I want to harm Harris Edwards right now.

"I can be back in New York by the morning?"

There's silence on the end of the phone, then she whispers, "Nate…"

"I mean it, Camryn."

"That's sweet, but you have too much going on to drop everything for me. Plus, I wouldn't want you to."

"I look after my friends, Camryn."

"I know you do, Nate. I'm safe, I promise. And if I don't feel safe, you will be the first person I call. Okay?"

"My apartment is free. I'll text you the address and code. I'll let them know you're on my list." Only my inner circle has access to my apartment, people I trust, like Sam. I don't bring women there, ever. I mean, I have clubs for that. It's *my* sanctuary. My place. But I think Camryn needs it more than I do right now.

"Nate, no. That's too much."

"Camryn!" I say her name, sternly. "I mean it. If anything happens to make you feel uncomfortable, and you can't get hold of Kimberly, Sam, or Harper, then use it."

"Thank you," she eventually gives in. "That's too kind."

"Like I said… I look after my friends, and you're in my circle now, sorry," I apologize, lightening the mood a little.

"I've made the Nate Lewis inner circle." She pretends to fake cry. "This is such a special day for me. I never thought this day would come," she continues carrying on, and it makes me laugh. "This is a dream come true."

"Fuck you!" I laugh at her antics.

"Maybe I might take you up on the offer of your apartment. I want to snoop through your drawers," she bellows with laughter down the line.

"Do you seriously think I would keep the good stuff at my home?" I challenge her.

"You probably have like a safe room somewhere in your home.

You know, like Batman. It hides all your deepest and darkest secrets."

Camryn's not too far from the truth. I do have a safe room. All my homes have a safe room. You don't own the world's most exclusive sex clubs, which are frequented by the world's high fliers and leave all that information lying around. I could bring down many of the world's biggest corporations with the information I have on my guests.

"You can ask me anything, Camryn. I'm an open book."

"You might regret that."

"Can't regret anything about you." My sincerity catches both of us off guard, and I sigh.

"What's your favorite color?" Camryn changes the tone of our conversation.

"Black."

"That's not a color."

"Fine… blue. The color of the ocean at the resort. It's calming."

"Just had to rub it in that you're on a tropical island, didn't you?" She chuckles. "What is your favorite food?"

This is hard. I like all food, so I have to think for a second or two. "Fresh seafood."

"Nate…" she growls at me. "Stop fucking rubbing it in."

"What do you like?"

"Cadbury chocolate buttons. The English kind because American chocolate tastes so different."

Well, that's not at all what I thought she was going to say.

"I do have to agree, nothing is like the chocolate from home."

"What the…" Camryn squeals. "You're fucking English?"

"Um, yeah. How do you not know this?"

"Because you went to school in Connecticut, that's why."

"My parents moved to Connecticut for a bit, then moved back to Europe after a couple of years. I didn't want to go back because

I was happy there. So, I went to boarding school with Sam, then college with him."

"Well, there you go. I thought you had that accent because you'd spent so much time in Europe." She chuckles.

"I have. The past ten years, I've been running around Europe building up the clubs we have there. The Europeans are a little more accepting of sex clubs than the Americans."

"Where were you born?" she asks.

"Kensington."

"Of course, you were." I can hear her practically rolling her eyes at me.

"And you?"

"Devon, but didn't stay long. You know, gold-digging mother and all." She laughs, but I can hear the sad undertones. "We traveled everywhere growing up. Thankfully, one of her husbands saw fit to put Ivy and me into boarding school, which gave us a sense of stability, but she never came and picked us up for holidays. Not even Christmas. Thankfully, the nuns at our convent took pity on us, and we would spend our holidays there."

"Oh, that explains a lot."

"What do you mean?"

"You were a catholic schoolgirl, raised by nuns. Those girls are always the kinkiest." Camryn's laughing again.

"I didn't want to end up like some of those cranky old nuns."

"You know, I'm getting all hot and bothered thinking about you in your schoolgirl uniform."

"Are you now, Mr. Lewis." My dick begins to strain against the seam of my pants. "Are you into a bit of naughty schoolgirl role-playing?"

"With you, yes."

"Duly noted, Mr. Lewis." She's killing me just by calling me that. "Might see what we can do in a couple of weeks when I'm down there."

"Can't wait."

"I better get going..." Camryn lets out a yawn, "... I'm shattered."

"Stay safe."

"I will. I promise. Night, Nate."

"Night."

The phone line goes dead.

Looking down at the darkened screen, I know what I have to do to protect her. Searching through my phone, I look for Jackson Connolly's number. He's Dirty Texas' security guy. His brother is in the band, he's also one of my loyal clients, and his security company also looks after my clubs in the states. I trust him. The man is ex-military.

"Nate, my man. How are ya?" Jackson asks.

"Great. I need a favor..." Jackson stays silent, waiting to see what I'm going to ask. "You know Camryn Starr?"

"Yes, she was at Vanessa and Christian's wedding."

"You know the story about her ex then?"

"I've heard the girls talking about it."

"She's just arrived home and looks like he's been stalking her."

"What?"

"She told me he's been banned from her building and her workplace for causing a scene."

"That fucking dick," he growls.

"I'd like to have extra security around her. But, Jackson, it needs to be discreet."

"Of course," he agrees. "I have a question, though. How do you know all this?"

Fuck! The line goes silent for a couple of beats.

"She told me."

"Hmmm, interesting," he adds.

"She's a friend," I quickly add.

"I'm sure she is."

"What the hell does that mean?" Instantly I get my back up, but Jackson simply bursts out laughing.

"You're so fucking busted, dude. You've been messing around with her, haven't you?"

"No." I am trying to sound convincing, but I think I am failing miserably.

"Bullshit! Plus, I saw her enter your room and leave early the next morning when we were at the castle."

Shit. Of course, he did. The man was looking after security at the castle.

"Fine. Yes. We hooked up during the wedding."

"Knew it." I can see his grin in my mind. "But you do know she also hooked up with someone else after you left. Just want to be really clear about that. Don't want you to get love hearts in your eyes or nothing."

"I know."

"And you're okay with it?" he pushes.

"Of course. We're friends. We are both adults. We both under-stood what it was." I can feel Jackson assessing me through the phone if that's possible. "Camryn isn't like the other girls."

"And you like that?" Jackson questions.

"She caught me off guard. Yes."

"Interesting," he adds. "I'll make sure nothing happens to your woman."

"She's not *my* woman," I argue.

"And yet, you're trying to save her from a shithead of an ex-boyfriend."

"It's the right thing to do."

"Your secret's safe with me."

Then he's gone.

He's hung up on me.

Shit!

19

CAMRYN

I t's been great being back at work for the past couple of days, getting into the swing of things. We have the first big gala of the society season coming up in a couple of months, the Rose Gala, which is hosted by Sam and Harper's parents. We have been organizing the event for the past couple of years. It really solidified us with the society women of New York when the first one was such an amazing success.

That changed everything for us business-wise, and we haven't looked back since. We donated over five hundred thousand dollars from the sale of all the presents Harris bought me to the Madagascan Hissing Cockroaches at the Bronx Zoo, in his name, of course. This seriously still makes me laugh. They were going to send Harris a shiny certificate of donation. I mean his donation is, after all, a tax deduction—he should be thanking me.

I haven't run into Harris since I've been back, but he's been prancing around town at every single event with his shiny new fiancée on his arm. He hated those events when I was with him, hated mingling with the people, sucking up to the old boys' club. Harris disliked it all, yet now, he's reveling in it. Go figure! Whatever floats his boat because he's not my problem anymore.

As the days go on, and the more I speak to Nate, which is every single night, the further from my mind Harris becomes. I know it won't be long until hearing his name, or seeing his picture in the news, doesn't instantly make my stomach churn.

I'm in the middle of making dinner when my phone begins to ring. Looking down at the screen, it's my sister. Quickly, I call her back, realizing my phone has been on silent, and I've missed a shit-ton of calls.

"Hey, what's happening?"

"Axel slept with Penny," Ivy curses down the phone.

Wait! What? There's no way Axel would have slept with Olivia's sister. No way! He's not that vindictive. Penny certainly is but not Axel.

"I'll send you the photo Penny sent, Liv." My phone beeps, so I pull it away from my ear and click on the message. There it is in color, Penny wrapped in a sheet with a sleeping Axel half-naked beside her. I always knew Penny was a bitch, and I've long suspected she's been fucking around with her sister's fiancé. I didn't know for sure, but they do hang out a lot in London partying together. The photographs I've seen online are pretty damning. Penny would have seen an opportunity to fuck over her sister, and Axel was probably thinking with his dick like most guys I know.

"We're heading to Olivia's parents' place in Mustique. She needs to get out of town."

"Is she okay?" Concerned for my friend, I know Olivia and Axel's non-relationship has been complicated, but still, she doesn't deserve this.

"She's devastated. Penny is the devil," Ivy hisses, and I have to agree. "I need to get her far, far away, so she can regroup."

I don't blame her, the change of scenery will do her good.

"Give her a huge hug for me and let her know I'm here if she needs me."

"Thanks. Sorry to dump this on you at the moment. How's things?" Ivy adds.

"Good. Harris seems to have forgotten about me. Work's super busy. I'm off to the Caribbean next week for work."

"With Nate?" Ivy asks.

"Yes. And a bunch of other employees."

"Okay." She doesn't sound at all convinced.

"I'm there for work."

My sister laughs. "Ah-huh... well, have fun. I'll be in touch when we get there." The phone goes dead.

Shit! The smell of my dinner burning pulls me from my thoughts.

I rush into the kitchen and ugh, it's ruined. There's no rescuing that charcoaled mess.

Think I'll order takeout.

****

Grabbing a glass of wine and my Chinese takeout, I sit in front of my television, but my mind's still thinking about Olivia. Picking up my phone, I call Nate.

"Hey, beautiful," he answers, which for some reason makes me feel giddy.

Maybe you need to slow down on the wine, Camryn.

"Hey, yourself."

"How was your day?" I like that Nate listens about my day in the same way I like hearing about his.

"Need to have a rant. Do you have a sec?"

"Yeah, of course. I'm in my villa looking at budgets. So, I could use the break and distraction."

"Your friend, Axel Taylor, is the world's biggest dick."

Nate's silence on the end of the phone speaks volumes—he's confused. "Did you just say Axel Taylor has the biggest dick?" he questions me.

I don't know, does he? Maybe. I don't think I've ever asked Liv. Oh, but Vanessa has told me Christian has a massive cock, and they're twins, so the likelihood is high. *Anyway, what were we talking about?*

"I don't know. But he is the world's biggest dickhead."

"Oh, I see." Nate laughs. "What happened?"

"You know how Olivia and Axel have been hooking up?"

"Yeah."

"Well, you know how I told you over New Years things blew up, and Eddie, her fiancé, rocked up throwing her under the bus..."

He agrees. "Well, Penny just sent Olivia a picture of her in bed with Axel."

"I don't believe it," Nate states.

I hear his phone beep. "Open the message," I tell him. The phone rustles as Nate opens up my text message.

"Okay. I agree it looks bad. But it could be a fake," Nate says in an attempt to stick up for his friend.

"Fake?" I raise my voice. "No. Axel's ego took a dent, and he's not used to that. Fucking rock stars." Not sure why I'm getting so worked up. *Stop the wine, Camryn.*

"I'm not defending Axel," he replies quietly. "But Olivia lied about having a fiancé."

I'm about to defend my girl to Nate, but he's right. Olivia hid the fact she had a fiancé.

"I know," I reply, calming down a little. "I told her what she was doing was wrong. I mean, me of all people, knows how much it hurts to find out the person you're with has a secret fiancée. But I didn't go off and sleep with Harris' brother when I found out. Not that he has one... but you know what I mean."

"I know. Men can be dicks," Nate agrees. "I also know that Axel isn't like that. He wouldn't hurt someone like that on purpose."

Maybe he's right.

"But the photo," I argue.

"I know it looks bad, but I swear there has to be more to it."

Dammit! I hate that he's making sense.

"Fine, you're probably right," I grumble into the phone, and he laughs. "Don't get used to me agreeing with you." This makes him laugh louder.

"Promise, I won't."

"It's one big mess."

"Yeah, but it's their mess."

Maybe he's right. Again. Damn him and his logic.

"Ugh… stop being so logical with your advice."

"Fine! How about this." Nate puts on a high-pitched voice. "Axel is the biggest douche in the world. Olivia doesn't deserve him. Penny is such a bitch." He has me laughing so much I have to hold my stomach.

"Stop it! I get it."

"I can be one of the girls when you want me to be." Nate's a genuine guy underneath all that bold exterior and uber sexiness.

"I like your dick too much for you to be a girl."

"Really! Tell me more about how much you like my dick."

"How about I show you how much when I get there."

"Can't wait." His voice has turned husky and needy.

"Thanks for listening to me."

"Anytime, babe."

I shouldn't like Nate calling me babe, but I do. I really do! More than I should. But friends can call each other babe, can't they?

"See ya soon." Butterflies swarm in my stomach, and I know that isn't a good sign.

"There are so many things I want to do to your body when you get here."

"You're going to have to make sure Sam's busy," I remind him of our mutual friend.

"He's not coming anymore," Nate tells me.

I shouldn't be excited, but I am.

"He's helping the Dirty Texas guys find some real estate in New York. Apparently, they're setting up an office."

"Harper isn't either," I let him know. "She's taking over the PR for Dirty Texas Records from Vanessa when she goes on maternity leave."

"Really? That's great." Nate sounds just as happy as I did about the Sam news.

"Yeah, I put her name forward knowing she'd be perfect."

"Kimberly's also staying. She has a last-minute event for one of her biggest clients."

"Bummer." He doesn't sound sad about that at all, which makes me internally giggle.

"I know. What are we going to do with ourselves?"

"I have so many ideas now that we don't have to hide," he muses.

I like the sound of that.

"Looking forward to it."

"See ya soon, Camryn."

20

CAMRYN

"Hey, ladies. Having fun in the Caribbean?" Ivy and Olivia's Instagram photographs have me seriously jealous.

"Yes, it's exactly what the doctor ordered." Olivia smiles. I can see her creamy skin is glowing, the bags under her eyes have almost completely disappeared.

"You both look relaxed. I'm freezing my butt off here in New York." A huge dumping of snow from a winter storm hit the city earlier, and it's chaos.

"We'll have a cocktail for you," my sister teases while waving her glass filled with some sort of tropical concoction in the air. *Bitch.*

"You're such a giver. Actually, I was thinking we could have a cocktail together in a couple of days."

"You want to come and stay with us?" Olivia asks, taking a sip from her fruity cocktail.

"Um… that's sweet, but no." I'm not sure how they're going to take what I'm about to ask. "I was thinking perhaps you ladies could come stay with me?" They both look at me strangely. "I'm organizing the soft launch of The Paradise Club Resort with Nate." I am hoping they remember my conversation about it that we had before Christmas. "And, well, I thought maybe you two lovely ladies would like to test out the facilities."

Nate asked me if I knew of anyone who might like to try it out for the first time. He was worried his loyal clients will love it no matter what. He wants to see what it will be like for someone new to the island, new to the whole Paradise Club thing. "When I say facilities, I mean have hot, wild sex."

The girls still, looking at me with wide eyes.

Crap! Maybe I've chosen the wrong two girls. I thought as they were in the area, it might be fun, but I don't know whether they are into that type of thing or not. "Hello? Guys... I can't hear anything. Did we lose the connection?"

"Um... no, we're here. Just a little stunned by your request," Ivy answers for the both of them.

"What? You don't want to come to a sex resort?" I remember back to my late-night conversation with my sister when she told me she wanted to try new things. Be more adventurous. This should be right up her alley.

"Of course, we do. We just weren't expecting that," Ivy adds.

"Um... so who's going?" Olivia asks tentatively. I know exactly what she's asking, and that's if Axel's going to be there.

"Don't worry, Axel declined the invite. He won't be there. Neither will the rest of the band. Something about expanding into New York, so they're here looking for office space," I state, putting Olivia at ease. "Come on! It will be fun... and wicked. The resort looks amazing. We're talking about seven-star luxury on an island. What Nate has built is spectacular. Plus, you both need some hot, wild sex as well, right?"

"Camryn," Ivy squeals with embarrassment. I love my sister, but she seriously needs to get some.

"Ivy, please. I know for a fact that it has been too damn long since you got your cage rattled."

My sister grumbles at me.

I turn my attention on to Olivia. "Come on, Liv, I know you

had fun at the club. I know things are shit right now. You don't have to do anything you don't want to do, but I would really appreciate two of my best friends helping me on this big project."

Yes, I will guilt them into coming if that's what it takes.

"Fine, we'll come," Olivia answers.

Yay! "Thank you both, so much. I promise you won't regret it."

* * * * * * * * *

"You're such a bitch," Kimberly tells me, looking up from her desk, which makes me laugh. "I'm stuck in the city when all I want to be doing is relaxing on a tropical beach, in the sunshine, with some hot young guy bringing me a cocktail and servicing me on the side."

"I'll make sure to appreciate the hot, young, pool boy and his cocktail for you."

"Bitch," Kimberly hisses again, throwing a stress ball at my head, making me clutch at my stomach with laughter.

"Love you." Walking over, I hug her. She grumbles but hugs me back anyway.

"In all seriousness, have fun, then report back all the naughtiness."

"Don't forget, in a couple of months, we'll all be there for the Grand Opening."

Kimberly smiles. "It can't come soon enough as far as I am concerned."

"I better go, have an early flight in the morning." Waving her goodbye, I rush out of her office before she can peg any more projectiles at me.

Stepping outside, I pull my coat around me tighter to hold back the bitterly cold night air. My driver's waiting for me, and he's standing by the door.

"Give me two secs, Damon. I want to grab something real quick."

He nods in agreement, closes the door, and hops back into the car to wait for me. Rushing up the street, sleet begins to fall toward the bright fluorescent lighting of the twenty-four-hour deli. I'll grab something quick for dinner, maybe some wine, and finish packing when I get home. It doesn't take me long to grab what I need and head on back out onto the street.

I'm not far from the car when I feel my arm being pulled, and hard fingers dig into my flesh as I'm yanked into an alley. A scream is on the tip of my tongue ready to be expelled until I hear the voice.

"Camryn," Harris says.

What the fuck?

Harris has dragged me into a darkened alley. My heart is thundering in my chest. My bags which were filled with my dinner and a nice bottle of wine are smashed all over the sidewalk. People are stepping around the mess, not even wondering why it's there.

"What the hell, Harris?" Catching myself, I say, "You scared the shit out of me."

"Baby, I'm sorry," he whispers. "I'm not allowed anywhere near you. It was the only way I could see you." He tries to reach out for me, but I take a step back.

What the hell does he think he's doing?

"You need to leave me alone, Harris." Folding my arms in front of me, I look around to see if there's a way to escape as Harris has the street blocked with his imposing body.

"I can't, Camryn. I miss you. I still love you." He reaches out for my hands, and I let him. I need him to think I'm complying, so he will let me go.

What kind of person acts like this? An irrational one, that's who.

I don't know what he's capable of.

I'm scared.

"What about Isabelle?" I gently remind him of his fiancée.

"What about her?" His words are like steel, and his eyes are dark and protruding.

"I don't think she'd appreciate you talking to me." My voice is calm. I am trying to use the most soothing sound I can without sounding frightened.

"She does as she's told. You don't have to worry about her."

Now that comment gives me chills and not in a good way. The way he said it was so cold and detached. I've never seen this side of him. Carefully, I pull my hands out of his grasp.

"Why did you sell your presents?" His tone turns accusatory.

"I didn't need them."

"You donated the money to the zoo."

"It's a tax deduction. Thought it might help." He eyes me suspiciously. It doesn't escape my attention that his hands are balled into fists at his sides. "I should go, Harris." I attempt to step around him, but he blocks me in.

"I miss you so much, Camryn." I can see that he means it, he keeps strong eye contact, and the look he is giving me is one of yearning and longing, and I am worried.

"I know."

"You don't miss me?" he questions.

"I miss what we had before it all fell apart."

There's hope in his eyes at my comment. Shit! That backfired.

"It wasn't my fault."

Grow a pair—you're a thirty-five-year-old man for fuck's sake.

"I had no choice, babe." He honestly sounds like a broken record.

"You *did* have a choice," I remind him. "You chose money over me."

Harris advances on me, pushing me up against the wall.

"I did it for us, you ungrateful bitch." My eyes widen at his venom. "Do you seriously think your little party business was going to be able to sustain *my* lifestyle."

Fuck him! At least I'm doing it on my own, not with Daddy's money.

"You need me. One false move, and I can destroy everything you've built here. I can make sure your little business disappears... just like that." He clicks his fingers right in front of my eyes.

My eyes narrow on him, and without thinking, I draw my eyebrows together and tilt my head. Harris is a fucking monster.

Without even thinking, I bring my knee up straight between his legs into his balls. Hard. He falls like a sack of potatoes to the ground.

"Don't you *ever* fucking threaten me, Harris. You have no idea what I'm capable of." Turning on my heels quickly, I rush back into the street.

"Miss Starr, Miss Starr... there you are." Damon looks frantic, his foot is tapping, and he's rubbing his chin when he sees me in the crowd. He rushes over, noticing I'm shaken and ushers me quickly into the back of the car. Slamming the door, he runs around to his side, starts the engine and speeds out into traffic.

"Are you okay, Miss Starr?" I can see the concern written on his face as he looks at me through the rearview mirror. "You're shaking." Looking down at my hands, I notice the visible tremor. The adrenaline must be wearing off.

"I lost you for a second and—"

"I'm okay, Damon," I reassure him. "Just take me home."

He does exactly that, and we don't speak again on the drive home.

I don't say a word as I get out of the car and rush through the foyer, ignoring the staff. Quickly, I punch my level and silently wait for the elevator. As soon as I enter my door, I rush to the shower, quickly stripping off and turn the faucet to hot. Standing under the boiling water, I attempt to clean off Harris' touch from me. I stay in the shower until the water runs cold, then I get out and into my pajamas.

My phone rings, pulling me from my zombie-like state.

Nate's name flashes against the screen and without even thinking, I answer because his voice is the only thing I need in this moment to help me through what's just happened.

"Hey, beautiful." I can hear the smile in his voice as he greets me. Biting back the tears that seem to have erupted and are now running down my cheeks, I don't answer. "Cam?" His voice turns serious all of a sudden. "Cam?" he says my name over and over again until I can't hang on anymore and burst into sobs.

21

NATE

No. No. No. No. What just happened?

As Camryn falls apart over the phone, I hear the uncontrollable sobs that are ripping through my chest like Wolverine's claws.

"What's happened, Cammie?" It's hard to work out what she's saying through her sobs, but I do catch the name 'Harris.' That fucking fuck, if he's touched a hair on her head, I will personally fucking kill him. I move to my computer and bring up my message app with Jackson, and shoot off a line about Harris getting to Camryn. He responds instantly letting me know he's on it. My main focus is Camryn right now and keeping her safe. My mind is rushing a mile a minute trying to work out how I can get to her, to get her to the island where I know she will be safe.

"Camryn..." I attempt to pull her from what appears to be a panic attack. "Babe..." I am trying to gain her attention. "Are your bags packed?"

"Yes," she squeaks out.

"Good. Good girl. You're leaving for the island tonight."

Silence.

"Nate…" My name is quiet as she whispers it, and if I weren't really listening, I wouldn't have heard it at all.

"No, Camryn. I have a jet on standby for you. Your driver has been alerted to the change of plans and will be back to pick you up in about twenty. He will be taking you to the airport to catch a private jet. You will be on the island by midnight tonight. Okay?" I don't want to force her into anything she doesn't want to do, so I wait for her reply.

"Okay."

To be honest, I'm surprised she's agreed so easily. "I'll see you soon. I promise you're safe with me."

"Okay," she says again.

I hope she knows I mean every word.

🌲🌲🌲🌲🌲🌲🌲🌲🌲

The fifteen-minute helicopter flight from the wharf to the island seems to be the longest part of the journey. I'm nervously waiting, the whole area is lit up like daylight waiting for the helicopter to land. Eventually, the sound of the blades echo through the night air, and I can see the lights of the helicopter come into view. It's not long until the chopper is landing on the grass, and I'm rushing toward it.

Opening the door, I'm relieved to see Camryn is safe. She gives me a sad smile. Her eyes are puffy from crying, and she looks so fragile sitting there. Without thinking, I unclasp her seatbelt and pull her into my arms, then carry her toward my villa.

Gary, the pilot, knows to leave her bags by the door. There's a buggy waiting for him to drive to his villa for the night. It's the least I can do for this late-night trip he's had to do for me. Camryn clings tightly to me, burying her face in my chest. I take the stairs two at a time to my bedroom. Gently, I place her on my bed. She gives me a small smile as I slide in beside her and wrap myself around her body. Moments later, she's sound asleep.

It took me a long time to eventually fall asleep. Stretching, I realize
Camryn isn't beside me. Panic laces my entire being as I touch
where she was, and it's cold.

Where the hell is she?

Jumping out of bed, I can't hear the shower running, so she's
not in there. I rush downstairs, my head flicking around. Then I
hear the sloshing out in the pool area. Looking out the glass
windows, I see Camryn's doing laps in the pool.

Relief.

Sighing, I step out into the sunshine and stand at the side of the
pool watching her.

She notices and stops in front of me and looks up. "Hey."

Camryn looks well-rested, fresh-faced, and is smiling. "Want to
join me?"

"Of course." Luckily, I am wearing a pair of shorts. As I jump
into the pool with a splash beside her, it makes her squeal. When I
pop back up through the surface, I have her in my arms. She lets
out a sigh, wrapping her arms around my neck. I can reach my feet
out to the floor of the pool as she wraps her legs around my waist.

"Thank you." The gratitude is written all over her face. "Thank
you for rescuing me."

"I didn't rescue you, Camryn. Selfishly, I wanted you
with me."

She smiles. "I don't think I would have woken well this
morning if I hadn't woken beside you."

Fuck! She's hit me directly through my protective heart.

Camryn leans forward and kisses me. Hesitantly, I open for her,
letting her set the pace. I am not going to push for anything more
than she's willing to give. Eventually, she pulls away, but I can't
help notice the fact that my dick is pressed squarely between her
thighs.

"I've missed you," she tells me.

"I've missed you, too, little one."

"Last night wasn't the grand entrance I wanted to make when seeing you again. I must have looked a mess."

The water is lapping between us when I answer, "I don't care as long as you are all right."

"I can't believe you organized all that for me last night." She seems in awe by the whole thing.

"I know people." Shrugging my shoulders, I smile.

"But you did this for me?" A frown mars her beautiful face.

"Of course. Remember... you're in my circle, now," I remind her of our conversation.

"Your circle feels safe."

Fuck! Jackson better be dishing out some kind of justice on Harris, otherwise I will be. She doesn't deserve this shit. Camryn leans down and kisses me again, this time with a little more heat. She finishes off the kiss with a bite to my bottom lip.

"I don't need to tell you what happened with Harris, do I?"

"Only if you want to," I state.

"You already know." My eyes widen with surprise as she continues, "You left your phone downstairs. I wasn't snooping, I promise. A message lit up from Jackson as I was grabbing a glass of water."

"What did it say?" Dammit! Knowing Jackson, it could have said anything.

"It said Harris won't be going anywhere near me again."

"Good." I can't hide my disdain for the man.

"He's going to fight back, you know," she warns me. "He said he would."

"Did he threaten you, Camryn?" My body tenses waiting for her answer.

"He's all bark and no bite." She shakes her head, but her eyebrows draw together in unease.

"Was it bark or bite last night?" As soon as the words fall from my mouth, I cringe. What was I thinking? Camryn lets go of me, putting distance between us. "Camryn…" The hurt is evident on her face as the sparkle dims in her eyes.

"You're right. It was most definitely, bite." Wrapping her arms around herself, she rubs her arms.

"Babe, I'm sorry." Walking back over to her, I state categorically, "I hate him. I hate him so much."

"I do, too."

Reaching out, I run my thumb along her cheek. "I promise you, Camryn, I won't allow him to ever come near you again."

"I know you won't."

"Is that okay?" I've totally crossed a major line between us, but how the fuck couldn't I?

"It's fine."

The tension slowly dissipates from my body.

She wraps herself around me again, and her hand disappears between us as she pushes past the band of my shorts before wrapping her hand around my cock. *Fuck me.*

"Camryn…" I give her a little warning.

"Please, don't treat me differently now, Nate. I'm not some fragile little woman who doesn't know the difference between an asshole and a good man when I see one."

"I know you're not," I reassure her. "I just need to know you're truly fine?"

"I am. I really am. And it's thanks to you." This puts me at ease. "Now, are you going to let me thank you properly or not?"

Oh, I like the sound of this.

Her hand continues to move up and down my dick. With great difficulty, I walk us to the shallow end.

"Get out of the pool and onto the bed," I demand while pointing to the large dome-like daybed beside the pool. Let's be serious, pool sex is not fun. With a giggle, Camryn stumbles out of the pool and begins to untie her red bikini, the top lands at my feet. Then seconds later, she's undoing the strings on the sides of her bikini bottoms that land with a wet whack on the ground. She jumps onto the large daybed with her face lit up in a large smile. She hurries by shuffling back to the middle of the large bed and watches me as I come to a stop right in front of her. Her eyes light up as I push my shorts down my legs and my dick slaps against my stomach, which makes her smile. She looks as hungry for sex as I now do. Her legs immediately fall open, inviting me in.

"No foreplay, Nate," she tells me.

"I need you inside of me."

If that's what the lady demands, that is what the lady gets.

One knee falls onto the soft cushion then the other follows as I crawl toward her, before stopping.

"Everything okay?" she asks.

"I don't have protection."

Fuck. Fuck. Fuck.

"I'm on the pill, and you know my test results."

Everyone who comes to the island needs to have an up-to-date sexual health check-up available.

"I've never…" I let the words fall between us.

"I haven't either." She bites her lip. "I can quickly run inside if you want?"

In all honesty, I don't want anything between us. I want to feel her bare against me. *What is wrong with me?* This is not like me at all. I am always so strict about protection.

"Are you okay if I'm bare?"

She nods her head slowly while biting her lower lip, and I'm nervous all of a sudden. Moving over her, I nestled between her legs. My dick rubs against her slit, making us both moan. I tease her with my dick, slowly letting it run between her folds, feeling her become wetter and wetter.

"Fuck me, Nate," Camryn demands, and before I have a chance to do exactly that, she grabs my hips and pulls me down and inside of her.

Shit.

Fuck.

We both hiss at the feeling. She's so wet, so warm, and so tight. God, this feels so good.

Looking down at her, her blonde hair is spread out like a beautiful angel. I slowly begin to move, and I can feel every movement like tiny little feathers running across my dick. The sensations are incredible.

Her fingers dig into my hips as I grab her legs and hoist them over my shoulders.

"Fuck, Nate," she blurts out as my dick slams deeper in her, hitting the spots I know are going to make her see fucking stars. Her tits bounce with each thrust, and they are mesmerizing me.

This feels so fucking good.

So right.

Camryn's here with me.

Mine.

All fucking mine.

"More, Nate. Please, more," she begs, and I give it to her, increasing my thrusts, stretching her, filling her. My thumb runs over her clit, and her cunt clamps down on me like a vice. Fuck, yes! Over and over again I play with her, teasing her, until she's begging for mercy.

I'm close, so fucking close, and with a little bit of pressure, I push her over the edge where she takes me right along with her.

22

CAMRYN

After a cleanup, we are tangled together in the daybed. "I could stay like this all day." I let out a long sigh.

"We can," Nate tells me. "We have nowhere to be until tomorrow." He nuzzles my neck, biting softly.

"Really?"

"Honestly. I've booked out today to spend it with you." Biting my lip at his surprise confession, he continues, "Before everything happened. I just wanted to spend the day in bed with you." He begins to rub the back of his neck nervously.

"Did you now?" I'm teasing him, and he rolls his eyes at me. "I'm glad," I reassure him. "It feels like we've had the longest foreplay since England."

"That feels like a lifetime ago." Nate runs his fingers through my hair, gently touching my face. My stomach decides, even though the moment is sweet, that it is the moment to assert itself, and we both burst out laughing.

"Sounds like you've worked up an appetite." He laughs, and I give him a friendly whack. "Come on, let's get you fed before you eat me."

Raising my brow at him, we burst out laughing again.

"Well, I hope you want to eat me." Giving my bare ass a slap as we slide off the daybed, it makes me squeal. He picks me up in his arms and rushes us back inside, then places me down at the foot of the stairs.

"Go... have a shower. I'll organize something for us to eat." He slaps my bare ass once again, and I quickly run up the stairs.

❦❦❦❦❦❦❦❦❦

Opening my luggage, I go to grab a cute sundress, but my naughty little schoolgirl outfit that I packed for him catches my attention. We might only have today to indulge in everything we want to do to each other, so might as well go out with a bang.

Coming down the stairs, Nate's busy in his kitchen and doesn't notice me. A couple of moments later, he turns around with a couple bottles of water in his hand and freezes. I stop just shy of the bottom stair.

"Mr. Lewis, may I have my lunch now, please? Before I have to return to the nuns."

Nate's sapphire blue eyes roam appreciatively over me. I'm wearing a pair of black Mary Jane shoes with knee-high socks, a tartan pleated skirt that basically doesn't reach my crotch, and a white button-down shirt that's cropped and tied with pretty much two buttons holding the material together with my tits ready to spill out. My blonde hair is pulled into pigtails with ribbons. Underneath this ridiculous outfit, I have a barely-there red G-String and red lace demi-cup bra, which hardly does anything except push my enormous boobs upward. Don't think I'll be wearing it for long, anyway.

"Miss Starr," he says without skipping a beat. "You are late for lunch."

Putting the water bottles on the kitchen bench, he continues, "You know what happens when you're late, don't you?"

No. No, I don't, but it better be something good. He opens one of the drawers in the kitchen, rattling things around with his hands, searching for whatever instrument he needs. Slowly, I make my way toward the dining room table, waiting for him. Nate pulls out a plastic spatula, and my eyes go wide.

What on earth is he going to do with that?

"Hands on the table. Back straight. Legs spread open," his voice changes with his commands. "You *will* take your punishment, like a good girl. Do you hear me?"

"Yes, Mr. Lewis." Smiling to myself, I love how quickly Nate has gotten into character. I always feel stupid roleplaying because the guys never keep character. As soon as they're turned on, that's it.

Assuming the position, I bend ever so slightly which exposes my ass to him. I can hear his footsteps as they come closer.

"Did you wear these panties on purpose, Miss Starr?"

"No, sir." Biting my lip, I dare not look at him.

"Don't lie to me. You wore these to try and tempt me, didn't you?"

"No, sir. I'm a good girl."

His hand runs over the curve of my exposed ass. "You most certainly are not a good girl, Miss Starr. I see the way you look at me in class. The way you suck on your pencil. You don't think I notice, but I do." He's standing behind me now, my chest is moving rapidly in anticipation for what he has planned next. "You're trying to break me, aren't you?"

"No, sir."

A whoosh through the air is the only notice I get before the spatula connects with my ass.

Fuck! That stings. I bite down through the pain.

"You're trying to get me to deflower you, aren't you?"

Another whoosh and crack against my ass.

"I bet you aren't even a virgin."

Another whoosh through the air but this time it connects with my pussy.

Fuck me! A tiny moan escapes my lips.

"Just as I thought. You're a hussy. You like me punishing you, don't you?"

"Yes, sir."

Another whoosh, and he gets me again across the pussy.

Fuck me dead! I move slightly forward away from the pain.

"I bet you're becoming wet with each one of my punishments, aren't you?"

Another whoosh, this time it's against my inner thigh which he rubs with his hand afterward.

Shit. Shit. Shit.

"Yes, sir." I am breathing through my nose.

Nate seems skilled with punishments. I mean the guy does own a sex empire, so I am sure he knows what he's doing. Trained with professionals and by professionals—he's an expert.

This is going to be fun.

Nate moves away from behind me and takes a seat at the end of the table. Lifting my head slightly, I don't dare move from my position. He looks like an arrogant king sitting on his throne as he pops a piece of fruit in his mouth.

"You must be hungry?" He raises a brow at me.

"I am, sir," I reply breathlessly. It's the truth. I am starving.

"What would you do for a bite of fruit?" He's holding up a slice of pineapple in his hand in front of my eyes.

"Anything you need, sir."

This makes him smirk. He seductively pushes the slice of pineapple into his mouth, then taps his thick finger against his bottom lip.

"Anything I need," he murmurs to himself. "Anything?" Raising a brow at me, he's now daring me, pushing me to see just how far I will take this role-playing.

I'll go all the way because I am having way too much fun to let an empty stomach get in the way of what might happen between us.

"Whatever you wish for me, sir."

That's the right answer because he gives me a genuine smile. "Stand up and come here, Miss Starr." His finger calls me over. Feeling a little lightheaded, I slowly move over to where he's sitting. He pushes his chair all the way back, leaving a large gap between himself and the table. "Stand here, please. Face the table." Pointing to the space, I do as I am told. "Now, lean forward and place your elbows on the table." Once again, I do as I am told, my face coming ever so close to the fruit platter.

A whoosh and a sharp sting across my thigh surprises me.

"Legs apart, Miss Starr." Moving my legs apart, I expose myself to him. "You may take one piece of fruit. But, stay on your elbows," he orders.

I take a large slice of pineapple that should fill me up a little. Slowly, I begin to eat, and he waits until I've finished before speaking to me again.

"Now, tell me... did you wear this for me, Miss Starr?" His finger slides between my legs and plucks my G-string before letting it slap back against me.

Shit, that was hot.

"Yes, sir."

"You may have another slice of fruit."

We repeat the same routine—I eat, he waits, then he begins again.

"You are tempting me, aren't you, Miss Starr?"

"Yes, sir." I am waiting for his next move, but nothing happens, he tells me again to eat something else, and we repeat that routine.

"Are you a virgin, Miss Starr?" he asks.

"Yes, sir."

His hand grips my ass cheek at that answer. "Oh, sweet girl, do you need help deflowering?"

"Yes, sir."

"Has anyone been inside of you?"

"No, sir."

That's when his finger slips between my folds and enters me, pushing me forward. My palms turn and slap the table at his intrusion.

"No one has slipped their finger inside this virgin cunt?" Dirty-talking Nate has come out to play as he curls his magic finger inside of me.

"No, sir."

"Do you like my finger inside of you, Miss Starr?"

"Yes, sir."

"Do you think you can handle more?"

"Yes, sir."

Nate slips another thick finger inside, stretching me. The burn quickly turning to pleasure. His fingers move ever so slowly, teasing me, taunting me.

"Eat, Miss Starr."

Grabbing a strawberry, I pop it in my mouth as he continues to torture me with his fingers.

"You're such a good girl." His hand rubs my bare ass. "I think you can take more." My eyes widen when a third finger slips inside of me.

Holy shit! I feel so full with the force he uses to push me forward against the table. The sensations are overwhelming.

"Look at your greedy cunt taking my fingers. Such a good girl," he continues to work me over, but each time he's careful not to touch my clit. He knows one touch and I'm going to explode.

Whoosh. A crack hits the side of my ass while his fingers are filling me, which makes me squeeze down on them.

"That's a good girl. Squeeze my fingers."

Whoosh again. Another crack. God, this feels amazing.

"Such a good little thing, aren't you?"

"Yes, sir."

"You've been waiting for someone to have their way with you, haven't you?"

"Yes, sir."

Nate's fingers don't let up during his questioning. His thumb slides against my back entrance with slight pressure being pushed against my hole. "I bet you've been letting the boys fuck you here, haven't you?" Pushing his thumb harder against my hole, I reply, "No, sir."

"Are you sure, Miss Starr?" he questions, pushing his thumb further past the puckered entrance.

Oh my God, my eyes roll back into my head.

"You seem to like it."

"I like it, sir."

"That's 'cause you're a hussy, Miss Starr." His fingers increase in speed inside of me. I feel like he's splitting me in two, but it's the most glorious feeling I've ever felt. "And hussy's like you, love their holes being filled."

Yes. Yes. Yes.

Then without notice, he pulls his hand away from me, making me whimper, and I feel desperately empty. My head turns to glare at him, but his hand is quicker with the spatula. Whoosh. Fuck! It makes me groan.

"Eyes ahead, Miss Starr," he commands. I do as I am told. "Eat," he orders.

With shaky hands, I grab a grape, this time popping it in my mouth. Nate's footsteps disappear, and after a couple of moments, they are back again.

Next thing I know, Nate's ripping my G-string from my body.

Holy hell, that's hot.

"Keep those legs open wide, Miss Starr." His tone is dark and commanding.

Then something cold lands on my ass making me jump.

"Stay still," he growls as his fingers begin to work over my hole. Over and over he massages it. Nate then leans over me and whispers in my ear, "The island's safe word is Paradise. Use it if you don't want to continue." He gives me a couple of moments to take in what he's said, but I don't flinch. I don't move. I want this so much.

"Good girl." His hand connects with my ass, hard. "I always knew you were a good girl, Miss Starr. You've always been eager to please."

"Yes, sir. I want to please you."

"Oh, you are." He caresses my behind, and then he's slipping inside of me. Not exactly the hole I thought he was going for but still feels so good. His thumb finds my other hole, and gently he begins to massage it while he moves slowly inside of me.

"You feel so tight. Taking me all in like a good girl. You like it, don't you?"

"Yes, sir."

A squirting sound echoes through the room, then something wet, cold, and hard nudges at my back entrance.

"You're taking me so well. Your cunt is greedy for more, I wonder if your ass is as greedy." *What does he mean?* "Relax, Miss Starr, I'm about to make you feel oh so good."

Slowly, he pushes something against my back entrance, working more and more lube against me all while thrusting inside of me. There's a slight burn as he pushes what I think is a butt plug past the entrance as my mind is diverted to Nate's thumb running over my clit. Who knew men could multitask? The butt plug finally slips easily in place, and I feel full. So very full as Nate continues to fuck me.

"You're not going to come, Miss Starr. Do you hear me?"

Hang on, what?

"No, sir," I defy him for the first time this session.

Whoosh. A slap against my ass. Fuck! The sensations are too much.

"You will *not* come until I tell you to, Miss Starr. Do you understand me?" His voice is sharp and menacing, which turns me the hell on.

"Yes, sir."

"Good girl, now you get your reward."

All of a sudden, my ass starts vibrating. What in the ever-loving fuck.

"Oh God." I cannot help breaking from character.

"He won't save you tonight, Miss Starr. The only name that you will be screaming is mine." He turns whatever it is up a little higher.

Holy fucking shit.

All while he's thrusting into me.

Don't come, Camryn.

Don't come.

I say over and over again.

I want to wait for him to tell me to because when he does, it's going to be spectacular.

Nate's slow, methodical thrusting keeps me at that heightened point as he slowly increases the power of the vibration of the plug. It feels strange, but oh so good. Nate starts to move quicker inside of me. Every so often there's a whoosh and a slap with the spatula, which simply increases the sensation. My mind's fuzzy with everything that's going on.

"You're such a good girl…" he caresses my ass, "… you have pleased me so much." Nate's words swirl around me, but my mind is in overdrive. "I think you deserve your reward now." His words slowly filter through the fog, while his thrusts become harder. He's turned the plug higher, then, holy shit. His thumb connects with my clit, and sparks begin to ignite.

"That's it, princess." Nate must notice the change in me. "You may now come." He puts pressure on my clit, lighting the fuse that has me igniting under his touch. I think I must blackout at some point because everything becomes foggy and dark.

Did I just pee myself? I feel liquid run down my thighs.

No.

Searching through the fog, I think he made me squirt—I've never done that before. Nate's grunting filters through the fogginess, and it doesn't last much longer before he's joining me in a liquified heap on the table.

The vibrating stops. The plug is removed. Now I feel empty.

Next thing, I'm in Nate's arms, and he's carrying me up the stairs into his room, past his bed, and into his bathroom. Still holding me, he turns on the shower, fiddles with the temperature, and places me inside. I'm unable to stand and slump onto the floor.

"Camryn?" Concern laces his voice.

"Give me a sec," I mumble through the water splashing over me. Next thing I know he's on his knees in front of me, and he appears concerned.

"Did I hurt you?"

Looking up into his handsome face, those sapphire blue eyes are darting back and forth over me, checking to see if he hurt me in some way.

"That. Was. Amazing…" I trail off while giving him a weak smile, and as soon as he sees it, the tension leaves him. "You've fucked me so good, I can't walk."

He chuckles. "That was the hottest thing anyone has ever done for me."

Reaching out, he caresses my face.

No one has dressed as a naughty school girl for Mr. Sex Empire. I'm shocked.

"Where the hell did you come from, Camryn Starr?"

23

NATE

We've spent the day lazing around my villa. We have gone for a swim and had a late lunch. We walked along the beach. Each time I have wanted to bring up Harris and what happened in New York, but I never wanted to spoil the moments we were sharing. But deep down, it's killing me.

Jackson told me he sent some guys around to Harris' place, didn't touch him, but most certainly warned him that the skeletons in his closet will most definitely reappear if he comes anywhere near Camryn again. Apparently, that didn't go over too well, which I'm not surprised because Harris has the ego the size of Manhattan.

"You okay?" Camryn asks, pulling me from my thoughts.

"Yeah," I answer while wrapping my arms around her tighter. We're currently lying outside by the pool with a nice bottle of red wine looking up at the stars. Millions of tiny shiny dots scatter the sky in their heavenly finery.

"You seem tense." Those jungle green eyes are sparkling with concern.

"I was thinking about Harris."

These words have Camryn sitting up and turning herself toward me. "Harris?"

"I can't stop thinking about what he did to you." My hand tightens around the wine glass stem. Camryn is silent for a moment while she assesses my words. Me? I am working out what her next words might be.

"He scared me," she says quietly. "I never thought he would go that far." She takes my hand in hers as if I am giving her the strength to continue. She entwines our fingers. "He brought me back to a time I want to forget…" She pauses for a moment taking a deep breath. "The night Vanessa was attacked, and all I could think about was is this going to happen to me?" Tears begin to slide down her cheeks.

"I will never let Harris Edwards near you again." My voice steels with anger.

"This isn't your fight, Nate."

Like hell, it isn't! Anger bubbles to the surface, and I can't help but let it pour out of me. "I protect my friends, Camryn."

"You hardly know me, Nate."

Her words hit me like a punch to the gut. Know her? What does she mean by that? I've spent every single night for the past couple of months on the phone with her, talking about anything and everything. How is that not knowing her?

"I know you, Camryn." Looking at her directly, she turns her head away from my intense glare. Lifting my finger under her chin, I turn her attention back to me. "I know you, Camryn," I repeat my statement for clarity.

"Nate…" The vulnerability on her face makes me think of her as someone who's exposed and defenseless.

"I've got you, Camryn." I need her to know that whatever's between us, no matter what, I have her back.

She leans forward and wraps her arms around my neck and hugs me tightly. Camryn begins to cry, which I know for someone as strong as Camryn, makes her feel vulnerable.

"I've got you," I tell her once more. She nuzzles her face into my neck. "I promise he will never touch you again."

She clings to me tighter, and we stay in this position for a couple of moments until she no longer needs my strength. "I'm sorry, Nate."

"You never have to apologize for being yourself in front of me."

She sucks in a deep breath. "What is this?" She moves her hand between us. "What's going on with us?"

I knew she might ask this question, especially after blurring the lines with my overprotectiveness.

"I like you... really like you," I reply, being honest with her.

"There's a but coming, isn't there?" She gives me a weak smile.

"I can't give you more."

"Never said I wanted more," she counters, surprising me. "Please know that I can tell the difference between friendship and sex. I'm so thankful you have my back when it comes to Harris because if I'm honest, I'm scared of him now. I thought he was just upset because he hates to lose, but now I think he might be crazy."

She sits up straighter. "I lost myself when I became involved with Harris. I'd been single for a long time before meeting him, and it was nice not to be lonely anymore." She shrugs. "My business is my first love, and after letting Harris take my focus away from it, I will *never* let that happen again. *Ever.*" She emphasizes the 'ever' making it abundantly clear she won't rely on a man again. "I like being with you, Nate." That's good to know. "But, I also like sleeping with other people."

I am definitely not a jealous man, but that stung. It's probably just my ego taking a hit.

"So, what you're saying is... you want to sleep with other people?" I am going to clarify this, so there's no miscommunication between us.

"And sleep with you... if you still want to, that is?"

"Of course, I do," I answer so quickly it makes her laugh.

"Good." She gives me a beaming smile. "Maybe we can have a 'friends with benefits' kind of deal. If that's what you want?"

Honestly, I don't want to give up her calls because this life, being consumed by work, it's a solitary life even when you're surrounded by workers.

"I'm not ready to give you up," I state categorically, my voice deepening with need.

"Same."

"When do your friends come?"

"Next week. Why?"

"Stay with me this week." Camryn's body freezes for a moment as her mouth falls open in shock, but she doesn't say anything, so I continue, "We can spend time together. Hang out. Work."

Camryn's quiet as she thinks it over. She's unsure about my request. I mean, I'm unsure why I've even asked the question because my villa here on the island is my sanctuary, but I like her in my bed even if it's only for the week.

"Okay," she eventually agrees.

"Okay?" I repeat just making sure I've heard her correctly.

"Yes." She crawls into my lap. "You might get sick of me, but I'm willing to risk it." Wrapping her arms around my neck, she begins to grind on me. My fingers grip onto her ass and dig in.

"You might get sick of me," I reply while nibbling along her neck.

"Honestly, I could never get sick of this." Camryn's hand reaches between us and grabs my dick through my board shorts. I know I will never get tired of her grabbing my dick, either.

She uses the thin material to slide up and down my shaft. *God, she's good.* Cam's wearing a white slip dress, no bra, and probably the tiniest underwear. I push the material of her dress up to find a tiny G-string and grip her bare ass. The sounds of the rainforest echo around us. This place truly is paradise, and so is the woman in front of me.

My hand moves between us and a finger slips between her wet folds.

"Yes," she hisses.

Her blonde hair is blowing wildly in the breeze. Her nipples are practically poking through the material of her slip dress. With my teeth, I pull one of the thin straps off her shoulder exposing a nipple. Leaning forward, I capture the puckered, pink bud into my mouth.

Camryn groans on connection, throwing her head back. Her fingers begin to unbutton my shorts, and slowly they fall apart exposing me to her. Sliding her hand over my sensitive skin, she grips me tightly. Nothing but the sound of crickets and a waterfall fill the void around us.

We continue exploring, touching, tasting one another in the darkness. Neither of us in a rush to take it further while we're savoring one another, enjoying simply being together.

"You're so beautiful, Camryn," I mumble into her chest while alternating between each of her nipples.

She moans at my compliment as my teeth connect with her sensitive skin. Camryn continues to ride my fingers in time with her movements across my dick. We continue teasing each other until I can't bear it anymore and pull my fingers from her cunt and move her over me, then thrust up into her.

"Yes, Nate, yes." Camryn moans when I enter her.

Her lips connect with mine as we become feverish with need. Our kiss is sloppy, teeth meeting teeth, lips missing each other, we're so caught up in each other that we don't care. Need has taken over, and we're both desperate to catch our orgasms.

Gripping her hips, I hold her tightly, forcing her pussy to grind across me as she rides me. Her cunt constricts around me as she becomes closer.

"That's it, Camryn, give it to me. Give me everything you have."

Seconds later, she's coming, and I'm not far behind her, pumping myself into her spectacularly tight cunt.

God, she's perfect.

I don't know how I'm going to let her go after this week.

24

CAMRYN

A fter spending all day yesterday screwing Nate, today we have put our professional hats on, and I'm exploring the island. Nate is waiting by the golf buggy looking like a sexy island snack. He's dressed in a white polo, khaki-colored shorts, deck shoes with a pair of aviators over his eyes. Hot!

The tropical heat is taking a little getting used to, and my hair has frizzed up so much I've thrown it into a messy bun. I've chosen a white summer dress with cute silver flats, and I'm ready to explore this fabulous island.

"Ready for a tour of the resort?" Nate hands me a chilled bottle of water.

"I'm so excited." I take a seat next to him in the buggy. Nate smiles at me before quickly leaning in and kissing me. As usual, it doesn't take long for the kiss to become heated, but we need to get this underway, so I pull back.

"Just had to kiss you one last time before we have to be professional," he says.

I hang on as Nate takes off, hurtling us through the jungle. Nate's being a professional tour guide explaining the history of the island. How it used to be overrun by pirates, which gives me all kinds of dirty fantasies, and I make a dirty joke about how he can plunder my booty which makes him laugh. He explains the process of getting the island to what we're seeing today, and how he hired one of his clients—who's a world-renowned architect—to help him design the ultimate fantasy island experience.

"The island has been split into sections, just like the levels of the clubs," Nate explains as we continue winding our way through the rainforest. "There are beginner, intermediate, and expert areas. We want people to feel comfortable in what they want from their experiences. Each section has signage indicating what level each of the zones are. White is beginner, black is medium, and red is expert," he tells me, then points out a couple of different signs with the colors displayed on them. It's all pretty cool.

"We have sections for couples where they have their own pool areas and bar. Not everyone wants to party all night. Some are simply after a relaxing holiday with a side of kink." Nate smirks at me. "We also have an area that's dedicated to singles. This area will be the party zone. They have their own pool and bars. It's a place for people to mingle. Couples, of course, can join in, but we ask singles not to go into the couples zone unless they've been specifically invited. Remember, clothing is optional at the resort." Nate smiles.

"Don't get any ideas, Mr. Lewis, I'm not about to swan around the resort in my birthday suit." Nate gives me an amused pout. "Clothes must be worn in the eating areas and bars, except in the swim-up bar areas."

The last thing I want to see is shriveled up balls as I pop a meatball in my mouth.

We continue through the forest. Nate explains to me the different types of accommodation you can stay in. There are stunning villas on the beach that are dotted along the shoreline and back into the rainforest. There are also luxury treetop houses set high in the trees which overlook the ocean and the resort below.

This experience is giving me sexy *Robinson Crusoe* vibes or naughty *Pirates of the Caribbean* parties.

Then there are the overwater bungalows which have see-through floors, where you can watch the fish swimming beneath you. Those bungalows also have private pools that jut out from the side of the bungalow and have infinity sides.

"Each room has its own private host. We choose the person based on the client's preferences they submit before they arrive. We make sure we select the right people to make their holiday the most enjoyable it can be."

"You've thought of everything."

"We have dedicated spa areas for massages... the sexual and non-sexual kind. People are here to relax and have a holiday, they don't necessarily need to have sex twenty-four seven. That's why we have so many activities for the guests like day tours, the best restaurants, luxury boutiques, bars, everything a normal resort offers. It's just that we have a little bit extra."

They most certainly do.

I mean, I'm sold.

Sign me up for a life membership.

"Over there..." he swings around, "... set away from the beach is a large glass room." Nate points between the palm trees to a large glassed off area. "This is made for the voyeurs and exhibitionists. They can come straight off the beach to the open showers. As you can see, there's enough space for more than a couple of people."

"That looks like a fun experience." I don't think I'd mind if people watched Nate give me an extra soapy shower between the palm trees.

"There's a whole section of the resort on the other side of the island which is dedicated to certain kinds of fetishes. Anything you could desire, within legal reason, is catered for with our state-of-the-art facilities. I scoured the world for the best masters I could find... they also helped me design the playground."

The place is huge. I'd be totally lost if Nate hadn't shown me around.

"As this is a resort, most of the areas are spread out across the island. We wanted people to get out of their comfort zones and explore. You never know what you might discover around the next corner."

"It's like a naughty scavenger hunt."

He chuckles as we drive a little more.

"I've also included a smaller version of The Paradise Club at the resort. The only catch is all the playrooms are open-door. We have so many closed-door areas on the island, so if someone wants to play away from everyone else, one of our staff will drive them to that venue."

Wow! How the hell has he come up with all this, and even more so logistically worked it all out. I'm impressed. I mean I knew he had a great business mind because you don't get where you are by not being savvy, but listening to him speak so passion-ately about his business, about trying to give people the best, safest experience that he can, yeah, it gets me hot. Not going to lie. Nate's brain turns me on.

After our tour, we spend the day in meetings finalizing organi-zation of the soft launch of the resort in a couple of days.

There's so much work to do, and so little time before the guests begin to arrive.

25

NATE

We've been working hard for the last couple of days concentrating on what we need to do for the Grand Opening. We haven't really had much time to explore the delights of the resort in its full capacity, not that Camryn and I haven't been having fun together. Most nights we come home to my villa, grab a bottle of wine, and talk business.

Yep. Talking work does it for me, and listening to Camryn speak about strategies really gets me going.

Once dinner is done, we might have a naked swim in the pool, which leads to lots of fucking on the edge, or a late-night swim at the beach with a nice outdoor shower, which leads to more fucking, or we could be watching Netflix and chilling on my couch, and next thing I know Camryn's riding my dick.

Not going to lie, I kind of like what's going on between us.

I enjoy coming back to my villa and finding her relaxing with no makeup on and messy hair, and a wine glass in her hand while hunched over her laptop. She might be humming to a song in the background or sucking on a pen. Then she will look up at me with those bright green eyes, and I can see the excitement register once she notices me. Sometimes, she will jump up and wrap herself around me, or other times I'm so overcome by her that I just kiss her. Nothing more, just a sweet tender kiss—one that takes both of our breaths away.

I know whatever's happening between us isn't going to last forever. I mean we're both on two different life paths which may cross over now and then, but mainly we are heading in opposite directions. Also, I can't give her the time she deserves, not with everything that's going on in both of our careers, and Camryn deserves more. She deserves to be treated like the goddamn queen that she is. She deserves a man who will give her everything this world offers. She deserves a man who will remain faithful to her.

How can I in this life?

It's not like I've been wanting to sleep with anyone else, but what happens if I do and things have progressed further in a relationship between us? I'm just going to be like all those other dickheads she's dated and break her heart. I'm going to be just like fucking Harris, and I don't want to do that to her.

Maybe it's good Camryn's friends are coming to the island to hang out with her. That way we can put some distance between us. She can explore the island with them and without me. While she's doing that, I can get my life back to normal before this blonde whirlwind has come in and messed everything up.

We are both living in a fantasy world, one I've created.

This, whatever it is, can't work outside of the island.

"Hey..." Camryn bounds into the living room. "Want to have some fun?"

"Continue..." I give her a smirk, wanting to know what she has in mind.

"It's late, but I was kind of hoping that maybe we could..." She bites her bottom lip as she nervously looks around the room. She has my full attention now, so I lean in closer. "Try that giant shower near the beach?" Her words are tumbling from her mouth so quickly it's hard to keep up. I know instantly what she's talking about. I remember showing her on the tour, and her eyes lighting up when she saw it. Her mind's probably filled with all sorts of sexy scenarios. "Before my friends come." She seems nervous about her friends coming. I'm not sure who they are, not that it matters because they have been vetted by the team.

"Of course." Reaching out for her, I pull her into my arms, and she comes willingly, straddling me on the couch. "Might have to get you nice and dirty first, though."

Camryn looks at me and smiles. "I like your thinking, Mr. Lewis," she replies while rubbing herself against me.

Fuck me, simply touching Camryn has my dick achingly hard.

Her hand pulls me out of my shorts, then she starts long, hard strokes, which has me closing my eyes. I'm going to miss her grip when this ends, no one has gotten me off so quickly and easily as Camryn can. She continues to tug on me, revving me up, teasing me. She likes it when I can't take it any longer and take her hard and rough. She likes it when I'm in control. She loves letting me take the lead but not all the time.

"I need you, Camryn." Want courses through my body, so undeniable, it's hard to control myself.

"Not yet," she whispers in my ear. "Save it for the shower," she purrs.

What? No! I need her now.

Camryn moves from my lap where all my blood has flowed into my dick, and I've lost brain capacity.

"Come on, Nate. I'll drive." She calls me with her finger, and I go, willingly. I would follow her into the depths of hell in this moment because all I can think about is fucking her into oblivion.

We jump into the golf buggy, my dick aching as we sit. I can't help myself as we hurtle the buggy through the rainforest, then along the beach path until we find the clear box which is illuminated in the dark, dense forest, like a shiny beacon. Camryn's out of the buggy and giggling as she skips along the sandy path toward it. She's shed her white slip dress, she's kicked off her flip-flops, and she's not wearing a bra or panties.

Damn, this woman.

Quickly, I follow after her. She's already in the shower as I reach the glass, and she has placed a sign up indicating 'Do Not Disturb - Viewing Only,' meaning she just wants me to fuck her, but everyone else can watch. I feel like this is our last hurrah before everything changes tomorrow with the arrival of her group of friends.

If this is what she wants, I'll gladly give it to her.

"Camryn…" I call her name as I open the door to the glass box. "There's a camera in here." I point to the tiny little black box in the corner, and she stills. "No one can record the stream. No one can hear what's going on inside the box, but they are notified via their tablet if they want to watch." Her eyes widen. "There's a button here…" I point to the button beside the door. "If I press it, it will cut the feed." She looks over at it and screws up her eyebrows. "Do you want me to stop it?"

Camryn doesn't move, her eyes continue to stare at the button, then she finally answers, "No. I want them to be jealous when they watch us. To wish they could be fucking either one of us. I want them to get off watching you with me."

My dick is frantically pushing against my shorts. Moving my hand away from the button, I drop my shorts and close the door behind me. She eyes me appreciatively.

"It's just you and me inside here." Biting her lip, she nods in agreement. "Sit on the step, Camryn." There's a seat to one side of the shower area, the perfect height to be used for practically anything we wish. "Open those thighs for me, sweetheart."

Camryn does as she is told, sitting on the cold step.

"Now, put on a show for our viewers because we have some." She tilts her head in a questioning way as I continue, "I can see how many people are watching via the tablet in the wall." She spins her head around spying the hidden screen, and she smiles.

We watch the numbers jump as people log on. "Show them just how beautiful you look coming all over my face."

Falling to my knees, my fingers grip her luscious thighs, spreading them wider for me. There's a slight back to the step which she lays against, angling her pussy toward me. Like the starved man I am, my head falls between her thighs as my tongue swipes across her slit, one, two, three times, and it makes her hiss. Her fingers dig into the skin of my shoulders while I'm lost in her scent, her taste, her warmth. Being on my knees before her is exactly where I'm supposed to be, even if it's for the short term.

"Nate," Camryn hisses as I continue my assault on her pussy. "More... more." Her voice raises meaning she's getting closer.

Adding a couple of fingers with my tongue has her practically growling, her tight little cunt squeezes my fingers as they move inside of her. I've mapped every inch of her body these past couple of days, and I know the exact route to her explosive zone. My fingers curl and caress that tight bundle of nerves which has her panting.

"Nate. Oh God, Nate..." she pants.

I have no idea if anyone is watching anymore because my sole focus is on her and her pleasure as I continue to get her off.

"Fuck, fuck, yes. Oh, good God, yes," Camryn screams as she comes all over my fingers and mouth. Her tiny convulsions continue as I slowly bring her back down to earth.

Sitting back on my heels, I give her a satisfied grin as I wipe her from my lips.

"I'm going to miss that tongue, Mr. Lewis." Camryn's cheeks are flushed, her pupils are wide, and a lazy smile hangs from her lips.

"I'm going to miss that sweet pussy, Miss Starr."

"Looks like we have some fans."

Looking over my shoulder, I see about ten people in various states of arousal watching us.

"Shall we give them a show?"

"Yes." She grins.

"Turn around."

Camryn does as she's told. Placing her against the step, she opens her legs wide for me. Standing behind her, I give her gorgeous ass a hard slap, making her gasp, and her cheek turns a nice shade of pink. She turns her head and smiles at me , so I do it again, which makes her bite her lip, but she continues watching me. I slap the other cheek now, jolting her forward an inch or two, while she hums with appreciation. I slap her again, this time my hand hitting her plump pussy lips, which makes her squeal because they're still sensitive from her orgasm. If only I had a whip, that would be perfect. Looking around the space, I spot her white slip dress made of linen. I am sure it will have a little bite to it. Grabbing the material, I roll it up until it's the perfect thickness.

"Open wide." I nudge her thighs apart with my knee then flick the material against her cheeks, working it out after each slap. Camryn is wriggling after each hit. Lining her up, the material hits her pussy at the right angle, and she falls forward on a hiss. I do it again and again in quick succession, which has her panting then collapsing forward on her forearms, exposing her wet pussy to me.

"Show them how much you like it, Camryn," I remind her of our audience.

Another succession of slaps across her rear have her panting and gasping with need. Her cunt glistens under the night stars as she tries to control the orgasm that's building.

"They can see how fucking wet you are, Camryn. They wish they could savor every last drop of you. But, they can't because you're mine." I'm determined to make her come now that I can see how much she likes it. Another couple of sharp strikes has her screaming out. "That's it, sweetheart. Give them more. Show them how much you love to be punished. That you're a bad girl."

Camryn bites her lip as another couple of swats connect with her skin, this time harder.

"You like it, don't you?" She nods her head. "You like me

showing them what a naughty girl you are." Her head jerks again. "You're mine to punish. You're mine to pleasure." Hitting her clit has her knees almost buckling. "No one knows what you want like I do," I continue talking, but don't let up on the strikes. "I'm the only one who knows how to please you... fuck you... to care for you."

Slap.

Slap.

Slap.

I continue until she comes undone with the next hard strike right across her pussy. My chest is heaving with exhilaration as the material falls away from my hand. I'm lost to the thrill of it as I step closer to her. My fingers dig into her hips as I line my dick with her swollen pussy and enter her.

Fuck! Yes.

She feels so warm. So slick. So tight.

I'm so lost inside her as I thrust, losing all semblance of decency as I fuck her wildly. Raw need has taken over, and it's uncontrollable.

I take and take and take until I can't anymore. Until I physically cannot hold on. Until she has taken everything from me that I willingly give. Until the fucking stars in the sky blur, and a wild roar leaves my body as I come.

Something inside of me cracks.

Shatters.

Something changes.

No. I can't do this.

Pulling myself quickly from her sweet cunt, I grab my shorts and put them on. By the time I turn back, Camryn has a concerned look on her face.

"Are we going to talk about what just happened?"

Dammit, it's as if she can read my fucking mind.

I don't like it, not one little bit.

"No." Grabbing my T-shirt, I throw her white dress over to her.

"Okay," she replies with a raised brow while slipping the material over her gorgeous body.

We silently pass the voyeurs who have either finished or are still going.

We don't say a word as we hop into the golf buggy and head home.

26

CAMRYN

"A re we going to talk about what happened?" I question Nate as we enter his villa.

"No," the stubborn fool answers me again.

"Nate." Grabbing his arm, I attempt to gain his attention. "I can handle whatever it is." He frowns. "If you don't want me anymore, it's fine."

Nate tenses. "You think I don't want you anymore?" His voice raises as he rakes his fingers through his thick brown hair. "That is so far from what happened."

"Then what did happen?"

"I realized all this..." he moves his hand around us, "... is over."

Oh. Realization hits me too.

"Do you not want *this* to end?" Hope springs in my chest because I've been feeling the same way. Our time together has been great, and I'm sad that it's ending.

Nate's face softens as he looks at me. "I will *never* be the man you deserve, Camryn." Crap! That's a sucker punch to the chest. "I can't be what you need."

"How do you know what I need?" My anger bubbles to the surface at his assumption.

"I know you, Camryn."

"No, you damn well don't." I raise my voice. "You have no idea what's going on inside of me. You have no idea what I want and from whom."

Nate doesn't seem convinced. I can tell by the shaking of his head.

Ugh. How did this night go from epic to crap in two point five seconds?

Storming off, I head toward our room.

"Camryn," he calls after me. "I wish I were the man for you, but I'm not."

Turning quickly on my heels at the bottom of the stairs, I say, "I know you're not the man for me." This has him pausing in his steps. "Because the way you're acting right now proves to me you don't really know me at all." His eyes widen. "Have I given you any indication that I want more?" He shakes his head. "Then why the fuck do you think I do?" Placing my hands on my hips, I keep going, "Why the hell are you giving me this bullshit speech of... blah... blah... blah? I'm not the man for you bullshit." Nate simply stares at me like a deer caught in the headlights while he says nothing. "Exactly! I didn't." Turning around, I stomp upstairs to our bedroom and storm into the ensuite and angrily undress before jumping into the shower.

"Camryn, I'm sorry. I thought after spending this week together..." Nate enters the bathroom, and I ignore him as I lather myself up. Goddamn men are dicks sometimes. "I..." He rubs the back of his neck nervously, and for the first time, Nate seems speechless. Wiping over the fogged-up screen of the shower door, so I can see his face before it mists over again, I angrily call out, "Get in the fucking shower, Nate."

Moments later, he's stepping into the cubical with me. Handing him the soap, he lathers himself up, and I help because even though I'm pissed at him, the man is fine. We bathe in silence.

"I wish things were different," Nate eventually murmurs to me beneath the water.

"What do you mean?"

"You're the kind of woman I could easily fall for." Damn him! "No." He shakes his head. "You're the woman I have fallen for."

Holy shit! My eyes widen in surprise at his admission.

"But I don't want more."

Well, fuck me, that was a bit of emotional whiplash.

"So, let me get this right... you've fallen for me, but don't want me?"

"Oh, I want you, Camryn. Don't think for one moment that I don't want you." Hunger burns in his eyes, and I can tell he means the words.

"You just don't want a relationship?" I finish for him.

"Yes."

"But I don't want a relationship with you, Nate."

His eyes widen with surprise. It's been incredible this week together, but that hasn't changed the way I feel.

"I like you. Actually, I like you a lot. Especially, your dick..." Reaching out wrapping my hand around it with a smirk. "I thought I made it clear from the start, Nate. My life is my business at the moment." My hand grips him tighter. "I'm not looking for anything more." Letting my hand glide over his dick, I feel it harden underneath me. "Am I going to miss staying here and being able to ride your dick any time I want? Yes." My hand grips him tighter. "I've liked living with you. I like coming home to you. I like having your dick on call twenty-four seven." Grinning as my hand keeps sliding against his velvety skin. "I like you... *a lot*." I emphasize the words. "But I'm going to be selfish this year. It's all about me and my wants. My needs. I'm not going to compromise for anyone."

"Fuck, Camryn." Nate's eyes roll back inside his head as I

continue to glide over him. "I've never wanted someone as much as I want you, and to be honest, it scares me."

"You're going to be a hard man to forget, Nate Lewis."

"Then don't," he's quick to answer, pushing me back against the wall. "Don't stop fucking me." His words are desperate. "I'm not ready to let you go."

"I won't be faithful, Nate. I've told you, I'm being selfish this year," I warn him.

"I can't either. Not in this world. Temptation is all around me."

"So what do you want?"

"You, when I'm in town," he suggests.

"Like a booty call?"

"Yes. Maybe even friends with benefits?"

"Will I be getting a membership to The Paradise Club?" I counter his offer.

"If you want. Free of charge. Call it a friends-with-benefits offer." He gives me a smirk.

"What happens if I'm busy when you're in town?"

"Then you're busy. When you can fit me in, I'll be there."

"You can have anyone in the world? Why do you want this with me?" I don't think I'm that much of a catch.

Nate's hands cup my face as he looks at me tenderly. "I don't want to let you go, Camryn. I'm being the selfish one now because I like being around you. I like being with you. I simply like you *a lot.*" Nate emphasizes the words which make me smile.

"Okay," I agree to his request, and for some reason, he seems surprised.

"Okay?" He double-checks with me.

"Nate, I like riding your dick. Of course, I'm going to be okay with fucking you any chance I can get."

"Is that so?" Of course, complimenting a man on his dick has him rising to the occasion.

"Yes, it is so. It's a fine dick."

"Fine?"

"Not as in okay fine as in fffiiinnneee." I wiggle my brows, which makes him chuckle.

"Well, how about you ride this fffiiinnneee dick one last time before I have to give you back."

"That sounds fine to me." I giggle as Nate turns off the shower.

27

CAMRYN

"I can't believe you guys are here," I state while wrapping my arms around Ivy and Olivia.

"This place truly looks like paradise to me." My sister looks around the island in awe.

"Wait till you get further in… it's a dirty paradise." I send them both a wink, and Olivia gives me a knowing smile, but my sister's jaw drops a little. I think it's going to be fun shocking her, and I am looking forward to it.

"Thanks, Steven." The concierge has laden up the golf buggy with their bags, and I give him a quick salute.

"He's cute." Ivy, my sister, elbows me.

"He's available to play." I wiggle my eyebrows at her.

"Really?" Ivy turns her head around to get a second look.

"You can tell by the colored bracelets they wear." I explain the meanings behind them to them both. "Yours are waiting at your villa for you."

"Thanks for inviting us. As much as I love my parents, being stuck on an island with them for too much longer would have had me jumping ship," Olivia groans.

"Thanks for coming. I know things are tough for you at the

moment." It's not like Axel, from Dirty Texas, and Olivia were ever going to be able to run off into the sunset with each other and live happily ever after. The girl is bound to some royal creep that her parents are desperate for her to marry. One thing you can say about Olivia Pearce is she's fiercely loyal, maybe to a fault, but each to their own.

"I never want to hear the name Axel Taylor, or listen to another Dirty Texas song for as long as I live," Olivia huffs.

That's going to be a little hard seeing as they are the biggest band in the world. At least my man-drama is wrapped up in the society pages of New York and not the world.

We continue on through the winding rainforest paths of the resort, while I point out the benefits of the different areas.

"Oh my God, that man is naked." Ivy gasps as we pass the beach area, where a tall, dark, and extremely well-endowed man is walking out of the ocean along the beach to his towel.

"Get a good look, did ya, sis?" I begin giggling while taking in her shocked expression.

"Sure did. You can't miss that thing hanging between his legs." She turns back to me and bursts out laughing, her cheeks pink with embarrassment.

"It was impressive," Olivia adds with a smile.

"Wouldn't mind giving it a bit of a test drive," I add.

"So, nothing's been happening with Nate, then?" Ivy asks.

"Of course not... I've been utterly professional." Keeping my eyes on the path, I dare not look at my sister because she will know instantly.

"Bullshit!" Olivia calls from behind.

"I call bullshit, too," Ivy adds.

"Come on, guys, I'm a professional." They both know me too well, though, and have guessed correctly.

"Professional at riding dick," my sister jabs.

"Hey!" Making her laugh, I give her an elbow to the ribs.

"Not saying there's anything wrong with that, though," she

quickly adds. "Nate is good-looking, and there's a spark between
the two of you. You're both single. You're at a sex resort. I mean,
hello... sex is flowing all around you. You can't tell me you
haven't slipped just once?" Ivy pushes.

I remain silent for a couple of beats. "Fine! Yes, okay? I
slipped a couple of times."

The girls squeal at my confession.

"It was good, wasn't it?" Olivia questions.

"Of course, it was. The guy owns a sex resort. He knows what
he's doing."

"And?" Ivy pushes, asking for more.

"And, that's it. We both had a need to scratch, which we did.
But that's it." Turning to look at my sister, she looks disappointed.

"Will you sleep with him again?" Olivia asks.

"Maybe. Maybe not. There are plenty of other men on the
resort who are up for a good time." Turning toward the beach
where the overwater bungalows are located and where we're all
staying, I continue driving.

"You're going to hook up with other people?" Ivy seems
shocked by my admission.

"Um... yeah. I don't have a ring on my finger. We're both
single, so why not?"

"You won't be jealous?" she continues.

"No. We aren't in a relationship."

Ivy has a frown on her face. I know this is hard for her to
understand because Ivy isn't like me, she thinks as soon as you've
slept with someone, you are monogamous. That you don't dare
look at anyone else, even if you don't have a commitment from
them. She gets her heart broken a lot. She can't change the way she
is. When the right man comes along, he will treat her right and the
way she deserves, but until then, she has to wade her way through
all the damn dickheads.

"Wish I was more like you." Her answer comes out quietly and
on a sigh.

"Oh, babe..." I feel sad for her, "... I'm sorry. But it is who you are. You're a good person, you don't have to change yourself for a guy."

"I lack confidence, that's my problem."

"You are the best interior designer in the world," Olivia adds.

"Thanks." Ivy sighs. "I'm so confident when it comes to work and dealing with men at work, even if I find them attractive. But when I step out of work mode, I turn into this wallflower."

"But, that's okay, too." I attempt to reassure my sister that being a wallflower is fine if that's who she truly is. She doesn't have to be something she's not.

"I think I'm missing out on things... on life... and on really good sex," she confesses.

Ah, okay, she's been thinking about this.

"Well, you've come to the right place to experiment."

"You wouldn't think I was weird?" she asks.

"What! No," I reassure her. "This is an extremely safe environment to test out being someone else. To experiment. To be free." Reaching out, I squeeze her leg.

"Thanks, Camryn." She gives me a small smile as we continue on in silence until we arrive at our destination.

"Here we are," I state as I pull up out the front of the overwater bungalows."

"Oh my... this is..." Ivy's eyes widen.

I know, it was my first thought too when Nate showed them to me. These large, luxurious villas are set out over the crystal blue of the ocean. The colorful fish are darting playfully around beneath the see-through flooring.

"Let me show you inside." We walk over a little bridge, and once we get to the villa door, I swipe my card across the lock, the light turning green, and it opens for us.

"This is gorgeous," Ivy says as she takes in the all-white and wood of the overwater bungalows.

"Oh my God, look at the pool," Olivia adds. There is a lap pool that juts from outside to inside the room. "Look at the fish." She points to the clear bottom of the pool, where you can see the tropical fish swimming around beneath the pool.

"Whoever designed these rooms is amazing," Ivy adds. "I'm going to need to know who did this?"

"I'll find out for you. Come on, you're next door," I indicate to my sister. Just as we're leaving, there's a knock at the door. Opening up Olivia's villa door, there stands a Scandinavian god— blond hair pulled into a man bun, a little bit of stubble on his jawline, his white polo shirt pulled tightly across his muscular torso and thick corded biceps. He's standing there with a bottle of champagne and a platter of chocolate-covered strawberries.

"Miss Starr, Miss Starr," he greets Ivy and me. "I'm Leon, Miss Pearce's villa host." We move away from the door to give Olivia a look, her mouth falls open in shock.

"Liv, this is your butler." Smiling from ear to ear, Leon enters the villa, putting the items down for her. Olivia's staring at him in awe. She also appears a little flustered.

"Miss Pearce, I'm your host, Leon," he introduces himself directly to her. "And I am here at your service day and night to fulfill any of your needs."

Ivy's eyes widen as she mouths to me, "Anything?"

I nod my head. Honestly, I don't think her eyes could widen any more than they are.

"Let's go." Ivy grabs my hand.

"Liv, dinner in a couple of hours. Meet you out front," Ivy yells out over her shoulder as she pulls me back over the bridge.

"Is that man for real, Cam?" Ivy questions me.

"Yes. Each villa has a host especially allocated to you, who caters to anything you want."

"You're not spelling it out, Camryn. Anything I want… like as in… sexually?"

"Yes." Chuckling at my sister's enthusiasm, I carry on with, "You can ask them to do anything you want, or they can arrange anything you want. You have a whole tablet filled with naughty requests."

Ivy simply shakes her head as we link arms, and I show her to her room.

It isn't long until Ivy has a knock on her door. She claps her hands excitedly as I walk over and open the door for her.

"Miss Starr, my name is Grange, and I will be looking after your guest during her stay," says the gorgeous golden-haired, South African god. He looks like he's stepped off the Rugby field, his uniform is seconds away from combusting from his taut muscles. He too has a bottle of champagne and chocolate-covered strawberries, so I move aside for him to enter.

"Have fun, see you in a couple of hours." My sister doesn't even notice me shutting the door, her eyes are transfixed on the demigod moving toward her.

Walking back to my villa that is directly across from them, with a smile on my face, I hope they both enjoy their hosts. Swiping my key to my villa door, I'm surprised to see someone already waiting for me inside.

"Miss Starr." The handsome dark-haired man grins at me. "My name is Massimo, and I will be looking after you during your stay. Thick jet-black hair is swept back in a perfect quaff, his dark tanned arms a stark contrast to his white polo. There is a little bit of scruff on his square jaw. The darkest eyes look down at me hungrily. I'm a sucker for an accent—Italian—and his is dripping in sex. "I've poured you a glass of champagne." He hands me the chilled stemmed glass. "Mr. Lewis…" I tense at the mention of Nate's name, "… he asked me to give something to you." Raising a brow at him, he has my attention. "He has asked if you're wearing any panties underneath your dress?" It takes me a couple of moments to comprehend what he's asked. "If you are, he has requested you to remove them, please." His request is dripping with need.

I'm wearing a short mini dress, so of course, I'm wearing

underwear, because if I bent over, you would be able to see what I had for breakfast. But, I do as I'm told and roll down my G-string, letting it fall on the floor beside me.

Massimo smiles. "Please, follow me." He holds out his hand and takes me outside onto the semi-covered deck. "Do not worry, your guests will not see you." Massimo presses a button, and the once clear glass walls on the outside turn opaque. "No one can see us now." He indicates for me to sit on one of the daybeds before getting on his knees in front of me. "Mr. Lewis said that this would relax you. That you would be anxious about your guests arriving, so he wanted me to help with that." My dress has ridden up my thighs where I am sitting on the edge of the daybed, exposing me to Massimo's hungry gaze. Slowly, I open my legs for him making him grin. "One last thing," Massimo adds. "Mr. Lewis will be watching." *Huh?* "He wants to make sure I am doing a good job."

"How is he watching?"

"He has set up cameras in your room to watch you," Massimo explains. "There's a remote beside your bed that you can press if you would like privacy, and Mr. Lewis will be unable to watch you."

"Where are the cameras?"

"They are everywhere in your villa except for the bathroom." *Well, that's interesting.* "He cannot hear you, he can only watch."

Most women might find this creepy, that a man would set up cameras to watch you get off with another man, and I guess outside of this setting, it would be. But to me, it's fucking hot. Looking down where an eager Massimo is kneeling waiting for my signal to start, I'm going to make sure that what Nate sees is worth it. You like watching, Nate, well, I'm going to put on a show for you.

"You may continue, Massimo."

As I lay back, I am feeling the prickles of his whiskers against my thighs.

28

NATE

This could possibly have been the stupidest idea I've ever had. Fucking creepy too. I watch as Massimo explains to Camryn what I've done. I watch as she looks around the room trying to work out where the cameras are. A small smile falls across her face, and that's when I realize she likes the idea. Letting out the breath I didn't realize I was holding, I then watch as she lays back against the daybed opening her legs wide for Massimo.

I do the same thing, except I'm in my villa.

"You may start," I let Tanya, one of my staff, know I'm ready for her. I chose Tanya as her hair color is the closest to Camryn's. I want to look down at her sucking me off while watching Camryn get off and think about only her. *I'm sick, aren't I?* Like that's not normal, right? I mean, I know the resort hosts heaps of different kinds of fetishes, but this one, the one that has me obsessed over a gorgeous blonde English event planner, has to be the craziest.

I watch as Massimo's face disappears between Camryn's creamy thighs, her eyes open, her back arching at the first swipe of his tongue against her slit. I don't even notice Tanya's wet mouth wrapped around my dick—I'm too transfixed on Camryn's reaction—the way her hand moves to her covered breast, her palm squeezing her flesh through the cotton of her dress.

Show me more, baby.

As if she can hear me, she lets the strap of her dress fall down her shoulder exposing her creamy skin. She then tugs the material further down until her strapless bra is showing. Slowly, she rolls the offending material down to her stomach, giving me a full view of her breasts. They're full, heavy, yet pert. She has the perfect dusty pink nipples that have a direct line to her clit.

Nibbling on the puckered skin sends waves of lust through her body.

I watch in fascination as she plucks them for me, her teeth sinking into her plump lip as she continues touching herself. Camryn's eyes are closed, enjoying Massimo's expert tongue, or so I've heard from the staff.

I can tell the moment his fingers enter her because she sits up, mouth now open on a gasp, eyes wide at the sensation of the sudden intrusion. She then settles back against the daybed, wriggling around as Massimo finds the bundle of nerves that drives her damn crazy.

Thick fingers continue to pump into her while I watch every little gasp and shudder as he brings her closer to climax.

Her fingers are now laced in his thick hair.

She's close. That's when you know as she holds you there, demanding more from you, demanding you to make her come.

I watch in slow motion the moment Massimo does. Her entire body shudders as she plummets over the edge, but he doesn't let up. I can see it on her face that he's doing some kind of pussy voodoo on her. Her body thrashes around, but he doesn't let up. He pushes and pushes her until she can't take it any longer, and I see her come again.

Good man, Massimo.

That's exactly how I want her to be treated.

My fingers now lace into Tanya's hair as she works me over.

I'm close. So very close. My eyes never leaving the screen as I watch Camryn place her foot in the middle of Massimo's chest, pushing him into the pool. He's surprised but has a smile on his face as he surfaces.

I place a hand on Tanya's shoulder, halting her. She looks up at me with concern as if she hasn't done something right.

"No sucking for the moment," I say, looking down at the beautiful blonde. "I'm not ready to come just yet." Nodding at my instruction, she does as she's told.

Camryn has now shimmied out of her clothes and is standing naked in front of Massimo, confidently. I watch her plump lips move as she talks to him. She must have told him to undress as his clothes disappear.

What are you up to, little one?

Camryn slowly enters the pool, then moves Massimo to the edge. She reaches out and wraps her hand around his dick and begins to stroke him.

"Now, you can suck," I tell Tanya.

Her wet mouth slips back over my aching dick, and I hiss at the contact.

Fuck, yes.

I watch as Camryn gets Massimo as hard as he needs to be, before reaching over and grabbing a condom from his uniform. She slides the latex over him, then pushes him back against the side of the pool before turning around. She slowly backs up against him until he's firmly inside of her. She begins to ride him, reverse cowgirl style. She looks up at one of the cameras and smiles— she's doing this for me. The naughty girl.

She widens her legs so I can see him entering her, watching as she slides over him, watching as his fingers dig into her hips as she fucks him.

Yes. God, yes, Camryn.

Her eyes never leave mine as she continues to fuck Massimo on the edge of the pool just for me.

I'm gone.

So far gone for Camryn Starr.

After my little voyeur party took a turn in a direction, I wasn't expecting it to go, I headed on back to my friend Axel Taylor, from Dirty Texas, to catch up. He arrived earlier in the day, and I left him to get settled in. I'm hoping he took advantage of all the amenities which were laid out before him.

"Hey man, are you ready for the tour of the resort?" I hand Axel a beer as he answers the door.

"Damn right, I am. If this place is as awesome as your clubs, I can't wait to test it all out," he enthusiastically tells me as we head toward the golf buggy. We tear off into the rainforest as I give him the full tour of the resort.

"So, did you enjoy Layla?" I ask about the gorgeous host I arranged for him, hoping to get his mind off of his woman problems.

"She fed me and brought me a beer, but that was as far as we took it." I'm surprised because Axel has been coming to our clubs for years. He was one of our original clients. I leave my questions well alone. Axel is a closed book, keeping his cards close to his chest.

We continue on our journey until we end up at one of our restaurants where we were planning on having dinner. I park at the long jetty where the restaurant is located and indicate for him to follow. He notices the overwater bungalows in the distance as we walk along the jetty.

"Pretty cool, aren't they?" He nods. "You might want to try them out later in the week. These are further away from everything going on at the resort, so that's why I started you off at the beach-side villa," I explain to him. "There is a restaurant and bar right on the point here... the sunset view is pretty spectacular."

"Aren't you romantic, Nate. Is this a date?" Axel cracks a joke, and I flip him off in jest. Eventually, we make it to the end where the maître d ushers us into the restaurant. I have a private booth set up for us looking out onto the deck where three beautiful women are sitting on the sofas enjoying cocktails. My footsteps still when I realize it's Camryn, then I notice Olivia, and I think Cam's sister, Ivy. Shit!

"Shit, man, I had no idea," I tell him. This was the last thing he needed to see—the woman he's trying to put behind him. "Camryn asked if she could bring two friends to the resort to test it out, I had no idea one of them was her." Dammit, I feel like the biggest dick.

"It's okay. I knew I'd run into her again at some stage. She's friends with Ness." That's the woman who married his twin brother. "I just thought I would have more time." It's been a couple of weeks since things blew up during New Year's.

"You sure? They haven't spotted us yet, and I have another six restaurants where we can relax." Axel shakes his head and tells me to continue. I'm guessing he wants to get this awkward meeting over and done with. Probably better to run into each other here than in the middle of an orgy or naked by a pool somewhere.

Camryn spots me, and her face lights up upon seeing me—she's going to flip out when she realizes who's with me, though.

"Hey, you." She gives me a flirty look as I lean in to peck her on the cheek. Her face falls when she sees Axel behind me. "Shit! What the fuck are you doing here?"

Axel ignores Camryn, moving past where she's standing and toward his target. "Evening, Olivia."

"What the fuck's going on?" Camryn whispers to me.

"I had no idea you were bringing Olivia here," I whisper yell back at her.

Camryn gives me a death stare.

"Evening, what a surprise." Olivia totally ignores Axel, which is probably a first as women don't turn him down.

"Certainly is. I'm surprised your fiancé would let you come to such a corrupt place," Axel fires back.

"Oh shit," Camryn mumbles beside me.

"He assumes I'm with my family in Mustique," Olivia states.

"Oh, that's right, I forgot how much of a skillful liar you are."

This is going south quickly.

"It wasn't the only thing I learned from you then," she bites back. Olivia gets up off the sofa and turns toward me. "I'm sorry I won't be staying for dinner. I've lost my appetite."

Ivy, Camryn's sister, stands with Olivia, and they walk out of the restaurant together.

"You're such a dick, Axel," Camryn adds. She gives me a curt nod and follows after the girls.

"Wow! Not sure what you've done, but they are three pissed-off women."

"Not sure why they're angry at me, I don't have a fiancée stuffed away somewhere." Axel sighs.

"Forget about them. They'll cool down soon enough. Look at the beautiful sunset." I point at the orange and pinks streaking across the sky because what else can I do right at this moment.

"Fine. But I'm not holding your hand under the table, you're not my type," Axel answers as he elbows me in the ribs.

29

CAMRYN

"Liv, wait!" I am rushing after my furious friend.

She whirls around quickly and spits, "You told me he wouldn't be here!"

"I had no idea he would be," I try to defend myself. "Nate said he declined his offer."

"This is a disaster. I want to go home. Now!" Olivia turns and rushes down one of the paths.

"Liv…" I call after her again. "Please… don't go."

She spins around with tears welling in her eyes. "I can't stay here and watch him fuck other people, Camryn." She wraps her arms around herself in a defensive nature.

"I know, babe."

We all stand there in silence for a couple of moments trying to work out what we should do.

"Fuck him!" Ivy states. "Seriously, Liv… fuck him!" Olivia's eyes widen at her best friend's reaction. "You're a good person who has been dealt a shitty hand." Ivy reaches out to grab Olivia's hand. "Don't kill me for saying this, but in all honesty, do you think Eddie isn't messing around on you while he's in London?"

I raise a brow at Olivia. Eddie's her asshole of a fiancé—they're only marrying because their parents want them to.

"I don't know." Olivia shrugs her shoulders.

"Come on, Liv. Are you serious right now?" I've never seen my sister talk to Liv like this before. "Cam?" Ivy turns to me for back up.

"Um..." I look between the two of them, "... I don't think Eddie can be trusted."

Olivia deflates a little. "I know I'm marrying the biggest dick on the face of this planet..." her shoulders sink further, "... but what choice do I have, guys? Dad's sick, and my wedding is bringing him joy."

"But what about you? What brings you joy?" I ask because I hate the fact she's putting her family's happiness before her own.

Olivia looks at me as if the question is so foreign that I must have asked it in Japanese.

"I don't know." She's looking very confused. "I..." She looks to the floor. "Axel... he made me happy." Ivy squeezes Olivia's hand. "And I messed it all up."

Now, I really feel for her.

"It doesn't matter, anyway..." she shakes her head, "... he slept with my sister. We can't come back from that."

We are all silent for a couple of moments, which gives Olivia the time to digest her thoughts and feelings.

"Did you at least try your host?" Ivy asks, breaking the silence.

Olivia's head swiftly turns to stare at her friend. "Um, no. Did you?"

Ivy nods her head quickly. "Oh my God, he was amazing." My sister grins, her cheeks are red just from thinking about the experience.

"Tell us more." I am surprised Ivy has already indulged in what the resort has to offer.

"You know... the usual." She shrugs her shoulders.

"Usual for you or usual for me?" I am questioning her because

I just fucked my host while my boss watched, so I'm pretty sure my sister didn't do that.

"Do I have to tell?" she whines.

"It's a long walk to The Paradise Club, which is where I think we should head next. We want to hear all the details."

Ivy sighs, but it's a happy one.

Twenty minutes later, we arrive at the club and are ushered inside. Security makes sure the girls have their colored bracelets on, so people can identify what they're into.

"Wow." Ivy's eyes widen as she enters the mini version of Nate's clubs. "I had no idea this world existed."

Ivy's story about the hot Southern African was pretty tame, but I'm proud of my sister for letting go of some of her hang-ups. Ivy has control issues, and they stem from her childhood, where we were shuffled all around Europe depending on whoever Mum was dating. Our life was so chaotic that the only thing Ivy could control was her weight. She eventually developed an eating disorder. Thankfully, Mum was dating a doctor who noticed the symptoms and organized her treatment in a world-class facility in Switzerland. I think those control issues have never truly gone away. She now channels them into being the best celebrity interior designer there is.

"Seriously, Cam, I want the name of the interior designer. I need to poach them."

Like I said, boss bitch that never switches off.

It's a family trait, what can I say.

We grab a couple of drinks and stay on the lower level, watching the people mill around before heading upstairs. My eyes assess the crowd, there are some exceptionally gorgeous potentials walking through.

"So, what happens upstairs." Ivy sips on her cocktail nervously.

"Fun. Lots of fun." I smile at her.

"You're going to see a lot of people messing around," Olivia adds. "At first it can be a little confronting, but … it can also be hot as fuck once you're accustomed to it."

"Is this sort of stuff really that much fun?" Ivy asks quite seriously.

"What do you mean?" I am a little concerned.

Ivy nervously plays with her straw. "Like …" I can see she's working out her words in her mind before she speaks. "Do you need all this when you go home?"

Oh, I see what she's saying.

"Are you worried you're going to like all this naughtiness and not be able to go back to normal sex?" I raise a brow at my sister.

"Yeah, I kind of am."

"I think for some people they need it."

My mind turns to Nate.

Does he need all this to get off?

Is that why he created this fantasy world?

But last week we had normal couple sex—we didn't need anyone else.

That was just one week, Camryn. Not a month. Not a year. Not a lifetime.

My stomach sinks at this realization. This is all fun for the moment, but I don't know if it's something I would want all the time in a relationship. I guess I'm two different people. There's single Camryn, who's crazy, wild, up for anything. And then there's in-a-relationship Camryn, who's more subdued, wants stability, and security. Quite the juxtaposition, really.

"I also think people come here for a holiday or their birthday for like a once or twice a year celebration."

Ivy nods her head, mulling it all over. "That makes sense."

"Shall we go upstairs and have a look around, then come back down for a drink? Sort of like easing you into it all."

Ivy nods, so we finish our cocktails and head on up to the next level. We continue up the stairs to the first level where there's a large see-through cube where exhibitionists are able to perform in front of a sea of voyeurs. It's utterly fascinating. Something's happening inside the cube as people are milling around.

"Oh my God." Ivy stops dead in her tracks. Her eyes widen as she watches two men pleasuring one woman in the cube. Her cheeks turn crimson, but she doesn't look away.

"Looks fun, don't you think?" Olivia adds.

"Have you done this?" Ivy points to the cube.

Olivia shakes her head. "I've had multiple men, though." Liv bites her lip, and I give her a high-five.

"Have you?" Ivy turns to me.

"Yes, not as many as dirty Liv here." I elbow my friend, who looks slightly embarrassed.

"Am I missing out?" Ivy looks at both of us.

We both nod our heads quickly, indicating yes, she is.

Ivy turns her attention back to the cube.

"Anyone can join them," I whisper in my sister's ear.

"Oh, hell, no, not in front of all these people," she quickly states, making me chuckle.

Ivy isn't an exhibitionist, but I wanted to let her know it was okay if she decided maybe she was.

30

NATE

We head on over to The Paradise Club needing to get Axel's mind off of Olivia. This wasn't what I had planned when I invited him here thinking I could help get his mind off of things. Instead, it seems like it's all turned into a bit of a shitshow.

One of the staff members from the restaurant gave us a lift on over to the club, and we breeze on through and up to the first level. The place is packed, and the cube is filled with people. Axel says he wants to hang back a little. He's lost inside his own head right now. I thought the copious amounts of beer would help him through it, plus a couple of gorgeous wait staff, but nope, not so far.

"Fellas." My younger brother, Alexander, comes over, surprising us.

"Bro, what are you doing here?" Clapping him on the back, I thought he was busy in Europe.

"I needed to check in on my investment." He chuckles, the asshole.

"Silent partner, remember?" I chuckle.

He's in the same boat as Sam Rose, having to be careful of the conservative board members of the company. Even though my parents still own the majority of the business, they have board members to satisfy, and even though they're okay with this, I promised them it wouldn't affect their business with my own. Hence, Alex is a silent partner.

"Hey, you remember Axel Taylor from Dirty Texas, don't you?" I introduce them again.

"Yeah, man… long time no see."

Alex smiles, shaking his hand. "Yeah, good to see you again. I'll tell you something, this resort is pretty amazing," Axel praises.

"I just flew in, so haven't seen much, but I'm pretty sure my night has just gotten better." Following the direction in which my brother is looking, something has caught his attention. My brother's a good guy, he puts on a front of being a playboy, but deep down inside, I know he'd love to settle down and have a couple of kids just like Mom and Dad.

That's when I notice he's talking about Camryn, Ivy, and Olivia, who are in the corner watching what's going on in the cube.

Axel's face looks like thunder. "They're nothing but trouble," he grumbles.

"Ignore him, he has a history with one of them." I give my brother 'the look' over Axel's shoulder, and he soon catches on.

"Hopefully, not the one in the pink dress?" Alex asks.

Looking back, I notice Ivy is wearing pink. Phew. I don't mind sharing Camryn, just not with my brother. I absolutely draw the line there.

"Nope, lady in white," I answer for Axel, who's scowling at the group of girls.

"Good choice." My brother chuckles as Axel shoots him a glare.

Maybe he didn't understand my not-so-subtle look after all.

"Your brother has a thing for his new event planner… the one in the red." Axel throws me directly under the bus, the dick. My brother whistles as he looks Camryn over.

"What about your motto? Never mix business and pleasure. Only make business out of pleasure?"

Yeah, yeah, I had a fucking motto, and that flew right out the window when fucking Camryn Starr walked into my damn life.

"Yeah, well, that one is biting me in the ass at the moment. When we first met, she had a boyfriend, and now... now she's single and trying to get over the douchebag who fucked her over. It's so hard because she's curious about everything." They always say lies are best told when dipped in truth. I know my brother will keep harping on about Camryn and breaking the rules if I didn't give him something, so I wanted to nip it in the bud.

"Stay strong, brother, stay strong." My brother slaps me on the back.

"I'm practically a fucking saint." The lie falls from my tongue so easily.

"Why don't we join them?"

Is Alex fucking serious, after what we all just talked about?

"Guys, come on... I want to meet the beauty in pink."

He's thinking with his dick, that's what's happening.

We follow after my brother toward the group of hostile women.

"Evening, ladies," Alex starts, really putting on his British accent. He spent half his time in America growing up like me, plus the three girls are English anyway, so they're not swayed by his accent, but I'm not going to tell him that.

"And who are you?" Camryn looks Alex over.

"My brother," I reply, hoping it will shut down any indecent thoughts she might have of him.

"Well, it's nice to meet you, Nate's brother." She gives him her most professional smile.

"It's Alex. My name's Alex," he introduces himself properly.

"If you will excuse us, I might show Camryn around. I haven't had a chance to give her much of a tour yet."

Lie. Lie. Lie.

I need her. This night has been one shitshow after another.

She smiles, taking my outstretched hand, and we disappear into the crowd.

The way Axel and Olivia are sending daggers at each other, the last place I want to be is being caught in the crossfire. Pushing one of the secret doors open, I pull Camryn into a darkened corridor. My lips are on her before the door is even closed. I've pushed her up against the wall, grinding myself against her.

"You look like a fucking temptress tonight," I growl into her ear.

"You told me red turns you on." Her hand reaches between us and grabs my dick. "I see my work here is done." Dimmed, fluorescent light falls across her face, showing me the smirk she's giving me.

"Your work has only just begun." My lips fall to the nape of her neck, and I pepper her heated skin with feather-light kisses before licking my way back up to her ear. She shivers beneath my touch.

"Thanks for sending Massimo today." Her hand tightens around me.

"You looked like you enjoyed him."

She gives me a coy look. "The real question is… did you enjoy it?"

"I did," I answer, looking down at her perfect face. "I crossed a line putting those cameras in your room."

"You did," she tells me.

My body tenses. Shit!

"I'm sorry, they can be taken down immediately." My hand reaches for my phone in my back pocket, but her hand tightens around my dick, gaining my attention.

"Never said I wanted them gone. Just that you crossed a line, a line I didn't realize I wanted to cross until it was presented to me." She arches a brow at me. "You want to watch me for the next week. You want to see me touching myself while I am thinking of you? You want to watch as Massimo fucks me again, all over the villa... over and over and over." My dick thickens with her words. "You want to watch as someone else bangs me until I come." Damn, this girl is torturing me to death. "I'll give it to you, Nate. I'll give you every single thing you desire."

Leaning forward, she bites my earlobe, sending extreme amounts of pleasure directly to my dick.

Fuck me, this woman's going to kill me.

"Was her mouth as good as mine on your dick," Camryn whispers into my ear.

It takes me a couple of moments to register what she means. "She was good, that's why I chose her."

"Excellent. Don't want you to have a sloppy blow job while watching me, that's not fair."

"I chose Massimo for you. I've heard he's the best."

"He was," she tells me, as a sharp fingernail runs down my jaw. "I can't wait to go home and have some fun with him." Camryn's hand releases my dick, and she pushes me away, then she begins to walk down the darkened corridor.

Hang on!

What the fuck.

Running after her, I grab her arm and push her back against the wall. Her eyes widen, and a slow smirk crosses her face.

"You testing me, little one?"

"No," she replies firmly.

"Do you want him over me?"

Her face softens as a tiny bit of vulnerability creeps through my hard exterior.

Camryn grabs my face between her hands. "No one can ever compare to you. Just know that," she states before she kisses me, gently, softly, slowly.

My hand slips under the short hem of her dress, and I find her pantieless. My fingers slip between her folds, and I enter her. Our kiss becomes heated as Camryn lifts one of her legs around my hip.

"I have something planned for you, little one." Pulling myself away from her lips, my fingers are still inside of her, working her up. "I think tonight is the best night to give it to you while your friends are occupied."

Her brows raise in surprise, heat and need swirls behind her green eyes. She moans as my fingers fall from Camryn, then one by one I suck her off them, which makes her smile. "Follow me." Grabbing her hand, I navigate the back corridors until we exit out of the club where there's a golf buggy waiting for us.

"Take Miss Starr back to her room," I explain to one of my staff members.

"Nate?"

"Trust me?" She slowly nods, slightly confused. "I'll see you at your villa in about ten." Leaning in, I whisper into her ear, "Leave the dress on."

Camryn nods and slides into the buggy, then she disappears off into the distance, only the red brake lights visible in the darkness.

Pulling my cell from my back pocket, I call Massimo to help me with my plan.

Ten minutes later, I arrive at Camryn's villa. Swiping my master key on the door, I let myself in. Camryn's staring at the fish swimming around underneath the pool. She looks up at me as I enter with a smile forming on her face.

"You are the most beautiful woman in the world." The moonlight illuminates her like some kind of goddess. She doesn't speak, she rushes toward me and into my arms, her lips meeting mine in a heated kiss. The need building between us is crazy like a damn tinderbox ready for the match to strike.

The beep of her door unlocking pulls us apart, and Massimo enters the room. He sees us together and hesitates, his dark eyes drifting between us.

"Please set up over here." I point to the living area. As Massimo brings in the swing, he attaches it to a concealed hook in the ceiling. Camryn watches in fascination as he puts it together.

Pointing at the black material hanging from the ceiling, I ask, "Do you want to have a look?" Camryn moves away from me toward Massimo.

"This is very safe," he explains to her. "You place your feet in here." He points to the footholds. "This will support your back and neck."

Camryn runs her hand over the black leather of the back brace. I like this kind, it's like a hammock. The backless ones you can't stay in too long before they start cutting into your skin, and Camryn's going to be in it a while. "You can place your hands here..." he points to the hand grabs, "... or they can be somewhere else." The inflection in his voice tells me he wants her hands *somewhere else.*

"This is for me?" Camryn looks over at me for reassurance.

"Yes."

"Just me?"

"As in being the only woman tonight, yes." I can see she's trying to figure out exactly what I'm up to. "Do you remember that fantasy you told me when we first started talking?" Pulling the blindfold from my back pocket, I let it dangle off my finger between us, and that's when realization filters across Camryn's face. She bites her lip as her head turns and looks around the room. At the moment, it's only Massimo and me, but more will come. I've planned it. "Would you like to get comfortable?"

"Should I?" She points to her dress, unsure about what she should be doing.

"Leave it on."

Camryn nods and places a nervous hand on the contraption in front of her. It does look confusing.

"Massimo..." He steps forward wrapping his large hands around her hips and places her against the swing. She lays back against the leather. Massimo settles her top half into position while I have the job of her bottom half.

Grabbing one of her ankles, I place it into the foothold, then do the same with the other. Her legs fall open exposing her pussy to me. It's too much, I can't not touch it. Reaching out, I run my finger along her slit, and she jolts in the swing, making Massimo chuckle.

Camryn sits up and looks down at me, giving me a smile.

"Lay back down, sweetheart. Let's get you into position."

She does as she's told. I angle her bottom, so it's hanging off the leather edge, but her back is supporting her weight. "Does this feel okay?" I tug on some of the lines. Her head is nestled in the correct spot as well. She's currently set high off the floor as it was the easiest place to set her up.

"I promise you, Camryn, I will take care of you." She bites her lip in anticipation while giving me a small smile. "You're going to need this now," I say, pulling the blindfold from my pocket again. "Everything is going to be heightened once you lose your sight," I explain to her. "But I've got you." She nods again as I place the blindfold over her eyes. "Say the word 'Paradise' at any moment, and we will stop. Okay?"

"Yes, okay." Her answer is loud and succinct, and I know she understands.

"Good." Nodding to Massimo, he unzips his shorts and drops them to the floor. He is commando, instantly hard, and ready to go.

"We are going to move you into position, and throughout the night we might move you up or down depending on what we want to do to you. Do you understand?"

"Yes," she relays confidently.

Again, I give Massimo the signal as he slides his dick into her mouth, which surprises her. Her hands grip onto the handholds as Massimo slowly begins to fuck her face.

Now it's my turn.

Walking around to her exposed legs, I'm able to stand in between them, she's angled enough that she's low enough for Massimo's dick, but high enough for me to either fuck her, finger bang her, or eat her out.

So many decisions.

Her glistening pussy has my mouth watering, so I know exactly what I'm wanting. Leaning down, I run my tongue along her slit, which makes her arch her back, pushing Massimo further down her throat, making her choke.

Massimo chuckles.

I bury my face between her legs, savoring her essence, savoring this woman who's giving herself to me. She's a fucking dirty little angel sent down from kink heaven just for me.

She's everything I could ever have wished for in a woman, and the fact that she loves sex, dirty sex, as much as I do, is like a fucking cherry on the top.

31

CAMRYN

This is torture.

The most beautiful torture that has ever existed.

Massimo's heavy, thick, dick is practically choking me. I mean, if I have to suffocate, I think on his dick is a pretty good way to go out. Then there's Nate going to town between my legs, all while in some medieval-style sex contraption.

Never in my wildest fantasies did I ever expect something like this. You can dream of crazy scenarios as you get yourself off, but having one of your fantasies come to life, it's inexplicable.

The first tingles of my orgasm begin to move over my skin, igniting every single nerve ending as if my body is a Fourth of July fireworks display.

Nate's thick fingers enter me, and it's game over. With each thrust of his fingers, he pushes Massimo further and further down my throat. The intensity is driving me crazy.

I'm close, so very close.

It's there.

The edge is ready for me to fall over into the abyss, my body is tense with need until it disappears.

What in the ever-loving fuck?

Nate, are you trying to kill me?

But I can't protest while I have a fucking salami down my throat. Moments later, Nate is entering me. Oh, sweet mother of God, yes. Fuck, yes. The swing moves with each of his thrusts. I don't care now that my eyes are watering, that I have saliva falling down my cheeks, that my makeup is probably smeared because I'm being fucked to within an inch of my life, and I love it!

Yes. Yes. Yes.

This is what dirty fantasies are made of.

I want it all.

Every little depraved thing these guys want to do to me. Sign me up.

This is a once-in-a-lifetime chance because once I'm off this island, reality will seep back in. I'm going to have to deal with being single in New York City.

I'm spacing out, the sensations are overloading every part of me. I'm lying here as if I'm their personal fuck toy, and I don't care.

Moments later, there's tugging at my top, hands are moving the top of my dress down. Quickly, I try and do the math about which body parts are where.

"Someone new, little one," Nate warns me.

Oh.

Warm hands caress my chest. Thick fingers pluck at my nipples. Fuck me, this is... I... then Nate's thumb connects with my clit, and I'm done for. Like fireworks, I've shot up to the heavens and exploded.

Massimo's dick falls from my throat, and I honestly feel bereft, but it's not long until a new one is there.

Holy shit! Who the hell is this?

My body is still convulsing under Nate's thrusts until he comes with a roar.

Yes. God, yes. I love hearing him come.

It's not long until Nate falls from my tender pussy, and

someone else is entering. Holy hell, that must be Massimo. It's like these men are playing musical chairs with me, which I am totally down for. His thrusts are frantic, I mean I've been sucking his dick for who knows how long, he's probably ready to combust, and by his forceful thrusts I can tell he is. Of course, the swing pushes me against the mystery man's thick dick, but Massimo must have warmed up my throat because I'm taking it like a fucking porn star.

"I'm taking a seat now, little one," Nate whispers in my ear. "Each new touch will be from someone new," he tells me. "First, there was me on your cunt..." his filthy words make me hum against mystery man's dick, "... while you sucked Massimo's dick like a champ. Then another came to play with your breasts." *Thought so.* "You're now sucking his dick like a filthy little girl." Holy hell, Nate, I can't take your dirty talk while all this other stuff is going on.

Massimo's finger runs over my sensitive clit which makes me jump. How the hell is my body ready again for another orgasm?

No. I am sure it's not, but then it is, and my orgasm rolls over my body like a fucking tidal wave. Holy shit.

"That's it, sweetheart. You made Massimo come as you squeezed the life out of his dick with your tight little cunt."

Nate! I scream internally, his words are driving me wild.

Massimo is still buried deep inside me as a new set of hands squeeze my breasts.

"Can you handle more, little one?" This time Nate's no longer whispering in my ear.

Is he going to be a dirty little voiceover through all of this?

Far out, I'm going to be pushed into some other world if he adds his brand of dirtiness to this whole scenario. The dick in my mouth removes itself, before quickly being replaced with another. Then I feel the mystery dick enter me. I shouldn't be liking this. I am trying to shake the slut-shaming thoughts from my mind. Women are told they can't like this kind of stuff unless they're sluts or porn stars. But I do like it. This is the third guy I'm letting fuck me in a space of, who the hell knows how long, and I have no idea how many more there are.

And I love it!

I want more.

I want to be used.

I want to make these men come.

New lips are on my lips. New dicks are in my mouth and pussy until I lose track of everything until I can't come anymore. Until I am nothing but a liquid mess of pure and utter contentment.

✸✸✸✸✸✸✸✸

Warm water seeps over my fully sated body. A cloth runs down my skin sending shivers over my body. I finally come to and feel a hard body against my back.

"Shh... don't move. I'm taking care of you." Nate's soothing words make me feel safe as I let myself rest against his hard chest. "You did so well tonight, little one," he whispers into my ear. "You were the perfect little toy." His hands pull my hair to the side as his lips caress my exposed skin sending tingles directly between my legs.

How the hell can my pussy want more? *Dirty whore.*

"Did you like it?" Nate asks, his tone soothing.

"Yes." My lips feel heavy. Maybe they're even a little bruised from the amount of dick I've sucked. Well, for the number of people who face-fucked me more like it.

"You are going to be sore tomorrow." His hand lazily glides over me.

"A good sore, though." I smile to myself.

Nate chuckles behind me, his breath sending goosebumps all over my skin.

"Nate?"

"Yes, sweetheart," he replies tenderly.

"You don't think any less of me because of what I just did. Do you?"

Water sloshes over the bath's edge as Nate turns me around, cradling me into his side. "Oh, sweetheart..." he runs his thumb across my cheek, "... I could never think any less of you for enjoying yourself."

Tears well in my eyes.

What the hell is going on?

I feel the first one fall down my cheek as I look into the concerned face of Nate. His thumb catches each stupid tear that falls.

"It's like the man upstairs has created my ideal woman and put her right here in front of me, in this moment."

Oh shit! The tears fall harder now.

This isn't me.

I'm not one of those kinds of girls.

"I'm all ..." I wave my hands around not really knowing what to say.

"I know. You entered some kind of subspace." Nate kisses my cheek. "But also know..." he kisses me again, "... I don't want to let you go, Camryn Starr."

My eyes widen as I say, "Nate." My heart thumps in my chest while my emotions are all out of whack from what just happened.

Pulling me to his chest, silence falls between us as he simply holds me. "You've been the best thing to walk into my life in a long time, Camryn," he mumbles into the top of my head. "Can I take you out for dinner when I get back to New York?"

"Like a date?"

Nate mulls my question over for a couple of moments. "Yes, like a date. But..." he bites his lip nervously, "... but we know that there isn't a future between us, right?"

Wow! That's like a punch to the gut.

"I want to be able to take you out, wine and dine you, take you home, fuck your brains out, then fall asleep beside you."

I swallow at his words. "You don't have to take me out, Nate. I'm a sure thing," I reply, trying to lighten the mood.

"I'm not explaining myself properly." He shakes his head and sighs heavily.

"Nate, I don't know what you want from me?" I'm becoming confused again.

"I've never done this before, Camryn." He genuinely looks confused as he rubs at his chin. "Usually, I meet women for sex or use my club to hook up." He's not telling me anything I don't already know. "But I kind of want more than a hook- up when I'm in town."

"You want my company?"

He nervously taps his fingers on the side of the tub. "Yeah. I'd like to call you up if I need a date for some stupid charity gala thing I have to go to." My mouth opens wide in shock. "I want to call you and catch up… for dinner or drinks."

"That's a friend, Nate."

"Yeah, but I want to fuck you, too."

This makes me chuckle. "So, what you're saying is, you want the girlfriend experience without the commitment."

Nate winces at my analogy. "Yeah, I do."

"What happens if I need a date for a stupid society gala, will you help me out?"

"Of course," he quickly adds.

"So, if I'm having a bad day and my girlfriends are too busy, and I need to go have drinks and whinge, I can call you?"

"Yes, of course, if I am in town," he quickly adds.

"So, I get all the benefits of a 'boyfriend,' but I don't have to answer to anyone?"

"Exactly. We are both busy, Camryn. We're cut from the same cloth. Our businesses will always come first. No one understands that better than us."

"No commitment. No jealousy. No drama."

He nods his head at my comments.

"And we're honest with each other. If something changes in our circumstances, then we have to tell the other."

"Of course," he agrees easily.

"Then we have a deal, Mr. Lewis." Grinning, I hold out my hand.

"I'm going to be the best non-girlfriend you ever had."

32

CAMRYN

I can't believe my time on the island has come to an end. It's most certainly been an experience.

Olivia left the island with Axel. She went back to LA with him after they sorted out that her sister never slept with Axel, that she crept into his room like a crazy woman, and took a picture with him. For what reason? Simply to hurt her sister.

I'm lucky Ivy's my sister because I probably would have murdered Olivia's sister by now if she was my own. Speaking of my sister, I haven't seen her for most of the week she's been here. Apparently, she's been hanging out with Alex, Nate's brother, for most of the time. Which is weird. Two sisters, two brothers, hooking up—that's like the start of a bad porno.

"The helicopter should be here at any moment." Nate pulls me into his arms and kisses me. It feels like a lead balloon has settled in my stomach, knowing my time here is now over. The island has been a kinky little bubble that I'm not ready to leave, but reality waits for me. We kiss one last time.

"I'll be back in New York in about two weeks," he tells me. "Then you will be back out here in what? About six weeks for the Grand Opening." I nod my head. "Plus, we have FaceTime." Wriggling his eyebrows, he's reminding me of the last time we Face-Timed each other.

"I'm looking forward to it." Wrapping my arms around him one last time, I sigh.

"Your membership to the New York club is in your email. Hope you have fun." He nuzzles the side of my neck. "I'll see you in a couple of weeks." Nate kisses me again, this time with urgency and need, both of us not wanting to let go of the past couple of weeks. I can hear the helicopter in the distance, so we head on down, but not before we walk in on Alex and Ivy making out like savages.

Nate clears his throat, and they both break apart.

"Didn't see you there, brother." Alex smirks.

Ivy's cheeks have turned bright red. I follow her embarrassment as it travels down over her throat and chest.

"Your ride is here," Nate tells the group.

We walk out to the grassy area. Alex helps Ivy onto the chopper. Nate slaps my ass hard as I walk away from him, then he gives me a grin when I turn around. Shaking my head, I head into the helicopter as Alex and Ivy finish another make-out session.

The doors shut, and we put on our headphones.

It's a quick trip over the ocean to the mainland where Nate's private plane will be waiting to take us back to the airport to take our planes home.

I watch as Nate and Alex become tiny little specks beneath us as the green of the rainforest makes way for the blue of the ocean. I'm sad to be leaving this gorgeous place. I'm sad I won't see sunshine for a couple of months because New York is going to be covered in snow. I am also sad that reality is going to set in. That whatever Nate and I have together will now fizzle out.

We settle into the private plane, and before we know it, we're off on the next leg of our journey.

"So, you and Alex, hey?" I question my sister.

"Yeah. It's been amazing."

"You like him?" I'm pushing for all the gossip.

"It was fun. But I think once you leave the bubble of that island, whatever you had on there doesn't exist anymore." Her words hit me hard right in the chest. "Don't you think?"

"I guess it's called Paradise for a reason."

"You think that's what happened to Axel and Olivia?" Ivy asks me.

"Liv's father has been sick, so I guess it's no surprise he's ended up in the hospital."

"Do you think Axel and her will survive it, though? She took a risk going to LA with Axel. She loves him." Ivy's looking hopeful for her best friend.

"Honestly, no. I don't think they're going to make it?"

Ivy seems shocked by my observation.

"Why?" she questions me.

"Olivia is loyal to her family. Plus, they come from such different worlds."

"Opposites attract," she adds.

"Yeah. But usually, it doesn't come with hundreds of years of family history and tradition, and a man who's the most famous man in the world."

"But they love each other," she pushes.

"Love doesn't conquer all, Ivy."

"That's so cynical, Camryn." Rolling her eyes at me as she flicks through her interior magazine, but I can tell she's not really taking any of it in.

"It's called being a realist." I'm becoming annoyed with my sister because she's seeking this happily ever after, but it doesn't exist. Especially not for us Starr women.

"So what about you and Nate, then?"

"What about it?" I can see my sister's getting frustrated with me.

"You were kissing him before we left. You both looked sad."

"I doubt he's that sad. There will be someone around to comfort him."

"And you don't care?"

"No. I don't."

"So, some woman is going to screw him while you're hard at work back in New York, and you're not going to care?"

"No, I'm not."

"Urgh... you're so annoying." She slams the magazine shut. "You like Nate. You just won't admit it."

"Oh, I'll admit it, Ivy. I like him. I like him a lot. The man is hot. He knows how to fuck. He has the best dick I've ever seen." Ivy is looking at me with wide eyes. "But that doesn't mean anything."

My sister has a couple of moments to regain her composure.

"So, you do like him?"

Of course, that's what she focuses in on.

"Why don't you believe me?"

"Because the way you look at him is different." This stops me for a moment. "The way you both look at each other... there's something there."

"There is something there between Nate and me, and we both don't deny that. But we also both agreed that we aren't looking for anything more." Ivy folds her arms across her chest and glares at me, calling bullshit on my statement. "Urgh, you're so annoying." Slamming my magazine shut, I state, "Fine! Nate and I agreed we would see each other outside of sex if he's in town." Ivy claps her hands excitedly. "Don't get too excited," I warn her. "We both will happily see other people." She frowns. "But, we still want to see each other with or without sex."

Ivy looks at me. "Sounds like you guys are in an open relationship."

"Maybe... but it's not really a romantic relationship as such. It's more than friends but less than partners if that makes sense?"

"Nope, not at all," she states. "But, if you're happy with the arrangement, then I guess it doesn't matter what I think, right?"

"You're my sister, of course, I want to know what you think."

"I worry that you're going to get hurt. That's all." A concerned frown falls across her face.

"Nate and I have played with other people in front of each other a couple of times now," I confess to her as Ivy's eyes widen. "And it was fun."

"And you weren't jealous?" she questions me.

"I thought I would be, but not really. Like there's the tiniest bit at the beginning when you first see them with someone else, but then everything fades away because it soon becomes so damn hot."

"I wonder if it's different if you're dating someone? Or like married to someone?" Ivy muses.

"Maybe." I shrug my shoulders. "Maybe that does change things," I agree with her. "But, Nate and I aren't, so there are no feelings involved."

Ivy isn't looking convinced. "Just be careful," she warns me.

"I promise," I relent while trying to reassure her.

After tearfully saying goodbye to my sister hours earlier, I am finally landing back in New York. Looking out the window, the city is covered in a light dusting of snow. It's dark already and gloomy, a stark difference to the paradise I've just left. Making my way through customs and out to the arrival area, I notice a sign with my name on it.

Huh? So I make my way over to the man holding the sign.

"Miss Starr?" he questions me.

"Yes."

"Great, Mr. Lewis has arranged a transfer to your home for you." Hearing Nate's name makes me smile. I follow the driver out to a black town car. After sliding into the back seat, there's a gorgeous bouquet of flowers waiting for me, plus a bag filled with groceries. There's also a card, so I open the small white envelope.

Cam,
   Welcome home.
   Thought you'd be exhausted after your trip
   So I included the basics to get you through the night.
   Sleep tight, see you soon.
   Nate
   xox

Damn him. My stomach starts somersaulting over his thoughtfulness. Without thinking, I pick up my phone and call him.

"Hey, beautiful," he answers the phone happily.

"Thank you so much for my flowers and groceries." Picking out a pack of Cadbury's buttons from England. Damn, he remembered my liking of the chocolatey goodness.

"Least I could do. Are you home yet?"

"No. Just landed and am in the car. The traffic is crazy. Wish I was back on the island, it's freezing here."

"Wish you were, too," he adds. Nate makes a pretty considerate man friend.

"Missing me already, are you?" I tease him.

"Of course," he shoots back quickly.

Urgh, I hate this feeling I'm getting in the pit of my stomach as I try and shake the butterflies away.

"Not, sure what I'm going to do with myself. My bed seems awfully lonely."

"Don't think it will be lonely for long." Chuckling, the man is literally at a sex resort with women on call, he's not going to be lonely at all.

"Not sure if it's going to be the same, though." His comment catches me off guard as silence falls between us.

What does he mean?

"Um… thanks again for the transfer, the food, and the gorgeous flowers."

"Anytime, Camryn. I better let you go. See ya soon."

"See you soon, Nate."

And with that, he's gone.

And a sudden unease fills me.

33

NATE

"I've missed you, Nate," Camryn's words filter through. "Let me show you how much I've missed you." Camryn looks up at me, need sparkling behind her green eyes. She pulls down my shorts and nestles between my legs, her ruby red lips wrap around my dick. "Yes," I hiss, running my fingers through her hair. "Yes. Yes. Yes," I shout as Camryn's lips slide up and down my shaft.

"More, give me more." Which she does, suctioning her mouth against me. God, she feels amazing. "Such a good girl."

"Thank you, Mr. Lewis."

That voice.

My whole body stills.

Why does Camryn sound different?

"Is everything all right, Mr. Lewis."

I sit up quickly in my bed and look down at the familiar blonde hair, but instead of green eyes staring back at me, they're blue. *What the hell?*

"Are you okay, sir?"

My heart is beating a thousand miles a minute. That isn't Camryn on her knees sucking my dick, it's Tanya, one of the staff from the resort.

"I didn't mean to startle you, sir." She looks at me with concern on her face.

What the hell is she doing in my room?

Pulling up my shorts, I cover myself.

"Miss Starr booked you in for a wake-up call," Tanya quickly explains.

"Camryn?"

Am I still dreaming?

Shaking my head, I try to clear the sleep fog that's taken over.

"Yes. Before she left, she organized a BJ wake-up call for you."

Falling back against the bed, placing an embarrassed arm across my face, I burst out laughing.

"Are you okay, sir?" Tanya asks.

Sitting back up again, I am still chuckling to myself. "I'm so sorry, Tanya. I was half asleep. I thought you were someone else in my dream and became a little confused when I saw you there."

"I'm sorry, sir. I thought it would be okay."

Running my hand across her face, I reassure her everything is okay. "Of course, it's fine. Just woke up surprised, that's all." I smile down at her.

"Would you like me to continue, sir?"

Do I? My dick's still hard, throbbing actually.

Should I? Camryn did organize the surprise, so she wanted me to enjoy it.

"Yes, Tanya, I would like it very much."

The tension falls from Tanya's shoulders as she resumes her position between my legs, and she pulls my shorts down again.

Falling back against the bed, I dream that it's Camryn.

"Hey, you," Camryn answers her phone.

"Thanks for my wake-up call."

She giggles. "Did you like it?"

"I near on had a heart attack. I was dreaming it was you, then Tanya spoke and woke me up from my dream and freaked me the hell out." Camryn's laughing uncontrollably. "It's not funny."

"Hope you were able to finish and didn't get stage fright," she continues chuckling down the line.

"Of course, I did. But it most definitely woke me up for the day."

"Good." I can picture her smile.

"What's your plan for the rest of the weekend?"

"I have so much work to catch up on. So probably going to be stuck inside in front of my laptop. The weather is shit, so not really in the mood to go anywhere," she grumbles.

"Guess you don't want to know how nice it is here, then?"

"Fuck you, Nate," she cusses down the line, making me laugh.

My phone beeps moments later.

"Sent you something," she tells me.

Pulling the phone away from my ear, I open up messages and see a picture of just her finger flipping me the bird in front of her rain-soaked window. This has me roaring with laughter. I quickly take the same shot, but point my camera toward the beach, where there's nothing but white sand and blue ocean in the background and send it to her.

"Fuck you, Nate," she screams, to which I can't stop laughing.

"Hope you have a great day, Camryn," I tell her through my laughter.

"Hope you choke on a dick, Nate," she adds.

"I'd rather suffocate under a pussy instead."

She groans at my lame joke. "Of course, you would. I better go. Hope you have a great day, too."

"Thanks for my wake-up call. After the initial heart attack, it worked out great."

She chuckles. "Bye, Nate."

"See ya, Camryn."

I haven't physically spoken to Camryn in weeks which, if I'm honest, I'm a little disappointed. We've both been really flat out, but honestly, I wouldn't mind hearing her voice even if it's just once.

What is wrong with me?

"The place is looking amazing." Sam Rose, my best friend and silent partner in this venture, greets me outside his beachfront villa. He flew in today to check on things for a couple of days. "It has come along so much since I saw it a couple of months ago. It is beyond anything I could have ever dreamed of, Nate." He slaps me on the back. "This truly looks like paradise, man." He's grinning from ear to ear, and it's contagious.

"I'm guessing you enjoyed the delights Willow had to offer?"

"She sure knows how to get the knots out of me." Wiggling his eyebrows, we jump into the golf buggy and head to the overwater restaurant for dinner and a catch-up.

We're shown to our private table on arrival just as the sun is setting over the ocean. I don't ever get tired of this view.

"This is truly beautiful," Sam says in awe, which is a high compliment as his family owns hotels in some of the most beautiful places in the world. "I see the feedback from guests who have stayed there, and it's always excellent." Most guests haven't found anything major to complain about, which for a soft opening is fantastic, but there are, of course, improvements still to be made.

"People are enjoying it, which is what we wanted." Sipping my beer, I relax into my oversized chair while watching the sunset. My phone beeps letting me know a message has come through. Picking it up off the table, I look down, and it's from Camryn. It's a picture of her flipping me off from the gym. Since our last phone call where she sent the original picture, every day we've been trading insults with each other. She's texted me photographs of her flipping me off in the snow, in Central Park, from her desk, on the subway, eating pizza, and they always make me smile. I, of course, have sent her back numerous photographs of me flipping her off all over the island.

"Never thought I'd see the day that Nate Lewis would smile like that over a text message," Sam tells me.

Forgetting who I'm sitting with, I still. Oh shit! Sam is close friends with Camryn, and we both agreed we wouldn't let them know.

"Was just a funny meme my brother sent me." I am trying to cover my tracks, but I know it's unsuccessful.

"Bullshit," Sam states. "That look on your face is not the one you have when you get something from your sibling. It's the one you get when someone you like sends you something," Sam notes.

Shit. Shit. Shit.

"It's no one, honestly."

Sam's eyes narrow in on me. "What are you hiding?"

Shit! I can't hide this stuff from my closest friend, he knows me too well.

"I'm not hiding anything." Placing my phone upside down on the table, I take a sip of my beer.

Sam swipes my phone and hightails it away from me. Fuck. Running after him, I think, *Are we in fucking high school?* Sam stops and turns slowly, his eyes wide, he even looks a little angry.

Dammit! He knows.

My shoulders slump.

"It's not what you think, Sam."

"You and Cam?" he questions, waving my phone in his hand.

"We're just friends." Grabbing the phone from him, Sam's eyes narrow on me. "You like her."

"Of course, I do. She's great. But not like that."

Sam pushes past me and slumps back in his chair. He grabs his beer and finishes it, then signals the waitress for another. Sitting back in my chair, Sam's silence is concerning.

"How long has this been going on?" he questions me.

"Nothing's going on."

He turns, glaring at me.

Fuck. Fuck. Fuck.

"Is that why Jackson is in New York updating the security at Starr and Skye Events?"

Not answering, I simply stare out over the ocean, wishing it would swallow me up, so I don't have to answer his questions.

"You want them safe, after all the stuff with Harris, don't you?"

"Of course, I do," he answers, but his tone is curt.

"That's all it is."

"Bullshit, Nate." He's angry. "Why are you lying to me? I can see it written on your fucking face."

"What do you want me to say?" I throw my hands up in the air giving in.

"The goddamn truth." His blue eyes boring into me.

"The truth? You want to know the truth about Camryn and me?" He nods his head. "I've never wanted someone more than I want her." Sam's sapphire eyes widen in shock with my honesty. "She is the most amazing woman I've ever met."

"I had no idea."

Rubbing my hands over my face, I continue, "How can someone like me..." thumping my chest, "... have a normal relationship?" Sam frowns at me. "Look around you, I'm surrounded by temptation."

"This is your job, Nate. It's doesn't define you."

"What happens if I'm too weak to say no to something or someone here?" Waving my hands around the paradise that surrounds us.

"I guess that's something you would discuss with your partner," Sam states slowly.

"I can't do that to her, Sam."

My best friend looks over at me, really looks at me. "You have actually fallen for Camryn, haven't you?" I don't answer him. "I've never heard you speak like this before. You've never cared about cheating on any of your other partners, but now, thinking about the possibility that you might on Camryn hurts you to your very core."

He knows me too well, the fucking bastard.

"How does Camryn, feel about this?"

"She doesn't want a relationship."

Sam seems surprised. "That's what she said?"

I nod my head in agreement.

"Do you want one?"

"I don't have time for one."

"That's not what I asked, man," Sam pushes. "Would you want a fully monogamous relationship with Camryn Starr?"

"Yes." The word is out of my mouth before I have a chance to realize what I've just said.

"Holy fucking shit, man." Sam runs his fingers through his hair. "This is fucking awesome. You two will be great together."

"Hold on..." I push my hand up to stop him, "... it's never going to happen. Maybe in some fantasy world it would be nice, but here in reality, I have so much going on with The Paradise Club. We have so many plans. I'm never going to be in New York. Her life is there. Her business is there." Sam frowns at me. "Why start something you know is going to end?"

"That's a little pessimistic, don't you think?"

"What about you and Kimberly, then?" I throw back at him.

"There's nothing going on between us," he answers quickly.

"But you want something?"

"When the fuck did we turn into women clucking about our relationships at a fucking sex resort," Sam states, annoyed at my line of question.

Exactly, man.

You want someone you can't have, and you know how much it

sucks, so you bury it deep down inside of you, pretending you're happy with your fucking life. When, in fact, you're miserable because the one person you can't fucking stop thinking about doesn't want you like you want them.

"Not so fun when it's about you, is it?"

Sam glares at me while finishing off his beer.

34

CAMRYN

"Miss Starr, there's a gentleman waiting downstairs for you," my porter, Barry, tells me. "He says his name is Nathaniel Lewis. I've checked his ID, it is him."

"Barry, send him up and add him to my list of approved people. Thanks."

What the hell is Nate doing back in New York?

I thought he was in London.

Why the hell is he here surprising me?

It's been a couple of months since we've physically seen each other, and our talking has been sporadic at best. I've organized Vanessa's baby shower one weekend in LA. Vanessa and Christian have been in town while Ness trains Harper up on everything Dirty Texas. I've just got back from the shitshow that was Olivia's wedding. We all knew that wasn't going to happen, but thankfully everything worked out in the end. We have the Grand Opening of The Paradise Club next month, not to mention the start of the New York charity season, which means most weekends we're booked for some kind of event through the Summer. The New York charity season kicks off with the Rose Gala, which is Sam and Harper's parents' annual charity event. We've been looking after this for the last couple of years, and thanks to them and the success of their event, they really elevated us into that upper tier of event planners.

I look a mess in my yoga pants, crop top, no makeup, hair pulled up in a messy bun. Quickly sniffing under my arms—yeah, that's not good—I race around my apartment like a madwoman.

There's a knock at the door, and it instantly makes the butterflies take flight in my stomach. Taking in a deep centering breath, I open the door.

Damn, he looks fine, dressed in jeans, a white button-down shirt, and navy blazer. His chocolate hair is messily tousled. He's holding the largest bouquet of flowers in one hand and a bottle of champagne in the other.

Are we celebrating something?

"Camryn." His handsome face lights up in a gorgeous smile, and I lose it.

Rushing to him, I grab his face and kiss him. I haven't been with anyone since Nate, I just haven't had the time, and it's not that I haven't wanted to.

He wraps his arms around me as much as he can with his hands full. "Missed me, huh?" He gives me a cocky smile.

"Yeah, I have." And it's the truth.

"May I come in?" he asks.

"Yes. Shit! Yes, of course," I welcome him into my home. I'm very proud of my gorgeous apartment. It's in a great location, just one block from Central Park, and one block over from Billionaire's Row. I'm near great shopping, amazing restaurants, with the subway close by. I even have a terrace which is hard to come by in Manhattan. It cost me a lot, but it's all mine.

"Wow! Your place is amazing." Nate's eyes widen as he takes in my apartment. "Is this the penthouse?"

It is a small penthouse compared to a typical penthouse in New York. Plus, this one was only a couple of million versus the tens of millions if I moved over one block.

"Yeah, it is," feeling very proud of myself, I reply.

"Look at your windows, there's so much light." One side of my apartment is floor-to-ceiling glass windows that look out over my terrace, which has stunning views of the buildings surrounding it.

"I have a full kitchen outside, too. In summer, I host the best parties out there, especially in the jacuzzi."

Nate's sapphire blue eyes sparkle with desire.

"There's another terrace off my bedroom that wraps around the other side of the apartment. Nate nods his head taking in my words. "Let me take these from you." Grabbing the flowers from his hand, I walk them into the kitchen.

"I love your apartment, Camryn."

"Thanks. It was my first big purchase when things started to take off for us. I'm pretty proud that I did it on my own." Nate's head is nodding as he looks around taking in everything. "There are glasses in the bar cupboard in the living room if you want to pour us some of that..." I point to the bottle of champagne he's still holding in his hand as I place the gorgeous flowers in a vase.

Nate walks off, and moments later, I hear the pop of the cork on the bottle. I place the vase in the center of my dining table and walk into the living room to take the glass from his hand.

"What are we celebrating?"

"We just finalized the purchase of another island."

My eyes widen. Holy hell, that's fantastic. Nate's really steaming ahead in his business pursuits.

"Congrats." We clink our glasses together. "Cheers! That's incredible news."

"I'm meeting Sam tomorrow to celebrate. He has no idea I'm here." His admission surprises me because those two are so close. "I wanted to see you first."

I smile at him. "Now, I know why Sam's called us all to his place for dinner."

Nate's eyes widen, I'm guessing he didn't know that was happening. "Guess we're both going to have to act surprised, then?"

I take a seat in front of the fire, and Nate joins me. He grabs my legs and lays them across his, which turns my body to him. We sip our champagne in comfortable silence for a moment.

"I've missed you, Camryn." Nate gives me one of his gorgeous smiles.

"I've missed you, too." Placing my glass on the coffee table, I maneuver myself so that I'm straddling him.

"I've noticed you haven't been to the club," Nate tells me.

Has he been checking up on me?

"Haven't had time," I tell him.

"Then who's been looking after you?" he questions.

"Me…" I leave it open, and he raises a brow. "I haven't been with anyone since you, Nate." I lean forward and kiss him.

"I haven't either since that wake-up call you left me," he murmurs against my lips.

Sitting back, I look at him in surprise.

"I've been busy." He shrugs his shoulders.

"I'm surprised, that's all," I tell him honestly.

"My business may be sex, but it doesn't mean I need it all the time. I'm a normal guy with normal needs." He grins at me, and for the first time, I see Nate Lewis, the man behind the mask of Nate Lewis, sex club owner.

Leaning in, I kiss him slowly. Nate follows my lead and savors me. We're not in any kind of hurry—we have all night. It's just the two of us again in our bubble. I didn't realize how much I missed his touch until now. The way his hand moves from the base of my neck, down my spine, to my ass. Those thick fingers digging in. Need pulses through my body uncontrollably while Nate keeps the same steady kissing tempo.

"I've missed you so much," he whispers into my ear as his lips find my neck. "I don't want anyone else, Camryn." His teeth sink into my skin, sending shockwaves over my body.

What did he just say?

"No one does it for me." Nate sighs heavily against my skin.

"Nate…" His words are like a potent elixir swirling through my body.

"Don't say anything, Camryn. Just feel." His lips capture mine again while his fingers tangle in my hair as he pours his feelings into every swipe of his tongue against mine and every press of his lips against me. Next thing I know, he's lifting me from the sofa and asking, "Where's your bedroom?" His voice is husky with need.

"Down the hall, to your right."

Nate looks over my shoulder and begins to make his way down the hall with me wrapped around his body. He doesn't falter with his kisses as he moves swiftly. I've never felt more adored than I do in this moment.

Eventually, he finds my bedroom, making his way to my bed where he lays me down gently against the soft duvet cover. He throws off his blazer without breaking our kiss, next is the thump of his shoes, the jingle of his belt as they hit the floor. Nate then moves me into the middle of the bed and hovers above me. He glances down, and the look that he's giving me, reaches deep inside my core and clamps around my damaged, frayed heart.

This wasn't what I was expecting. I wasn't looking for anything, but there's something in the way he's looking at me tonight that's changing the way I feel about him.

"How did I get so lucky that you've allowed me into your bed, Camryn." His large palm caresses my face in a loving manner.

"I think I might be the lucky one, Nate."

His face softens at my compliment.

Things are changing between us, and I don't think either one of us has the power to stop it.

Nate leans down and softly kisses me again, my hands begin to unbutton his white shirt until it slides off him. My hands run over the strong planes of his body. Nate pushes my top up and throws it to the side exposing me to him.

"So fucking perfect," he mumbles as he takes a nipple between his lips.

Closing my eyes, I enjoy the sensation of Nate's warm breath across my chest, his wet lips wrapped around my nipples, his sharp teeth teasing me, his strong hands caressing me.

My hands find the button of his trousers and urgently try to get them off. He helps by kicking them off, along with his boxer briefs. His hands roll down my leggings and underwear in one fell swoop.

Nate falls to his elbows, bringing his body closer to mine, while my legs fall open, letting him rest between them. I feel his velvety skin rub against me.

"I need you inside me, Nate."

Without a word, he slowly rubs himself between my legs, teasing my folds with his shaft, never losing eye contact with me.

Opening my legs wider, I wait for him to push inside of me, but he doesn't, he simply continues working me over, never giving me what I need.

"Please, Nate…"

My begging makes him smile, so he reaches between us and glides himself into me.

Oh my goodness, he feels so good.

"I've never wanted anyone more than I want you, Camryn," he groans into my ear. His thrusts are slow, even torturous. "I can't stop thinking about you," he confesses.

"Me, too."

It's his face, his lips, his hands, his mouth that I use and picture to get myself off.

Nate thrusts deeper into me. He likes knowing that I'm just as affected by him as he is me.

"When I touch myself, I think only of you."

"Camryn…" he moans the word into my ear, making him misstep with his thrusting.

"No one fucks me like you do." My hands grip his taut ass, pushing him further inside of me.

"Your tight little cunt... it drives me wild," he growls as his thrusts begin to become more frantic. His words make me squeeze down on his dick. "Holy fuck, woman."

I love making a man like Nate Lewis lose control, it's the biggest aphrodisiac. So, I squeeze him again, and he practically loses his mind. Next thing I know, he has us flipped around, and now I'm riding him.

"I want to watch your tits bounce." He grins up at me.

Sitting against him, I give him exactly what he wants as I ride him. Those sapphire blue eyes are mesmerized by the movement of my breasts. Leaning back, Nate's thumb slides across my clit, making me squeeze down on him again.

"Yes," he hisses as he continues to let me rub myself against his hand, his thumb, his knuckle. "Use me, Camryn. Get yourself off," he tells me, and I do, riding him, while rubbing myself until I feel the tingles begin to shoot over my body.

Yes.

Oh, yes.

I'm feverish with need as I chase the edge, chase the fall into the abysses.

A couple more rubs against him, and I'm gone, my body contracting around him as an almighty orgasm rips through me.

"That's it, baby, ride me. Milk every last bit of your orgasm from me." His fingers grip my hips, holding me in place, pushing him deeper inside me, pushing my sensitive clit against his hard pelvis. I'm becoming delirious with need as another orgasm follows soon after.

This spurs Nate on. His thrusts become wild and frenzied until he can't hold on any longer and comes inside me. I've missed the sound of Nate coming, the manly grunts and groans, the sigh of utter contentment once he comes.

It takes a couple of moments to calm ourselves down. I'm plastered across his bare chest and am unable to move.

Nate chuckles, moving my hair to the side. "I've missed that." His dick twitches inside me.

"Me, too."

"I don't want to move, I like being inside you." Nate kisses my forehead, making me sigh.

Nate picks up my liquid state, making sure we stay connected and rushes into my bathroom. My legs are still wrapped around his waist as he fiddles with the shower faucet getting the water temperature just right. Then he steps us under the warm water. Slowly, I slide off of him, and he falls out of me. Instantly, I feel empty, so I wrap my arms around his neck.

"I already miss you being inside of me."

"Give me twenty minutes, and I can go again."

35

NATE

Last night I spent all night making love to Camryn, if that's what you call it. Doesn't mean we did missionary all night, though. We christened the entire apartment, twice over.

Waking up to her this morning was great. Rolling over and wrapping myself around her, slipping into her hot little cunt, waking her up with a couple of orgasms, I could get used to that. We spent the morning walking hand in hand around the farmers' market, chatting and laughing about mundane things. We blended in with the hundreds of others doing the same thing.

Once it became too cold outside, we headed home and warmed ourselves up in her jacuzzi. Not going to lie, fucking her in it with all those buildings looking down over us was fucking incredible. They couldn't see anything as Camryn had her bikini top on, but they would most definitely have had an idea by the way Camryn was moving above me. This woman—she's so fucking beautiful.

I like being with her.

I like fucking her.

I like waking up next to her.

I simply fucking like her.

I sound like a lovesick fool, and maybe I am. That's why it's a

major pain that we couldn't come to Sam's together. Camryn
insisted we arrive separately, and not act like we have just spent
the past twenty-four hours fucking the soul out of each other. I'm
not sure if I am not that good of an actor.

The elevator opens into Sam's penthouse apartment. He has the
traditional rich-person penthouse in New York—it overlooks
Central Park, views to the Hudson, walls upon walls of glass with
spectacular views. His aesthetic is very *Architectural Digest*.

Walking out of the foyer, I turn left directly into the entertaining
area. What I wasn't expecting to see is Camryn wrapped in Sam's
arms. *What the fuck?* My stomach sinks to the marble floor. His
arms are around her, they are way too close, and they are laughing
and joking. Sam eventually looks up and sees me standing there.

"Nate, you made it," he calls out as Camryn curses against him.
"You wouldn't be able to help us, would you?"

That's when Camryn turns around, and I see her hair is stuck
on his wrist.

What the hell's been happening here?

Placing the bottle of expensive champagne on the marble
kitchen counter, I walk over to where they're huddled together.

Camryn's green eyes look up at me, and she mouths "sorry,"
and that's when I put my damn ego to the side and help.

"I was a little enthusiastic about our news when I gave Camryn
a big old bear hug and got my button caught in her hair," Sam
tells me.

I can see it on his face that it isn't what I first thought. I feel
damn stupid that the first thing I thought of as I entered was that
Sam and Camryn had hooked up.

This isn't good.

Eventually, after a lot of tugging and pulling, they're finally
apart. Sam with some of Cam's hair still attached, but they are
separated now.

"I'm going to get changed." Sam waves his shirt sleeve in the

air with the hair waving in the air. As soon as Sam has disappeared, Camryn grabs my face and kisses me.

"Just wanted you to know nothing's going on between Sam and
me." She's biting her lip which tells me she's concerned.

"I know, little one," I reassure her.

"I saw your face when you came in, and—"

"Well, it certainly looked bad," I tell her but smile.

"I know. I was hoping it was Harper or Kimberly who was
going to walk through those doors."

"It's fine, Camryn. Let's face it, one tiny moment of insecurity
is not going to ruin what happened between us last night." She
shakes her head and closes her eyes. "Just so you know, you're
coming home with me tonight."

She raises a brow as if she might defy me, but my steely eyes
are determined and need not say another word.

"Fine." She crosses her arms over her chest.

Now that the shock has worn off, I take her in. She's dressed in
an animal print blouse, tight, black pencil skirt, and sky-high heels
that bring her up to chin height. Her blonde hair is straight. She's
wearing bright red lipstick on an otherwise makeup neutral face,
and she smells like berries.

Sam steps out and interrupts us.

"I'm going to freshen up." Camryn points in the direction of
the bathroom. As soon as she's disappeared, Sam punches me in
the stomach.

"You should have seen your face, man. You were ready to kill
me." He laughs hard.

"It looked shady as fuck," I say through gritted teeth.

"You still have feelings for her."

"Leave it," I warn.

Sam's face changes, and he becomes more serious. "I've been
messing around, but you are serious, aren't you?"

"Yes. Just… let me work it out, okay?"

Sam slaps me on the back. "Will do, man. Last time I'll push you on it." And with that, he moves back into the kitchen.

"You better have champagne ready, I need a drink," Harper bellows through the apartment. She's just come around the corner with Kimberly by her side. "Nate didn't know you were coming." Walking over, she greets me with a kiss on the cheek. Harper stays wrapped around me as Camryn walks out of the bathroom. Her face sinks a tiny bit seeing her best friend wrapped around me.

Tonight's not our night.

"Cammie." Harper lets go of me instantly and rushes over to her friend, greeting her. "You look positively glowing." Harper stares at Camryn while she looks her over. "Do you have a new man?"

I freeze.

Sam shoots me a look of 'oh shit.'

"You look like you're getting some."

"I wish." Camryn laughs lightheartedly. "I just touched up my face. I bought a new bronzer." She smiles at her friend, and Harper's eyes narrow as if she doesn't quite believe Camryn, then she laughs.

"That is some good shit. You need to tell me about it later."

Phew! Okay. This is good.

"What are we celebrating?" Kimberly asks Sam.

"Hold on, let me pop some champagne quickly." Sam grabs a chilled bottle from his fridge, popping it, then pouring out glasses for each of us and gets into position. "Okay, Nate and I have just purchased another island."

The room's silent for a couple of minutes before the girls all cheer.

"So, another Paradise Resort?" Harper asks.

"Yes. This time in Asia." She nods her head. "It's going to take a couple of years till we open the doors, but it's great news."

"I'm so proud of you two." Harper grins, which is nice, but all

I care about is Camryn's thoughts even though she already knows about it.

"It's going to be spectacular." Camryn raises her glass, and I mouth, "thank you" to her.

"Also..." speaking up, "... I bought a superyacht." The room goes silent. "Next summer will be the launch of The Paradise Club on the ocean."

Everyone gives me a round of applause. Last night I didn't know if the sale had gone through, I only found out a few minutes before I arrived.

"Christian and Ness' bachelor and bachelorette parties were awesome last year on the yacht." Camryn smirks.

I forgot she was there for that. I keep forgetting that our lives are so interwoven together.

"I love her so much," Harper coos. "I've had the best time hanging out with her in New York. Christian and Vanessa are so adorable together."

"They are the best people," Camryn adds, her eyes fluttering over to me.

Sam's phone dings, and he rushes out of the bar area and comes back with bags of food.

"I'm starved, let's set up in the dining room."

We all move around, placing the Italian food containers on the table. Harper grabs some plates, and we all sit. I, of course, sit next to Camryn—I want to be able to touch her under the table. I'm only human, after all.

We're all happily chatting as we hand over plates of pasta to one another.

The night is filled with way too much wine and pasta, and my hand hasn't left Camryn's thigh under the table. It feels good. Right even.

"You guys all ready for the opening?" Sam asks the girls. There's a little slur to his words after all the alcohol we have consumed.

"Of course, we are," Kimberly fires back.

"Are you going to use any of the facilities?" he asks.

"When the job is over, of course. It would seem cruel to be sent to Paradise and not be able to try anything out."

The daggers being shot back and forth between these two is about to collect collateral damage, meaning us.

"Stop being so overprotective, Sam." Harper points her long red nail at her brother. "If Kimmie wants to fuck a million men on the island, she can. I mean it's not like *you* aren't going to be fucking a million women while you're there." My head ping pongs between the three of them. "Double standard much?" Harper questions her brother.

It's a common argument between Harper and Sam all the years I've known them. Sam is protective over his sister which really pushes her to go a little crazy.

"Don't you have anything to say?" Harper turns on me.

"Nope," I reply, shaking my head nervously.

"So, you'd be fine if Camryn fucks a million guys while on the island?" Sam adds, and the room falls deathly silent.

I send my friend the biggest motherfucking glare known to man. He just threw me under the bus.

Realization hits him, and he zips his mouth and turns away.

"I'm a professional, Sam," Camryn begins. "You've hired Kimmie and me to do a job, and that's to make sure the Grand Opening is a success. Which it will be," she tells him. "Once our job is over, I'm sure both you and Nate will be perfectly happy for us to relax and enjoy the island, no matter what that is."

Sam looks well and truly scolded. He's almost sulking.

"You tell him, girl." Harper high-fives Camryn.

Sam grumbles in his chair and continues drinking his wine.

"And with that… I'm out." Camryn stands and places her napkin on the table. "Nate, do you mind if I share a ride with you. It's late, and I don't want to get a cab at this time of night by myself.

"Of course," I answer, knowing full well she's coming home with me.

Camryn says her goodbyes.

I flick Sam on the back of the head. The dick.

We leave. Together.

36

CAMRYN

"Sam knows, doesn't he?" I question Nate as soon as we slide into his car.

"He worked it out."

"What did he say?"

"He thinks it's great," Nate adds.

I can see he's trying to work out if I'm bothered by it or not, so I add, "And that's all?"

"We are guys, Camryn. We don't probe." He smirks.

Maybe I'm freaking out for no good reason.

"I wish I were able to touch you freely tonight, instead of under the damn table." Nate reaches out and caresses my face.

"I had to catch myself a couple of times," I agree, reaching out and taking his large hand in mine and linking our fingers.

"Do you think Harper and Kimberly would freak out if they saw us together?" Nate asks.

"Maybe shocked at first. But they'd get used to it, I guess."

"Then maybe we shouldn't hide what we have anymore?" Nate suggests.

Looking up, I see how serious he is, and it surprises me.

"We should tell them we are what? Exactly?" I am wondering where he's going with this.

Nate stares off in front of him for a couple of moments. "That we're dating," he states before looking back at me.

"Dating as in…"

"I've fallen for you, Camryn," Nate confesses, which utterly throws me. "These last couple of months apart from each other has made me realize that I might want something more with you."

My heart is beating madly in my chest as he pulls in front of a luxurious apartment building. An immaculately dressed doorman rushes out and opens the door of the car as Nate rushes around the car to my side.

"Come on." Nate takes my hand and helps me from the car. He greets everyone in the building when we enter. The elevator is waiting for us, and we step inside. He presses a couple of buttons, and we're moving quickly. Nate pushes me against the glass wall then runs his fingers through my hair and rubs his nose against my cheek and neck. "The things I could do to you in this lift," he growls into my feverish skin. "But I'm not prepared to give my security free porno." His teeth sink into my neck.

Moments later, the doors open, and he pulls me into a marble foyer. I don't get a chance to see anything before he picks me up and throws me over his shoulder.

"Nate!" I slap his ass as he runs through his apartment. All I can see is the gorgeous tiles underneath his feet. Next thing I know, I'm flipped upright, but I am falling, my back hitting the soft duvet of his bed. He throws his jacket off, next his cufflinks, socks, and shoes then his belt. I'm simply lying back admiring the view.

"So," he states as he begins to unbutton his dress shirt, one by one. "You think you could handle dating me?" He raises a brow at me.

"Maybe," I reply while admiring the tanned skin that's slowly becoming exposed to me.

"I'm going to make my base in New York for the near future."
Okay, this has my attention. "I can work from anywhere in the world,
why not in the same city as the most beautiful woman I know."

Fuck, he's good.

His shirt flutters to the floor, and I take in his gorgeous body—
the deep 'V' of his hips, the bumps of his abs, the tight muscles of
his shoulders, his thickly cut arms. This man is the most handsome
man in the world, and he wants me.

"Can you handle that, Camryn?" He raises a dark brow in my
direction.

"I think I can." Biting down on my bottom lip, his fingers
begin to unbutton his suit pants.

Show me the dick, show me the dick, I chant to myself.

"I want you and only you," he confesses. "I want us to be
exclusive unless we are playing at my clubs or the resort."

"So, nothing outside of that?" I double-check, I mean it's not
like I'm going to have time or anything, anyway.

"Exactly."

"But what happens if you're at the club by yourself?" This
seems like a gray area to me.

"We play together or not at all. Is that okay?" His fingers
unzips his trousers, and they fall to the floor. His dick is sticking
out the tip of his boxer briefs as I run my tongue over my lips.

"Yes. Yes, that's fine." I'll agree to anything in this moment.

He grins before pushing his underwear down and kicking it
across the floor.

"Hang on..." He pauses. "Are you sure?" Shaking the lust from
my brain for a couple of moments, he kneels on the bed and moves
closer, then he stops and hovers over me.

"I'm going to show you that I can be the man for you,
Camryn." This man is chipping away at the ice around my heart.

"Okay," I agree to it all. "I trust you, Nate."

This makes him smile.

"I have to run, or I'll be late for a meeting." Nate kisses me quickly but thoroughly. My whole body is sore from us consummating our new relationship multiple times. I feel giddy and lightheaded for him. "I have a car waiting for you downstairs to take you home." He smiles. "Breakfast is on the table, too."

This man is really upping his game.

He kisses me again. "My place or yours tonight?"

"Um... I..."

"Text me. I'm happy with either. Got to go." And with those last few words, he's out the door. Wrapping the duvet tighter around me, I scream excitedly into the bed.

I have a spring in my step walking out of Nate's apartment not that long after, even if I'm technically doing the walk of shame. I know I feel no shame about it whatsoever.

"Miss Starr." The driver opens the door for me.

"Do you mind if I walk home instead? I could really do with the fresh air."

The driver frowns at me before saying, "Mr. Lewis was specific. He would rather you take the car."

I know the guy's only doing his job, but I need some exercise to stretch my tired muscles. "It's fine. I promise. Mr. Lewis will be fine with it," I reassure him.

The guy relaxes, then he agrees and lets me leave.

The world looks fantastic this morning. I feel great, happy, content, and most definitely satisfied. This morning, I checked Google Maps to see how far I am away from my apartment. It's a ten-minute walk, which is only a block away. It's so strange that Nate and I have so many friends in common, live a block away from each other, but have never met until now.

I'm heading in to grab a coffee from a local café to keep me going. Lost in my little world, my great mood comes crashing down around me when I hear two simple words.

"Hello, Camryn." Harris surprises me while waiting in line for my coffee.

The hairs on the back of my neck stand to attention.

Ignore him, Camryn. You're in a busy coffee shop, he can't do anything to you in here.

"Saw you coming out of Nathaniel Lewis' apartment this morning. You're looking very happy with yourself."

I turn and glare at him. "Are you following me?"

He shakes his head. "Just a happy coincidence."

How did I ever fall for him? He has sleazebag written all over his face.

Ignore him, Camryn.

I am looking desperately at the barista willing him to hurry up.

"I knew it wouldn't take you long to start fucking him. He likes my sloppy seconds," Harris hisses at me.

Ignore him, he's trying to get to you.

Mentally I count to ten, ignoring his ass.

"You know he's not going to stay faithful, don't you?" Harris pushes.

I make a conscious effort to shuffle away from him, but the damn asshole follows.

"The man has women falling at his feet daily. I mean, he owns a sex resort for God's sake."

How the hell does he know about The Paradise Club?

"I thought that would get your attention. If I'd known you had wanted to explore your kinky side, Camryn, maybe I wouldn't have had to go elsewhere."

What the fuck is he saying? That he cheated on me before?

"I have friends in high places." He smirks, and I shudder.

"Camryn," the barista calls my name, and it's not soon enough. I grab my coffee and hightail it out of there.

"He will never love you like I do, Camryn." Harris chases me through the busy morning commute.

"Leave me alone, Harris."

"You're mine, Camryn. Do you hear me? I will not lose you to that man," Harris curses.

Pushing his threats from my mind, I know I need to get to safety. I look around, and he's gone.

Thank God!

Falling against a brick wall down a side street, the tears fall down my cheeks, my coffee drops from my hand as I begin to shake, and I come to the realization that Harris is never going to leave me alone.

37

NATE

"Welcome to The Paradise Club," I greet Sam, Harper, Kimberly, and Camryn as they step off the boat from the mainland. I haven't seen Camryn in a week since leaving for the resort to get ready for our Grand Opening.

Without thinking or consulting with Camryn, I stalk over to her, grabbing her face and laying one directly on her. She is a little taken aback at first but then opens wide for me.

"What the?" Harper stares.

Sam's clapping excitedly, and Kimberly is smiling at the two of us.

"How long has this been going on for?" Kimberly points between the two of us.

"A while." I tuck Camryn underneath my arm.

"You dirty bitch. You never told me," Harper states.

"That was my fault," I exclaim, taking the blame. "I didn't want anyone to know about us until I was certain."

"Certain?" Kimberly asks.

"Certain that I could commit to one woman."

The girls gasp in surprise over my candid words, a reassuring smile falling on each of their lips. It's the truth.

"I'm happy for you both," Sam tells us.

"Enough about us, let's take you to your rooms." With my thumb, I point over at the golf buggies that are all lined up. "You're staying with me," I whisper into Camryn's ear.

"I'm happy to take over from here," Sam interrupts.

"You sure?" He nods, throws us a wave, and heads on over to the buggy.

"See you later... I want *all* the details," Harper tells Camryn as Kim waves goodbye.

"Well, that went well." Camryn wraps her arms around my neck.

"I couldn't help myself. It feels like forever since I've seen you." Leaning in, I kiss her again.

"It's been a week." Camryn smiles at me.

"And I have blue balls."

"Sounds like I'm going to need to do something about that, aren't I?" Her hand disappears down my shorts, gripping me hard, making me hiss.

Oh, yes, she most certainly does.

"We're alone. I've tightened security so no one is allowed in unless they call me first." The resort is extremely busy at the moment, and I don't want unwanted guests wandering into my private compound, or for that matter, our nosey friends.

"Really?" Camryn sinks to her knees, and within seconds she has my dick out and her mouth wrapped around it.

Holy shit. Fuck. God, yes.

She takes me all the way back into her throat.

Looking down, I see those green eyes staring up at me as I run my fingers through her blonde hair.

I'm gone for.

I am done!

This woman on her knees in the middle of the back lawn of my villa in fucking paradise, no one else will ever compare to her.

Pulling her mouth away from me, and as much as I want to come down her perfect little throat, I miss her pussy much more.

"I need inside of you, Camryn."

Helping her up from her knees, she gives me a knowing smile as I lead her back around to the daybed beside the pool. She's dressed in a gorgeous magenta kaftan. I wonder what she has underneath? Undressing quickly, I lay back on the daybed.

"What you got on underneath all that fabric, Miss Starr?"

Camryn gives me a knowing smile as she slowly rolls up the fabric, bit by bit, exposing her beautiful tanned skin. She stops just short of her pussy.

"Don't tease me, Miss Starr. I'm on the edge as it is," I warn her, which makes her laugh.

In one smooth action, she whips off her kaftan and shows me she's bare underneath the dress. Instantly, I grab her, pulling her onto my lap. "Please tell me you haven't been traveling all day with no underwear?" I growl. "Are you wanting me to lose all control?"

Camryn leans forward and distracts me with her tits, rubbing them in my face. "I took them off before boarding the helicopter," she whispers in my ear. "I wanted to be ready for you."

"You know me so well."

She slowly sinks onto my dick, and I bury my face into her breasts as she begins to ride me. "You feel so good."

Wrapping myself around her, holding her close to me, skin to skin, chest to chest, neither one of us takes their eyes off the other. We are totally connected in this moment. We both feel it, whatever it is that's happening between us. And it soon turns from primal fucking to something more, some might even say, making love. Yeah, I know it's cringeworthy to say, but that's what it feels like, out amongst the rainforest with both of us connecting as one.

How the hell have I become poetic and shit?

Camryn continues riding me until both of us can no longer hold on, and in perfect harmony, we come together.

"That was…" Camryn kisses my cheek not finishing her words.

"Different?" I add.

"Yeah. It was." She obviously felt it too. I'm glad I'm not alone in this.

"I'm happy you're here."

"Well, you're kind of paying me to be here," she cheekily jokes as I roll her onto her back, making her laugh.

"You know what I mean."

Camryn's legs wrap around my waist. "I knew what you meant, I'm just teasing."

I run my nose along her cheek and neck until my mouth wraps around one of her exposed nipples, giving it a gentle tug making her groan.

"I could stay here all day with you," I state, then nuzzle into her chest.

"Well, you do have a fantasy island to open. Unfortunately, you have things to do."

Groaning, she lightly pushes me away.

"You're such a slave driver," I grumble as I pick her up from the daybed. "Can I at least clean you up before I have to entertain people?"

"I'd love you to."

After spending our time in the shower lathering each other up, having way too much fun with bubbles, we eventually emerge from the shower after giving her a thoroughly good cleaning. Lying down with her on the bed, it's not long until we both must fall asleep.

***

"Nate. Wake up, Nate." Camryn's voice pulls me from my dirty dreams.

"You're here!" I forget for a moment that she's here with me.

"I am." Leaning over, she kisses me.

I want more, so I pull her on top of me.

"As much as I would like thirds, why is Massimo downstairs with a massage table set up?"

Oh, that's right, I organized something for her as I have to run off to a meeting. Looking down at my watch, damn, in about twenty minutes.

"I organized that for you." Rolling her to the side as I jump up from the bed, I make my way into my walk-in closet.

"Me?"

"Yeah. I have a meeting I need to get to." I change into a linen suit as quickly as I can. "I want you to have a nice massage before the chaos starts." Walking over to her, I kiss her.

"But I…" She seems a little confused.

"Unless you don't want it?" I turn back to her with questioning eyes.

"Um… I…" Camryn becomes flustered.

We're sort of in a 'no man's land' at the moment.

"Babe…" Grabbing her face, I say, "I've organized a happy-ending massage for you. I thought you'd be comfortable with Massimo." She nods her head in agreement. "Now, he can finish you with his fingers or his mouth. But…" Camryn stays silent waiting for me to continue, "… I don't want him to fuck you. Not while I'm not here. Is that okay?"

"Of course," Camryn agrees.

Leaning forward, I give her a deep kiss. "I'm okay while you're here on the island sleeping with someone else, just as long as I'm in the room with you. Is that okay?"

"I understand. That goes for me, too," she quickly adds.

"I feel more comfortable that way."

"I think that's a perfectly acceptable request."

I'm relieved. I've never really put restrictions on a partner, not even when it comes to sex. I know most people wouldn't want to watch their partner fuck someone else, but I will feel more comfortable, more in control, if I am there knowing how she's enjoying it. Otherwise, I think the not knowing might mess with me more.

"You are enough, just so you know," Camryn adds, stopping me.

"What do you mean?"

"I'm happy to play around, but I'm also happy if you don't want me to. That you, and you alone, are enough. Only when you're ready for it."

My heart stops for a couple of beats before rushing back to her. "When there's a ring on your finger, my baby in your stomach, that's when there will be no more sharing."

I'm serious as I give her a passionate kiss, letting her know my full intentions before I have to leave.

38

CAMRYN

W hat the hell just happened?

"When there's a ring on your finger, my baby in your stomach, that's when there will be no more sharing."

What does he mean by that statement?

I walk down the stairs in a daze.

"Nice to see you again, Miss Starr." Massimo's timbred voice gains my attention.

"Massimo, nice to see you, too." I give him a warm smile.

"Mr. Lewis said you've been working very hard organizing this Grand Opening, and you need to relax." Massimo waves his hand across the massage table. "He also advised that the happy ending should be via my fingers or tongue. Is that okay with you, Miss Starr?"

My mind's still trying to compute the bombshell Nate just dropped on me upstairs.

"Yes. Of course.," I answer, feeling distracted.

"Are you okay, Miss Starr? You look tense."

"I am." All of a sudden, I feel the weight of the world on my shoulders. I haven't told Nate about my run-in with Harris yet, and I know it's the last thing he needs just before his big opening. The way he feels about that man, he would kill him. It's best we get through this opening, and then I will tell him what happened.

"Please, take your clothes off," Massimo tells me.

Distracted, I do as I am told and lay face down on the massage table. I wriggle around getting comfortable, closing my eyes as I lay my face in the hole.

Massimo moves my legs apart, splitting the massage chair open. The sound of his movements, the squirt of liquid onto his hands before they descend onto my body, warn me before strong fingers begin to work my tense muscles over and over again.

This is an amazing massage. I can feel all the stress and tension I've been holding in my body slowly drift away.

Those strong hands concentrate on my body not a happy ending. He works my muscles over and over for a long time, nothing sexual just pure and utter relaxation.

Once my body has become liquid, his fingers begin to slide up and down my thighs moving further and further toward my center. The first swipe of his finger along my slit makes me jolt, but then I soon relax into it. His hands move over my body until they finally slip between my folds. A thick finger enters me while another runs over my clit. He continues to slowly and methodically work me over until I'm unable to hold it in anymore, and he pushes me over the edge.

"Enjoy your stay, Miss Starr," Massimo tells me as he leaves the villa.

I stay there for a while until I'm able to move again.

"Hey, guys," I greet Harper and Kimberly for drinks at the bar. They both hug me.

"You have so much explaining to do." Harper's eyes narrow on me as she hands me a glass of sparkling champagne.

"That was very public what he did as we arrived earlier," Kimberly adds.

"I know. He kind of caught me off guard."

"But in a good way?" Harper asks.

"Yeah, I think so." I'm smiling at my best friends.

"You two look so good together." I can already see Harper has love hearts in her eyes.

"You know she has you walking down the aisle already," Kimberly adds sarcastically.

"I know, I can tell." I turn to her. "Harps, it's still new."

"You two would have the most gorgeous babies." She giggles.

How much has she had to drink?

Kimberly chokes on her drink beside me over Harper's comment.

"Oh my God, Harps. Calm down. You do realize we are at a sex resort. There is no talk of babies or anything like that."

Harper simply rolls her eyes at me.

"So, do you like him?" Kimberly asks. Thankfully, she hasn't lost her mind.

"I do. I actually really do. But, we both work long hours, so not sure how well it's going to work out."

"But you're trying?" Harper questions.

"Yes. We have both agreed to try *our* version of a relationship."

"What does that mean?" Harper questions.

"We are together unless we want to play."

My friends all have wide eyes.

"You would share Nate?" Harper asks.

"It's not about sharing, it's just that we both agreed when we're in his clubs, we can explore things with others."

"Makes sense. The man does have a sex empire," Kimberly adds.

"Don't you get jealous?" Harper pushes.

"No. We've had many encounters where we have watched each other with other people, and to be honest, it's hot."

Harper's shocked face is almost laughable. "I don't think I could do that. Not with someone I'm dating." Harper shakes her head, over-exaggeratedly.

"I wasn't looking for anyone after Harris," I tell the girls. "Nate kind of just crept up on me."

"I can see it on your face you really like him." Kimberly nudges me.

"I think maybe because we've built up whatever we have via words not just physical, that things have moved a lot quicker than I was expecting."

"How so?" Harper asks.

"We chat most nights."

"So, it's been months then?" Harper seems surprised.

"It started out as a drunk text message which led to more, and now we talk all the time," I reply with a shrug of my shoulders.

"So, you kind of got to know him for him, not for all this." Kimberly waves her hand around the bar.

"Yeah. I think that's what is different. I also have no idea how this is all going to work, but he's moving back to New York to give it a chance."

"Nate is moving back?" Harper questions.

"That's what he said."

"That man is done for. Nate doesn't like staying in one place for too long. He calls it 'itchy feet,'" Harper explains. "So, for him to want to stay and pursue things with you, Camryn, he means it." She gives me a genuine smile.

"Enough about me. How did you guys go with your villas?" Wriggling my brows at them both, I smile.

"I had the best massage." Harper giggles.

"So did I." We high-five each other. "What about you?" I ask Kimberly.

Her face turns a shade of pink, one I haven't seen before.

"Nothing... I just ordered some food and had a nap."

Harper and I stare at her with drawn brows.

"Nothing?" Harper places her hands on her hips. "You are at a fucking sex resort, and you did nothing?" she states, her voice rising as she speaks.

"We are here to work, not to mess around," she counters.

She is right with that statement. But that's tomorrow, today's for just a little bit of fun.

"I need to pee." Harper huffs, walking off.

"You better not tell a living soul." Kimberly tugs on my arm seriously.

"Of course not." I am a little confused, so I don't say anything else and let her continue, "Sam popped over." My eyes widen. "We're just having fun." Well, I totally get that. "It's nothing serious."

"As long as you don't get hurt, then what does it matter?"

"I knew you'd understand. As much as I love Harper, Sam is her brother. We both agreed we are 'friends with benefits.'"

"How long has this been going on?"

"A while." Kimberly shrugs.

"And you're seeing other people?" She nods. "And if you see him with someone here, are you going to be okay?"

"I don't know… I mean I know he's hooked up with people before, but if I have to physically see it, I think it might be a little much for me to handle," she confesses.

"Things might change after here, then," I warn her.

"Yeah, I know. I just… I just never saw him as anything more than a friend, and now… now I can't get enough of seeing him naked."

We both burst out laughing. I totally get what she means.

"Speak of the devil." Looking over Kimberly's shoulder, Sam and Nate are walking into the bar like two male models down a runway. Women and even a few men stop to watch them pass by. The two of them command attention when they're together.

"Hey, ladies," Sam greets.

I notice Sam catches himself as he was about to reach for Kimberly. *That's interesting.*

"Hey, babe." Nate kisses my cheek.

"Babe?" Sam's screws up his face. "I never thought I'd see the day Nate Lewis, babe's someone," Sam teases him.

Nate flips him off before grabbing my face and kissing me hard, just to fuck off his friend.

Sam makes gagging sounds behind us, and it makes me laugh, breaking off the kiss.

"Where's Harper?" Sam asks.

"She went to the bathroom," Kimberley tells him.

Nate turns and gives me all his attention. "How was your massage?"

"Satisfying."

"Not too satisfying, I hope?"

"Not as satisfying as you." Reaching out, I wrap my arms around him.

"Good to know." He grins.

"Seriously, are you two going to be like this the whole time we're here?" Sam groans behind us.

39

CAMRYN

The official Grand Opening night went off without a hitch. It was perfect, everyone came out and attended. People were genuinely happy for Nate, Sam, his brother, Alex, who is also a partner in this venture. Nate announced the purchase of their next resort in Asia, and also the summer for The Paradise Club on the sea with his luxury yacht. All the guests were excited about their news and were ready to party, and now things have started to get a little crazy.

"You did it." Nate wraps his arms around me when we finally get a moment alone together.

"No, you did it! You created all this, Nate. I just created a cool party."

Nate kisses me ever so gently. "Thank you." I can see his sincerity. "You have been a lifesaver working up to tonight. You've helped me with so many other things outside of just a 'cool party' as you have termed it." He's sweet to say so. "I've organized a very special way to say thank you tonight."

Now I'm intrigued.

Nate takes my hand and leads me off into the rainforest to a special cabin. "This is the dark room," he tells me before we head inside. "Do you remember me telling you about this room?" he asks.

"Yes. It's completely dark except for a couple of lights that flash on every now and again. You don't know who is who."

This room has me intrigued.

"I have organized for a couple of special people to be inside with you. People you trust."

"You're going to be with me, aren't you?"

"Yes, I wouldn't miss it for the world." Grabbing my face and pulling me into a kiss, he says, "You sure you're okay with this?"

"Yes," I answer with nervous anticipation because the last surprise he organized for me was incredible.

"Good. I don't ever want to push you to do something you don't want, Camryn." He holds me tightly.

"As long as I am with you, I know I'm safe."

"I'll never hurt you, Camryn. Never." He kisses me slowly again, and I know in this moment, he means every single word he says, and that I'm safe. He opens the door to the dark room where there's a brightly lit foyer. There is a luxury change room off to one side with lockers to place your items.

"Get undressed Camryn, and I'll set things up." He places another reassuring kiss on my temple before leaving the locker area. I get undressed and see a sheer robe waiting for me. Nate's thought of everything. He knows I would be self-conscious walking from here to the room. He comes back in, his eyes blazing with heat when he sees me standing before him.

"You look like a goddamn angel, Camryn." He shakes his head in disbelief. "I will never understand what I did to deserve you." He kisses me again, this time with more heat. "I promise I will cherish you for as long as you'll have me."

Damn this man and his words.

"Shall we?" He takes my hand and pushes open the door.

The lights are on, there's a bed in the middle of the white room, with some bean bags scattered around it, an armchair, and a bench.

"I wanted you to see what the room looked like before the lights go out."

Looking around the room, it's sparse, but it doesn't look as intimidating as it probably would have in the dark.

"Let me take your robe, little one." Nate slides the sheer material off my shoulders and lays it across his arm. "Now, go lay down on the bed for me." His hand gives my ass a little tap which pushes me forward. I do as I am told and crawl onto the oversized bed. Turning around, I watch as Nate places the robe on the chair by the front door.

"You ready for this, little one?"

"Yes." My answer is breathless.

"Remember, the safe word is Paradise."

"Okay," I verbalize my understanding.

"The lights will be going out in three… two… one…"

I'm plunged into darkness.

The room is silent.

I hear shuffling, then Nate curses as I hear him run into the bed. This makes me giggle.

"Not funny, little one. It's dark in here," Nate groans.

I can't wipe the smile off of my face.

It's pitch black. I can't see anything at all, and I can already feel my senses heightening.

A hand runs along my body, then a bright flash of light filters through the room, and I see Nate standing there next to me before we're plunged into darkness again.

"That was just a test to show you what the room looks like when the light switches on."

This is going to be fun. It's not scary at all, and in that millisecond of a flash, I was able to see so much. The bed dips, and I can feel Nate's body heat near me. His hands push my legs open as his face dips between my thighs.

In the distance, I hear the door creak open, then the patter of bare feet in the darkness. The room lights up, and I see two men have entered the room.

"Everyone's been vetted by me, Camryn," Nate tells me from between my legs. This calms my beating heart. I could think of nothing worse than some random person, even though that's the point of the room.

A hand runs up my side as Nate disappears between my legs again.

The door creaks open again as a flash of light shows me another two gorgeous guys entering the room.

Yes. This is going to be so much fun.

It's too long until there are multiple hands all over my body. Nate's still between my legs, but there's someone sucking on each of my breasts, and there's a dick in my mouth.

I'm in heaven.

I don't even register the light flashing on and off anymore, I'm so consumed by need, by the sensations of what these men are doing to me. The orgasm given to me by Nate catches me off guard, my entire body arches against his tongue, but pure and unadulterated need fills my body.

I'm not sure who then enters me, I don't even know if I care. I let my mind go blank as I savor every ounce of what these guys are giving me.

"Ouch," Nate says beside me, which makes me smile.

He must have run into the bed again as I heard a thump.

So, Nate mustn't be fucking me as he sounded like he was beside me. Next thing I know I'm being flipped over onto all fours. Someone is underneath me, their mouth connects with my clit. Someone is also inside of me slowly moving. Someone shoves their dick in my mouth, while another two guys grab my hands and have them wrapped around their dicks. I don't have any idea how I'm sitting up, but this is crazy. This is insane.

One by one, the men move around until I don't really feel

anyone anymore. A hand runs along my body making me shiver, over my nipple, down my ribs to the juncture of my thighs but doesn't go anything further. Their finger then travels down my thigh to the tip of my toe.

My legs fall open for them, even though it's pure darkness. I can feel their radiant heat around me. The bed dips as they put their weight on the mattress.

The light flashes on, and I catch exactly who's between my legs.

A deep-seated scream echoes through the room.

How?

No. No. No. No.

His hands grab my knees, keeping my legs apart as I try and to scramble away from the man who has threatened me over and over again.

"If I'd known you were such a whore when we were dating, I wouldn't have cheated."

"Leave me alone." I try and scramble away from him, but he's too strong. "Help, help," I scream through the darkness.

I feel his warm breath on me.

No. Please, no.

"I've had to watch as all these men have their turn with you. Now, it's mine."

He yanks my legs apart, and it hurts.

No. No. No.

Punching him.

Pushing him.

"Would you stop fighting me, Camryn. And let me fuck you."

My heart's racing, fear laces my body. *Is he seriously going to rape me?*

Next thing I know, I'm bringing my head back, and with as much force as I can muster, I throw it forward and hope to God I connect with something. The deafening crunch of bone-breaking echoes through the darkness.

"Fuck. Fucking hell," Harris screams.

It gives me enough time to scramble off the bed. Another flash, and I can see his nose is broken and bleeding. His eyes are filled with hatred, and then we've plunged into darkness again.

"You fucking bitch," he curses through the room. "Wait till I get my hands on you. I'm going to show you no fucking mercy."

I'm so disorientated that I try and find my way to the exit. The tiny slither of light is the only indication of the doorway. Rushing toward it, I open the door, which bathes the room in light. Spinning around, I see Harris bent over, blood dripping everywhere. His head lifts, and he notices I'm escaping, so he rushes to the door.

Slamming it shut behind me, I grab a towel that's hanging on a hook and wrap it around my body.

My legs are like jelly as my instincts kick in, and the adrenaline begins to take over. Pushing myself to the limit, I run as quickly as I can through the rainforest. Sticks and stones dig into my bare feet, but I hardly feel the pain because all I am focusing on is getting to Nate's villa.

"Nate. Nate," I scream the place down.

Where the hell is he?

He told me I was going to be safe.

He told me he would look after me.

Where is he?

Why did he leave me?

Why did he let Harris in there?

I'm so confused.

Running through the quiet villa, it doesn't look like he's here. Taking the steps two at a time up to his room, I run along the hall until I get to his closed bedroom door. Opening it, I rush inside and pause at the scene in front of me.

There's a woman riding Nate's face, while another is sucking his dick.

What in the actual fuck?

Did he set this all up, so he could mess around with other women?

Running back out of the room, I throw up in the hallway.

40

NATE

"**W**hat in the fuck?" A male's blurry voice curses in the distance.

"You fucking bastard," a female's shriek fills the air. "Get out, you fucking whores," she shrieks.

The bed moves and the patter of feet filter through my consciousness.

"Something's not right," another male voice adds.

"Of course, something isn't right. Harris was on the fucking island, and now Camryn's missing," the female voice yells.

Hang on, what?

Trying to clear the heavy fog that's swirling around my mind.

Harris is here?

No. That's not right.

Camryn is gone?

My stomach rolls and decides in that moment to unload itself as I puke over the side of my bed.

"See, I told you something isn't right... my brother never vomits."

Alex? Why is my brother here?

"What…is… goin' on?" My lips feel like lead bricks as I try and talk.

Why the fuck can't I talk?

"See," the male voice says.

"He's probably just hungover, the fucking dick," a female voice adds.

"I think we need a medic," someone says as I black out again.

☘ ☘ ☘ ☘ ☘ ☘ ☘ ☘ ☘

When I wake up again, there's something in my arm, and I can't move.

"We're trying to flush the drugs out of your system, Mr. Lewis."

Blinking a couple of times because my room seems overly bright.

Drugs?

I try and focus on the object in front of me, but it's a blurry mess.

"Security is looking for the man who did this," the doctor tells me.

Looking for who?

I slip away into the darkness again.

☘ ☘ ☘ ☘ ☘ ☘ ☘ ☘ ☘

Feeling much better this time when I open my eyes, I look around.

"You're awake." I am looking up at the concerned face of my brother.

"Wait! What is going on?" I am feeling awfully confused as I try to sit up. My brother instantly stands and helps me with a pillow.

"Good, you're awake," Jackson Connolly, good friend, guest,

and the man who looks after our security is here, but he looks the most serious I have ever seen on his face.

"He doesn't know yet," my brother tells him.

Know what?

They both stare at me looking mighty uncomfortable.

"What?" I scream at them both.

"It looks like Harris Edwards made it to the island."

He did what? Sitting up, my heart races a million miles a minute.

"Where's Camryn?"

The two guys look between each other with concern on their faces.

"You need to calm down, brother," Alex tells me.

"I will not fucking calm down until you tell me where Camryn is."

"She's gone," Jackson tells me.

Jumping out of my bed, I grab at him, but Jackson's ex-military and takes it easily.

"Where the fuck is she?" I shake him, but he barely moves.

"She's disappeared off the island sometime last night."

She what?

A headache claws at my brain as I draw my brows together not understanding what they are telling me.

"It looks like Harris planned all of this."

"All of what?" Am I missing something?

"He drugged you, brought you back to your room. Set up two women to fuck you so Camryn would see," Alex tells me.

"Camryn wouldn't leave over that?"

Would she? I mean if it's true, it's a dick thing to do but not to disappear like that. Surely, she'd give me a roasting first.

"There's more, and you're not going to like it," Jackson explains.

"More?"

"You were drugged in the dark room. One of the guys you had

in there had a needle. Harris paid him a million dollars to drug you," Jackson tells me.

"He told them he wanted access to your office to get some info. They didn't know it was to—" Alex stops what he's about to say and looks over at Jackson.

"Harris paid all the men to leave him alone with Camryn in the dark room."

No. No. No. No.

My world begins to crumble around me.

"No. He… no…" I'm going to fucking kill him.

"She broke his nose," Jackson adds. "Then rushed to your villa to find you."

"Except you had company," Alex adds.

Wait! What?

Jackson presses play on the security camera in my room that only I have access to. There, clear as day in black and white, are two women having their way with me. Camryn rushes in looking disheveled in a towel. The women see her, stop what they're doing, and then Camryn's gone.

"Fuck!" Screaming, I run my hands through my hair.

Fuck. Fuck. Fuck.

As I fall back onto my bed, the realization hits me. "He raped her, didn't he?"

Alex and Jackson look at me. I can see it on their faces they're going to tell me something horrible.

"We don't believe that he did," Jackson adds.

"But you're not sure?" Jackson shakes his head. "Fuck, Camryn… I… fuck. Fuck!" My heart is slowly being ripped out of my body knowing I put her in that position when I told her I would protect her.

"We are going to find her," Jackson tries to reassure me.

"What about him." A sneer falls across my face. "Where the fuck is Harris?"

"We are on it," Jackson tells me.

"I want him destroyed. I want everything he owns destroyed. Harris Edwards needs to die."

"Bro, no," Alex butts in. "That's murder."

Turning around quickly, I glare at my brother. "He's going to fucking pay. That man tried to rape my girlfriend. He drugged me. He doesn't deserve to live."

"Nate," Jackson grabs my attention. "Death is too easy for a prick like him. I have other ways to destroy him that won't land you on death row."

"He fucking touched her," I scream at them both. Do they not understand what I'm saying? "And who the fuck knows where she is now? She is out there thinking I set her up with that monster, all so I could fuck two fucking women who mean nothing to me. No. He doesn't deserve to get off lightly."

Jackson places two hands on my shoulders. My chest is heaving. My heart's leaping out of my chest.

"I promise you... I will find a way to destroy him and keep all our hands clean." There is an edge to Jackson's tone that tells me he means it.

"I don't care what it costs," I tell him.

"Noted." Jackson nods his head.

"Where's Camryn?" My stomach churns at the possibility she's gone.

"Sam, Kim, and Harper have gone back home to look for her."

Fuck! I run my hand through my hair.

"They hate me, don't they?" I question my brother.

"The girls, yes. Sam's borderline."

"I've passed on all the information about what happened to Sam. They know that this isn't your fault," Jackson states.

"But it is." I thump my chest. "I promised her I would keep her safe. That I wouldn't ever let Harris near her again. I failed her. I've fucking failed her." My heart is being ripped out of my chest, knowing Camryn's out there all alone and thinks I fucked her over in the vilest of ways.

✿❀✿❀✿❀✿❀✿

"You okay?" Alex asks me once we're alone.

"No, I don't think I am." Looking up at my brother, I continue, "I love her, man." The realization hits me like a sucker punch to the gut.

"Once we find her, and she realizes that Harris set this all up, everything will be fine."

Shaking my head, I answer, "I don't think so. I don't know if we will come back from this."

"Don't say that, man."

"Love doesn't always conquer all."

My brother frowns at me.

✿❀✿❀✿❀✿❀✿

It's been a couple of weeks, and no one has seen Camryn.

It didn't take long for Jackson to locate her, he even hacked into her phone. I know it's wrong, but I'm desperate. She's been in contact with the girls but has asked for them to respect her needing some time alone, which is good. The last thing I need is for them to try and push her further away from me.

Men like Harris Edwards, entitled assholes, who think the world owes them everything because of who they are, always have secrets, and those secrets are the ones they wish to stay buried. Once you start digging deeper into people's lives, the skeletons soon rise to the surface.

Who knew we would hit the jackpot so quickly? One little hack and Harris' world is all about to crumble to the ground, and I didn't have to plant a thing. Jackson started looking into the Harris' family business. Our forensic accountant was able to find some discrepancies, and the next thing we knew, we uncovered the motherlode.

Harris's father was the leader of an international underage girls' escort ring. Once we picked the first thread, the whole elaborate scheme unraveled. We obtained as much evidence as we could legally because most of it was obtained illegally, and handed it over to some friends in the FBI.

We had no idea that they too had been investigating the leader of this ring for the last two years, and we just handed them all the evidence we had.

Watching Harris and his father taken away in cuffs with all of their assets frozen, and the whole of New York society turning on them once everything was flashed across the nightly news, gave me some joy.

Honestly, I wish he was dead, but we can't always get what we want.

Now that the arrests have happened, it's time for me to see Camryn.

41

CAMRYN

I'm staring at the news highlights on my phone about Harris and his dad. I can't believe that they were both involved in something so insidious. A shiver travels down my back just thinking about Harris.

How do I always pick the worst guys in the world?

Lance, Harris, Nate.

Damn if that last one doesn't hurt my soul just thinking about him. I thought Nate was different, but he's just as bad as the other two. The difference with Nate is, I fell for him. I gave him all of me, and he still threw me away like yesterday's trash. I haven't heard from him in the two weeks I've gone underground. I mean I blocked his number, but still, that's not the point. I am sure with his abilities and people he could have found me easily.

I'm nestled up at Vanessa's parents' health retreat in Byron Bay, Australia. This will be the last place anyone will think to find me. I couldn't get any further away than here. I have been doing yoga daily, eating vegan food, and I've done some crystal healing, but above all, I have seen a therapist. The therapist has been helping me work through my trauma. Of course, I didn't tell them exactly what had transpired that evening, just the points which didn't make me seem like I might have deserved what happened to me because I let multiple guys sleep with me. I know they're meant to be unbiased, but still, I don't trust them.

It's nice being here. It is quiet, the views are spectacular, and I've been hiking through the bush just trying to process everything. It's been hard.

I've spoken to Ivy, Harper, and Kimberly a couple of times letting them know I am safe and okay, just working shit out. They wanted me to tell them where I am, but I didn't because I knew they would be on the next plane to Australia. And in all honesty, I don't want to see anyone.

I'm embarrassed.

Ashamed.

I don't want to see people's pity when they look at me or their damn judgment. I know my sister and close friends won't be like that, but I am working on myself, getting myself stronger to go home and tackle my life again.

I'm walking back from a session in the pool, taking in the songs of the birds around me, listening to the serenity as I walk along the pathways back to my cabin. I still when I see a figure standing near my cabin. My hands become clammy, my heart rate increases, and for a moment, I feel like I'm seeing Harris, but the closer I get, I realize it's Nate.

Shit. How the hell did he find me?

He looks good dressed in shorts and a casual tee with his avia-tors on. He stops and turns, he sees it's me, but my steps slow. There's probably a couple of hundred feet between us when he lifts his hand and waves. I simply stand there, unsure how I feel about him invading my personal space. He then turns on his heel and walks away from me. *Weird.* I mean he's flown all this way to see me, yet he walks away? Once he's gone, I rush toward my cabin and race up the stairs. There's a bouquet of Australian native flowers waiting for me, and a thick envelope with my name on it. Picking up the flowers, I bring them inside and place them on the dining table. I pull off the envelope and turn the white paper in between my fingers. I'm not really sure what to do.

I've stared at the envelope for the past hour with every single scenario flashing through my mind, and they all come back to Nate being here.

Curiosity finally gets the better of me, and I open the envelope and pull out a letter addressed to me.

Dearest Camryn,

I'm not sure where to start with this letter. I feel like there are not enough words in the English language to convey how sorry I am for everything.

I let you down.

I promised I would keep you safe. That you could trust me. That I would never ever let that man anywhere near you again.

I failed you.

Everything I promised you, never happened.

I let that monster back into your life.

I don't know if there's anything I can say for you to ever forgive me, and I would completely understand if you never did.

Tears begin to fall down my cheeks onto the handwritten pages.

I guess I'm being selfish in my reasoning for writing this letter. I simply want you to know the truth about that night. It doesn't absolve me from anything, but maybe it might help you, and that's more important than my own pride.

That night was supposed to be a celebration, a thank you for everything you had done for me. I wanted to give you the world, instead I sent you into a nightmare.

Everything was going great until one of the staff members in there stabbed me with a needle.

My hand flies to my mouth in surprise.

Apparently, it was filled with a date rape drug, but in an extremely high dosage. Enough to kill me if I'd been given the full dose.

Wait. What? I reread that sentence.

I'm not saying that to make you feel sorry for me, Camryn. Just that I blacked out, and they were able to remove me from you without a fight.

They knew I would have fought until the end to protect you if I'd known.

I was taken back to my villa, where I was placed on my bed unconscious. Apparently, at some point, someone organized for the two women to have their way with me.

The image of Nate with those women in that moment is burned deep in my soul.

I had no idea what they were doing to me. It took me two days to come around after many, many treatments.

That was when I found out about what happened to you.

I lost it, Camryn, and I was ready to kill him with my own bare hands. I didn't care if I went to jail for the rest of my life. Just the fact he was able to get to you again was enough for me to want him dead.

Biting my lip, I continue reading Nate's angry words.

Thankfully, I was talked out of murder. It's still on the cards, just say the word then burn this letter.

This makes me smile. I shouldn't, but his semi-joke in between the seriousness of everything gets to me.

I'm hoping now you have seen the news. It took us a while to find all the information on Harris and his father, but we did it. Jackson told me that it would be better to see him taken down this way than the other. For me, the jury is still out on that one. But, the case is solid, we made sure the evidence could never be disputed. We wanted a rock-solid case, so they got what was coming to them. Seeing him disgraced, his reputation in tatters doesn't feel like it's enough, but I know it has to be for my own sanity.

I'm not sure if this news will help you heal, but I'm hoping it does a little.

I'm sorry I let you down, Camryn. My heart feels like it's been ripped out of my chest since you left. I feel lost without you around me, but I understand why you left. I understand why you needed time to begin healing. I know things may never be the same between us, but just know that I love you, Camryn.

I suck in a surprised breath.

. . .

I know this is a shitty way to tell you through a pathetic apology letter, but I need you to know that.

    I know it won't change anything, because I've hurt you, maybe beyond repair.

    I'll wait if you let me.

    Even if you don't, I still will.

    You are the first thing I think of when I wake, and the last thing I think of when I fall asleep.

    You haunt my dreams, Camryn.

    I'm selling my stake in The Paradise Club Resort.

Hang on, what?

I can't stand to be there anymore. I hate it. I never want to go back there again. My brother and Sam are going to purchase my stake in the business. I trust them to keep my vision alive.

    I'm not sure what I want to do next, but maybe it's time for me to leave the sex empire behind.

He's going to give it all up?

Pass it on to someone else. It's not really a good business to have if you want to settle down one day and have kids. I'm sure the PTA moms might not want me around their husbands.

This makes me laugh. Damn him. Even on paper, he's fucking charming.

     . . .

I'm rambling now.

I just want to know if you are okay? You can text me that you're okay and to leave you alone, and I'll respect your wishes. If you want to curse me out to my face, I'm staying in room 308. Whatever you want, I'll respect your decision.

I love you, Camryn Starr.

You were going to be my end, Camryn.

My happily ever after.

I am so angry that Harris destroyed what we had before we had a chance to explore more of it.

I'm sorry I couldn't protect you, Camryn.

If there is a slim chance that you might ever want anything with me again, know this... I would give up everything I have in this world to have a second chance with you. To wake next to you. To kiss you. To make love to you. To sit around binge-watching Netflix. To be the man you want in your life.

I know you need time, so I will give it to you.

Love Nate.

xoxo

I'm a blubbering mess, but my heart aches for him. My head is telling me he's no good, and I have no idea what to do.

42

NATE

C amryn looks like she's lost an awful lot of weight when I saw her walking along the path. She looked so sad, so damn vulnerable. Then she saw me, and the look that she gave me chilled me to the bone. I know I have broken her. There's no coming back from this, I saw it written plainly on her face. That's why I had to walk away. And as I did, my heart shattered into a million pieces.

All night I hoped for a knock on my door, but it never came. Eventually, I fell asleep sometime in the early hours.

Maybe I should go? It's clear Camryn doesn't want me here.

You're just going to give up? It's only been twenty-four hours, you dick. My stupid subconscious kicks in. But maybe it's right. I just don't want to cause her any more pain by being here.

I need to go for a run, clear my head. Grabbing my workout gear, I open the door and find a letter addressed to me in Camryn's handwriting. The thumping in my chest echoes in my ears. Slamming the door behind me, I rip into the letter.

Nate,

I've hated you for weeks now.

. . .

This is not a good start.

I could never get my head around how you let him into the resort, or into that room. How you could have betrayed me like that?

Was I not enough for you that you needed to distract me to fuck those girls?

Shit.

None of it made any sense in my head. I didn't think you were that cruel. I believed in you. I trusted you. And I just didn't understand how you could throw me into the lion's den with him.

Since I left the island, that's what's been plaguing me. How did things go south so quickly?

But then I saw you looking miserable at the end of the path, halfway across the world. Somehow you found me.

There was still a moment I was afraid that maybe you were not the man I had spent months with, getting to know.

Then I read your letter.

Hope suddenly blooms deep down inside of me.

In my mind I was punishing you, but I realized it wasn't as badly as you were punishing yourself. I can't let you give up everything you have worked for all of these years because of my ex and his inability to let me go. I won't allow you to give up your business. Please, don't put that on me.

Shit. She's right, that is a lot of pressure. How the hell did I mess this up so much?

. . .

I did see the news, and I can't tell you how happy I am that karma is heading Harris' way. I would have been fucking angry if you had been charged with murder. You know you're too pretty to make it in jail.

This makes me chuckle. Maybe there is hope if she's cracking jokes.

Things are a little mixed up for me at the moment. I don't know how I feel anymore.

Well, that line's like a punch to the gut.

All I can ask is, please, give me time.

That's fair enough.

What happened on the island has brought up some past issues for me, and I have to rework through things. If you're going to stay here in Australia, I'm okay with that.

So that's good, isn't it?

But, I understand if you need to go home.

. . .

There is nowhere else in the world I want to be. I told you I will wait, Camryn, and that's exactly what I'm willing to do.

Thank you for getting justice for me.
  Camryn
  PS: I've unblocked you.

Okay, that wasn't as bad as I thought it could have been, especially now that I'm unblocked. I guess that's why none of my messages were going through.

I'll stay the course because she's absolutely worth the trial.

❖❖❖❖❖❖❖❖❖

It's been twenty-four hours since receiving Camryn's letter, and I somehow feel lighter. Even if things don't go the way I want them to go, and we can only be friends or acquaintances, I'm okay with that too. Because I get it, I get where she is coming from.

I've decided to throw myself into everything this luxury health retreat has. Maybe it's good that I take some time out for myself. Maybe all this hippy stuff is starting to rub off on me.

I'm up early for a yoga session on the hill watching the sunrise. There's a couple of people scattered around. I roll out my yoga mat and attempt to follow the instructions of the trainer. I'm stretching my body in all kinds of unnatural ways, attempting something called the half-moon pose, and I end up overcorrecting myself and falling on my ass. I've totally embarrassed myself, and for the first time in my life, I think I'm blushing.

Then I hear a giggle off to the side. Looking over at who's laughing at me, I see Camryn, and everything stops around me. It's like the world ceases to exist, and all I can see is her. She stops laughing when she notices I am looking at her. She's dressed in a white sports bra and black leggings, her blonde hair is pulled up in a high ponytail, and she looks awfully thin.

I can't do this.

I can't be this close to her and pretend that she isn't the love of my life.

Rolling up my mat, I cut short my yoga lesson and head on back to my cabin.

"Nate," Camryn calls out behind me. "Nate. Wait! Please." Her plea makes me stop and turn around. There she is striding toward me, her ponytail bouncing from side to side. "Why did you leave?"

"I can't be that close to you..." hurt falls across her face, "... when all I want to do is reach out and touch you, but I know I can't." I let out a long sigh. "You asked for space, so I'm giving it to you."

Turning on my heel, I start to head back to my cabin feeling utterly defeated.

"Nate," Camryn calls after me again, but I don't stop.

My heart is breaking, and there's nothing I can do to stop it. Her hand reaches out and touches mine, and when she does, sparks fire under my skin.

"Do you hate me?"

Tentatively, I reach out and cup her face with my palm. "I could never hate you, Camryn. Never."

"Then why are you walking away from me?"

My hand falls away from her face. "I'm too brokenhearted to stay."

Tears well in her eyes. "Nate, I..."

Shaking my head. "Sshh... you don't need to say a word." A solitary tear falls down her cheek. "I'll always be here for you, things are just messed up at the moment." She nods her head in agreement. "I don't know if you're going to heal if I'm here. I don't want to get in your way of recovering from what happened, Camryn."

"I don't know how I feel," she confesses.

"I think you should stay and work through what you need to. Maybe ask Harper and Kimberly to come down. I know they miss you." Camryn's steely façade begins to crack as more tears fall down her cheeks.

"I don't know what to do anymore." Reaching out, I pull her against me, she wraps her arms tightly around me as she breaks down and sobs.

"I've got you," I tell her, kissing her temple. "I've got you."

We stay wrapped around each other for who knows how long until Camryn pulls away from me. She tries to straighten herself out.

"I'm sorry, Nate."

Shaking my head, I reply, "You have nothing to apologize for." She sadly nods. "I wish nothing but the best for you, Cam. Just know that."

"I do." She gives me a weak smile.

"If you need anything, I'm a phone call away."

Then I watch as she walks off down the path giving me a wave over her shoulder.

Then she's gone.

43

CAMRYN

It's been four months since I've seen or spoken to Nate. Not because I haven't wanted to, but because I didn't know what to say, and then so much time had passed, and I let the window of opportunity slip by me. Not that I haven't been busy or anything.

My good friend, Vanessa, had her twin girls, Ruby and Sadie, in LA, so I flew out to catch up with the new parents. That was so much fun, especially seeing her poor husband, Christian, this rock star, utterly besotted with these two tiny little girls. Not going to lie, my ovaries exploded watching him cuddle the tiny bundles— I'm only human.

Olivia and Axel are engaged, which was exciting. It's going to be a short engagement because, let's be serious, Axel is over waiting for his woman. Kimberly and I are organizing the wedding for her in one of her châteaus in France. It must be great to be royal.

That's where you find me now, as one of the bridesmaids in Olivia's wedding. We are currently in Paris for their bachelor and bachelorette parties. It's going to be the first time seeing Nate in a long time. Thankfully, he wasn't at the Eiffel Tower dinner with everyone. That would have been too much of a romantic place for our first meeting.

I'm walking around in a bundle of nerves waiting for him to arrive. The girls thought it would be a great idea to surprise the boys at Moulin Rouge, doing a can-can routine. Honestly, how the hell do I get pulled into these crazy things by my friends.

"Okay, the lights have gone down. Everyone's leaving, the boys have been asked to stay behind, and we go on in five," Kimberly tells us. I'm dressed in a ridiculous costume—it's what you do for friends. "You look like you're going to puke," Kimberly tells me.

"I'm nervous."

"Don't worry, people won't be looking at you." She smiles, elbowing my side. She's right, all the men sitting in the audience are taken by the gorgeous ladies surrounding me.

"Two minutes, ladies," Kimberly advises. We're all messing around with our costumes with last-minute nerves.

"Go time, ladies," Kimberly tells us.

The lights turn on, the stage flashes, the music starts, and off we go.

The whole thing lasts maybe five minutes, and we're all in fits of laughter afterward.

Once the music stops, the boys rush down from the VIP section, and that's when I notice Nate is with them. He looks tanned, he's toned up a little more, and he's grown a bit of scruff. He doesn't look as polished as he used to, though. Everyone is distracted by their significant others, kissing and hugging them.

"Have you been moonlighting on the Moulin Rouge since I last saw you," Nate breaks the awkwardness between us.

"My secret's out." Both of us smile at each other.

"The gang's heading over to my club afterward." He shoves his hands into his pockets, obviously not knowing what to do with them.

"Oh… Yeah, I might head home."

"Okay."

Well, this is awkward.

"I like the scruff." I am not sure what else to say because I'm feeling awfully nervous.

He scrubs his hand against his jawline. "You're looking well," he compliments me back, and I give him a little curtsey which makes him chuckle.

"Looks like we're going." Nate points to the couples heading on out to the limousines.

"I'll let you go then." I give him some sort of pathetic wave.

"It really was good to see you again." And with that, he's gone.

"How did that go?" Kimberly asks, wrapping her arm around my shoulder.

"Awkward as fuck."

"Well, it's over now. You can relax."

Maybe she's right.

❋❋❋❋❋❋❋❋

We've arrived at Olivia's family's château, and it is spectacular. The whole crew is here getting ready for their wedding. Kimberly and I have spent the entire day getting everything ready for the wedding tomorrow. It's late. I can't sleep. So I am prowling the château's corridors by myself, maybe with a ghost or two. I sneakily walk into the kitchen to grab something to eat, maybe another eclair, which is probably not a good idea because I won't be able to fit into my bridesmaid's dress in the morning. Opening the refrigerator, I stare long and hard at the eclair weighing up the pros and cons of eating it.

"If you don't eat it, I will."

"Holy shit!" I scream at Nate's voice behind me. "You scared the hell out of me." I lightly slap at his chest. His super hard chest. Shit. Not a good idea.

"I just arrived and am starving, so thought I would sneak in and

grab a bite to eat. Then I saw you staring into the fridge for what
seems like an eternity. It was then I realized what you were looking
at."

"Wanna go halves?" I quirk a brow at him.

"Sure," he agrees.

I grab the plates, and he fetches a knife from the drawer and
slices the éclair in half. We both bite into the pastry goodness, and
both of us moan in appreciation of the baked good.

"It's amazing," Nate states with a mouth full of dessert.

I just nod my head in contented agreement.

"Want some wine?" Nate asks, spying the opened bottle of red
on the counter.

"Sure."

Grabbing two glasses from the cupboard above, Nate pours the
ruby liquid into the glasses, we cheer, and take a sip. I jump up and
sit on the large island bench in the middle of the kitchen, the wine
now relaxing me, but an awkward silence falls between us.

"How've you been?" Nate breaks it first.

"Busy. Planning a million weddings." I roll my eyes. "And
you?"

"About to launch Paradise Club by the Sea for the summer."
He shrugs. "So, I've been in Monaco for most of the time."

I bet. Surrounded by stunning French women, I internally
groan.

"What's that face for?" Nate catches my reaction before I have
a chance to hide it.

"Nothing." Taking a sip of my wine, Nate's sapphire blue eyes
stare me down. "Fine! I thought of all the gorgeous French women
that probably have been keeping you company."

I'm such an idiot.

"No one has been keeping my bed warm," he adds. There's a
slight smirk. It's as if he knows I was wondering if he's slept with
anyone since we last spoke.

"You don't like sharing your bed, so doubt they stayed long."

Why, do I give a shit?

"Why don't you just ask me if I've fucked anyone, Camryn?" He seems annoyed with my question.

"Fine. Have you then?" My heart thunders in my chest, waiting for his reply.

"No."

Huh? What! As if. I don't believe him.

"Have you?"

"I haven't had time to."

"So, you would have if you had the time?" Anger laces his voice.

"I don't know," I answer, feeling very confused.

He throws his wine back, his glass slams onto the counter. "Good night, Camryn." Nate turns and walks out of the kitchen.

Throwing back the rest of my wine, I follow after him. "Excuse me." Grabbing his arm, I turn him around. "Where do you get off getting angry at me?"

"I'm not."

"You sounded like it."

"Maybe wishful thinking on your behalf," he shoots back at me.

"No. You're the one who sounds jealous, not me." I'm poking my finger in his chest. His damn hard chest.

His nostrils flare. "Of course, I'm fucking jealous, Camryn."

With that, he turns on his heels and storms up to his bedroom leaving me shocked in his wake.

44

NATE

I couldn't hide it anymore, my feelings for Camryn. Finding her all alone in the kitchen was a blessing and a curse. I wanted to spend time with Camryn, but then, on the other hand, things are so awkward between us.

Then I caught a flare of jealousy telling her about opening my club in Monaco. There was every opportunity to have hooked up with someone, but in all honesty, nothing felt right. Then I had to know if she had moved on.

Honestly, I don't know if I'd be able to cope if she has met someone else.

You know she hasn't.

Fine. I've been keeping tabs on Camryn, wanting to make sure she's okay because I can't stop thinking about her. Even after all this time, I reach for my phone to call her and realize she isn't in my life anymore. This is all so fucked up.

Taking my seat next to the aisle, I watch and wait for the wedding to start. Sucking in a deep breath, I turn and look just as Camryn begins to walk down. It's been about eight months since the last wedding we were both at when I watched her walk down the aisle, and in all honesty, my feelings haven't changed one bit.

She is still the most beautiful woman in the world. I guess my feelings have only intensified because last time we were still flirting around the issue.

As she passes me, her green eyes meet mine. There is a tiny smile pressed across her lips, and then she's gone.

What does that mean?

Camryn's been avoiding me all night. The last straw was when Johnny from Sons of Brooklyn asked Camryn to dance, and she accepted. I couldn't watch any longer because he was looking at her the exact same way he did at Vanessa and Christian's wedding when they hooked up. The way they're dancing, he's probably going to take her back to his room and fuck her. He won't make her come like I do. I'm sure it will be good, but he's not me. It might take her a while to realize that, but I am confident she will.

I walk outside, taking a seat, and just stare up at the stars trying not to think about what's happening back inside. I'm out here for a long time, just not feeling like socializing.

"Is this seat taken?"

Looking up, I see Camryn standing there with two glasses of wine in her hands.

"No."

She hands me a glass of wine and takes a seat beside me, then she stares up at the stars too.

"Someone two maybe three hundred years ago stood in this same spot and looked up at these exact stars," she murmurs to herself.

"If these walls could talk," I add, taking a sip.

"Imagine all the gossip. The liaisons…" Camryn smiles at me. "All those years ago, me sitting here in the middle of the night with you would have been a scandal."

"Still would be a scandal nowadays, too."

"Do you really think that?" She questions me, then turns her body toward me.

"My business is hardly… traditional."

"It's probably one of the oldest, though."

She surprises me with her answer. Silence falls between us as an undercurrent of sexual tension wraps around us.

"I miss you, Camryn." Reaching out, I place my hand on her leg.

"I miss you, too." She places her hand on top of mine.

"Are you taking Johnny to bed?"

Camryn shakes her head. "I wanted to make you jealous," she confesses, which surprises me.

"I was. That's why I came out here."

Now Camryn seems surprised by my confession. She intertwines our fingers together.

"Do you think we can get back to the way we were?" she asks, looking at me in the moonlight.

"I think too much has happened to go back to the way we were." Her shoulders deflate at my comment. "But I think we can start again."

"You do?"

"These months have been torture, Camryn. I haven't stopped thinking about you. I've wanted to call you so many times when something has happened in my life, and then I realize you're not there anymore. It kills me every single time."

"I've wanted to call you for so long, but then days turn into weeks turn into months, and I thought I'd missed my chance." Those green eyes look up at me with so much vulnerability shining through.

"I thought I might have missed mine." My heart is practically beating out of my chest.

She shakes her head. "I'm miserable without you," she confesses, a tear falling down her cheek.

"Me, too." Reaching out, I swipe the tear away.

"You wanna try this again?"

Hope flutters in my chest. "I don't want to share anymore," I tell her. "You're mine if we do this." I pull her into my lap.

"Agreed. You're mine, too." She looks up at me.

"I still love you, Camryn Starr."

"I love you, too," Camryn finally confesses as she leans forward to capture her mouth with mine.

45

CAMRYN

Six Months Later

"Merry Christmas, gorgeous." Nate rolls over and wraps his warm body around me. It's our first Christmas together as a couple. It has taken a lot of therapy for both of us to be where we are now.

We both suffer from PTSD from the events of that night. I had no idea all those months apart that Nate thought Harris had physically violated me. It wasn't until one of our joint sessions that it came out, and I was able to tell him that he didn't get a chance to touch me, that I was able to break his nose before that was able to happen. When he heard those words, it was like a dark cloud had lifted off him, and we were finally able to put that horrific time behind us.

It was the fresh start both of us needed in our relationship, and it solidified us even more.

A week later, he was moving into my apartment. I know? Surprising. I mean his apartment is so much more luxurious, but Nate told me he felt more at home in mine.

We couldn't be happier.

Yes, we're both still workaholics.

Nate has chosen to hire more people to take over most of his hands-on roles, so now he stays in New York most of the time. He's learned how to delegate, just like me. This personal growth stuff is pretty liberating.

Starr and Skye Events has exploded—our business has doubled this past couple of months, especially leading up to the Christmas season. We had to move out of our old offices into a much larger space. Funny thing is, Nate just happened to have space in his office building. Yes, we have turned into that couple. You know the one joined at the hip. The one that makes you sick with their love. Most days, it makes me gag too, usually around Nate's dick.

What I am trying to say is, I'm happy. We're happy. Happily, monogamous. Both of us don't feel like we are missing anything from our old world. Although, you would hardly call what we get up to vanilla.

"Morning." Nuzzling into Nate's hard chest, he's nice and warm.

"It's still snowing outside."

Lifting my head from his chest, I stare out the large picture windows of our cabin and watch as the white flecks fall from the sky across the glass. We are spending Christmas in Sam and Harper's ski chalet in Aspen. Ivy and Alex have flown in from England to join us too. Kimberly's here also.

"It's going to be a white Christmas." The inner child in me jumps up and down with excitement.

Nate kisses my cheek. "I organized that just for you."

"Just because I scream 'oh my God' every night doesn't mean you are one."

He chuckles as his arms wrap tighter around me. Then he presses his impressive morning wood against my ass. "You sure about that?" He lets himself slip between my ass cheeks.

"Maybe you'll have to remind me?"

Yes, morning sex is my favorite thing.

White Christmas morning sex—even better.

Nate's hand slips between my folds and slowly works me over, making me wetter and wetter. He lifts my leg and hooks it over his, spreading me open. Nudging my entrance a couple of times before slipping inside of me, we both hiss at the joining. His hand grabs my breast as he pushes into me from behind.

"I love you, Camryn Starr," he whispers into my ear, the prickles of his jaw tickling my cheek. "I want to fuck you for the rest of my life."

Me too, without a doubt.

My eyes roll back in my head as he begins to get into the perfect rhythm.

"I can't wait to knock you up."

This stills me for a moment, especially as we don't use any protection.

"Don't worry, not until there's a ring on your finger."

This makes me smile because I can't wait for the day until there is one. I know, me the woman who's all independent hear-me-roar crap, what can I say, good dick is hard to find. I'm locking it down.

Then I feel something cold against my skin. Nate's doing something weird with my fingers, but I'm too mesmerized by his dick to care.

"Marry me, Camryn?"

Now that statement has me stopping what we're doing, and my eyes widen.

"I want to spend the rest of my life with you, Camryn. I love you so much." My eyes automatically begin to prickle with tears. "Would you do me the honor of becoming my wife?" Nate lifts my hand in front of me.

Holy shit! That diamond is fucking huge. How the?

Silence falls across the room as I stare at the diamond on my finger.

"Camryn?" Nate questions, trying to pull me out of my shock.

Pushing him away from me, so I can turn around and look at him, I think for something this serious, we should be face to face.

"I can't believe you just proposed while your dick was inside of me?"

"Thought it was a good idea at the time?" A frown crinkles across Nate's forehead.

"You sure you want to marry me?"

Nate reaches up and cups my cheek. I can see his love for me written across his handsome face.

"I love you so much, Camryn. It's always been you."

Damn him as tears begin to fall from my eyes. Shit!

"Yes," I answer—the word falling easily from my lips.

"Yes?" Nate's sapphire blue eyes widen, but he still isn't sure if he heard correctly.

"I want to spend the rest of my life with you, Nathaniel Lewis."

Nate's eyes widen in understanding as he captures my lips with his own.

THE END

ACKNOWLEDGMENTS

Thank you so much for reading this book.

Finally Camryn and Nate got their happy ending.

It's exciting to see the very first spin off from the Dirty Texas series live and out into the world. Don't worry there will be more. We have the Dirty Texas Records Series because I know you all want more rockstars . There is Jackson's security series because we have seen him in the Dirty Texas series, Paradise Club and also the Playboys of New York series. Derrick will finally get his happily ever after so stay tuned.

Want to send out a big thanks to my amazing Beta's. Thank you to all the bloggers and readers for sharing the book. And a big thanks to my author buddies for helping me too.

ABOUT THE AUTHOR

JA Low lives in the Australian Outback. When she's not writing steamy scenes and admiring hot cowboy's, she's tending to her husband and two sons, and dreaming up the next epic romance.

Come follow her

Facebook: www.facebook.com/jalowbooks
Twitter: www.twitter.com/jalowbooks
Instagram: www.instagram.com/jalowbooks
Pinterest: www.pinterest.com/jalowbooks
Website: www.jalowbooks.com
Goodreads: https://www.goodreads.com/author/show/
14918059.J_A_Low
BookBub: https://www.bookbub.com/authors/ja-low

ABOUT THE AUTHOR

Come join JA Low's Block
www.facebook.com/groups/1682783088643205/

www.jalowbooks.com
jalowbooks@gmail.com

ALSO BY JA LOW

Timeline for interconnected characters in this series.

Dirty Texas Series

Suddenly Dirty

Suddenly Together

Suddenly Bound

Suddenly Trouble

Suddenly Broken

Paradise Club Series

Playboys of New York

ALSO BY JA LOW

The Dirty Texas Box Set

Five full length novels and Five Novellas included in the set.

One band. Five dirty talking rock stars and the women that bring them to their knees.

This collection includes:

Suddenly Dirty

He was everything she wasn't looking for.

She was everything he wasn't ready for.

A workplace romance with your celebrity hall pass.

Suddenly Together

She was everything he always wanted.

He was everything she could never have.

A best friend to lover's romance with the one man who's off limits.

Suddenly Bound

He was everything she could never have.

She was everything he couldn't possess.

An opposites attract romance with family loyalty tested to its limits.

Suddenly Trouble

She was everything he wasn't allowed to have.

He was everything she couldn't have.

A brother's best friend romance with a twist.

Suddenly Broken

He was everything she wasn't looking for.

She was everything he wasn't ready for.

A friend's with benefits romance that takes a wild ride.

One little taste can't hurt; can it?

If you like your rock stars dirty talking, alpha's with hearts of gold this series is for you.

ALSO BY JA LOW

Chloe Jones is trying to put the scandal of leaving her Super Bowl legend fiancé at the altar behind her. No better way to escape than to turn her island honeymoon into a much-needed vacation with her girls. What she wasn't expecting was to meet a hot stranger. Don't they say to get over somebody you need to get under someone else?

Chloe's ready for a fresh start, shame her vengeful ex is making it difficult for her. That is until she lands the job of her dreams.

What she wasn't expecting was to come face to face with the hot stranger from her island escape—Noah Stone, New York's biggest playboy, and her new boss.

Chloe can be professional even if all she can think about is those lips. And the way he fills out his suit pants.

He's totally off-limits, and she's signed the paperwork that says so.

ALSO BY JA LOW

International Bad Boys Set

Book 1 - The Sexy Stranger

Book 2 - The Arrogant Artist

Book 3 - The Hotshot Chef